OF ASHES

BY

STEPHANIE HUDSON

Rise of Ashes
The Transfusion Saga #4
Copyright © 2020 Stephanie Hudson
Published by Hudson Indie Ink
www.hudsonindieink.com

This book is licensed for your personal enjoyment only.
This book may not be re-sold or given away to other people. If you would like to share this book with another person, please purchase an additional copy for each recipient. If you're reading this book and did not purchase it, or it wasn't purchased for your use only, then please return to your favourite book retailer and purchase your own copy. Thank you for respecting the hard work of this author.

All rights reserved.

This is a work of fiction. Names, characters, places, brands, media, and incidents are either the product of the authors imagination or are used fictitiously. The author acknowledges the trademark status and trademark owners of various products referred to in this work of fiction, which have been used without permission. The publication/use of these trademarks is not authorised, associated with, or sponsored by the trademark owners.

Rise of Ashes/Stephanie Hudson – 2nd ed.

ISBN-13 - 978-1-913769-39-0

Dedication

I dedicate this book to my dear friend, Caroline Fairbairn, who is one of the most talented and warmhearted people I have ever known. A strength she may never truly believe she possesses, but to me, it is one that is offered daily and given without question. She is one of the most selfless and giving souls, who puts all those before her and never questions why she should. She is fierce and protective of those she loves and kind and warm to those fortunate enough to know her. She is funny, and silly and full of life, that makes you want to be around her and miss her terribly, when you are not. She is loved and adored and valued for being all that she is. She makes you want to be a better person, just so you are worthy of her friendship. And a hundred reasons more why I am utterly honored to not only call her a business partner, to not only call her my friend, but also to call her a soul mate, for I truly would be lost without her.

She is my rock and the silly string that surrounds it.

I love you dearly my forever *clumsy* friend x

WARNING

This book contains explicit sexual content, some graphic language and a highly additive dominate Vampire King.

This book has been written by an UK Author with a mad sense of humour. Which means the following story contains a mixture of Northern English slang, dialect, regional colloquialisms and other quirky spellings that have been intentionally included to make the story and dialogue more realistic for modern day characters.

Thanks for reading x

PROLOGUE

GLASS HEART

Is this how it ends?

The second I pressed the start button I was gone. I was gone to the sound of a twin-turbocharged V8 engine kicking out 986 horsepower. This was thanks to the Ferrari SF90 Stradale I had just stolen, which was now my getaway car. And I was doing all of this, not only to the sound of a powertrain engine, but also to the sound of my glass heart breaking as Sam Tinnesz hauntingly sang the lyrics that mirrored my own shattered soul…

'It's waiting, in shadows, my every turn feels haunted.
It hits me, like arrows, so deep, the blood is scarlet.
Is this how it ends? Is this how it ends?
This glass heart, is shattering to pieces, shattering to pieces…
This glass heart, is shattering to pieces, shattering to pieces.
Cold waters, too shallow, to keep me from the fire.

*The harder, I swallow, the more it paralyzes.
Is this how it ends?'*

And I really wanted to know as I ran from everything I knew and everything I thought I'd ever loved…

Is this really how it ends?

CHAPTER ONE

COCKTAILS AND PARTY GIRLS

"*The blood was the key,*" I uttered in a breathy whisper the second I heard the click of a mechanism being released and sure, there was an inner voice that was screaming at me as to whether this was a good idea or not. It was one that was near begging me to question if this was worth it...*worth the risk*. My mind said no and was in fact battling against the driving force behind my actions. Actions many would have thought were being led by the hand of curiosity. But they would have been wrong.

It wasn't curiosity that drove me to recklessness. No, it was,

My Heart.

I could barely explain it. Barely explain why I felt this way, a sense of empowerment that overtook me, powering me well beyond the realms of rational thought. Every clue, every symbol and text had been translated as a warning against opening the box, yet in that moment back in that silent garden I had felt something else. As if the box had been communicating directly to me. It had started when the small amount of blood-soaked snow had touched it. The whole thing had started to pulsate with life as if it held inside it a beating piece of heart.

Looking back now and no longer shadowed by the terror I was experiencing at the time, it almost told a story. Like 'The Tell-Tale Heart" by Edgar Allan Poe, it was beating at me, where no one else could hear it. But instead of a story of the guilty pounding soundlessly against the floorboards, it was telling me not of the death I would cause but instead of the lives *I could save.*

So, I had opened it and now here I stood, faced with the option to trust in my heart or in the logic I had depended on for most of my life. Lucius' little scholar, the Dravens' good girl, the heart of an historian. Facts. Dates. Evidence. Science. This had been my life so far.

But now?

Well, now I was the girl who had defied logic for love. I had chosen danger over safety. I had picked his world over my safe mortal one. All had been a leap of faith and this was just another one that I had to trust in. So, I took hold of the top of the box and after taking a deep breath and pushing my glasses up my nose, I started counting down,

"Three, two, one...fuck it!" I shouted and lifted the lid, praying unlike ever before to every God in Heaven and Hell that may be out there listening to me that I wasn't bringing on the end of days! Lucifer's blood, but I even had my eyes closed and I swear that every muscle in my body was tensed so hard, I wouldn't have been surprised in that moment if the first thing I heard was a fart before the destruction started. And wouldn't that have been fitting for the shit show of a girlfriend I was being right now.

Holy Hell, but Lucius was going to fucking kill me!

But then, as I waited with my mind going a million miles around the Armageddon tree, I was awarded with nothing but silence. There was no sound of the world crumbling around me. No signs that the belly of a mountain was erupting with me as its seed inside it, asking its forgiveness for causing its destruction.

This meant that after a very tense few minutes of waiting for nothing visual, I actually braved opening one eye, doing so in that slow and uncertain way.

"Well okay, can anyone say anticlimactic much?" I muttered as I now stared down at a folded piece of parchment inside. Now I knew better than anyone that to just dive right in there and grab it may end up contaminating it in some way.

Hello, but of course I had seen the Da Vinci Code. Which meant that these things could often be booby trapped to releasing all number of contaminants that would erase the contents should I accidentally trigger something inside when trying to retrieve it.

Besides, I was still bleeding from my self-inflicted injury that, looking at it now, was most likely a little overkill. Something I was also wondering on how to explain to my overprotective bloodthirsty boyfriend who, let's just say, was going to notice shit like that quicker than I could say 'hello honey'.

I quickly located a tea towel that, damn it, just had to be white.

"But of course, why not just wave a blood-soaked flag at him, stupid Fae...stupid," I said chastising myself as I wrapped the thing around my palm, hissing with pain the second I fisted it to keep it in place. Of course, before deciding on the tea towel I had first looked for a first aid kit, which made me laugh at how pointless that had been. As why would Lucius have any need for one, even with me around? Hell, but cutting myself was only going to end up as foreplay when I came screaming his name as he healed me, something that would no doubt end with him spreading me wide and filling me up, inciting another scream from me. Well, at least I could class my clumsiness as a plus when that was the outcome to look forward to. But then how he would feel about self-inflicted injuries didn't take much guessing as I was pretty sure he was going to be pissed at that as well.

Either way, the towel would have to do for now but at least it was my left hand, something I wisely decided was best to keep far from the box at this moment in time as who knew what would happen. Maybe it would be like the demonic plant in Little Shop of Horrors and grow massive and start demanding chopped up body parts. Fortunately for me I didn't know any biker singing dentists that liked to cause pain, so that was off the menu if it did. I did, however, at least have one name on my list I would be happy to feed to it... *first name Bitch, second name Face.*

"Zeus' balls, Fae, where is your head at?" I muttered as I started looking for any utensils I could use to extract the paper without touching it. In the end I found a pair of metal cooking tongs like you would use to turn meat on a BBQ, to use to remove the paper. I was then assaulted with a mental picture of what I looked like right now and the word 'overkill' came screaming to mind! I swear if any of my peers at the museum saw me now, I would die of nerdy shame.

"When means must and all," I said talking to myself as I usually did when working. I took hold of it in a feather-light hold and then lay it carefully down on the kitchen counter before tossing the tongs into the sink scared that my clumsiness might strike at any minute. Because even though I was normally fine with keeping it on lockdown for most of the delicate parts of my job description, there was also a first for everything. Gods, but what I wouldn't have done to get my hands on my kit right about now. Gloves, tweezers, brush in every size, flashlight, Hell, I even had a toothbrush in there for those really stubborn bits.

"God Fae, just man up would ya!" I told myself and rolled up my sleeve, if not a little awkwardly thanks to my bleeding hand. Then I rolled my shoulders, licked my dry lips and took a deep breath,

"Let's do this," I said aloud before I started to unpeel the folded paper that I couldn't yet age, but knowing it was at the very least a good few hundred years old. Nothing as old as the 11th century, when papermaking was first brought to Europe and nothing as refined as it was by the 13th century when paper mills utilized waterwheels in Spain. Which instantly told me that the box and the paper inside didn't match in age, meaning only one thing…

I hadn't been the first one to open the box since its existence.

"Erm…okaaayyy," I said stretching out my very confused words as I finally got the paper unfolded and flat on the worktop. Because no matter how much I squinted my eyes or spun it around, flipped it over and stood back and glanced at it, there was no mistaking what it was and that was…

"Utterly useless," I muttered as it literally gave me nothing. Okay, so that wasn't being completely fair to the seemingly pointless piece of paper. But then, in my defence, it was only one step away from being completely blank, as all it held was nothing more than a painted image of a mountain view that could have been literally anyone of the million mountains we had in the world!

It was done in a very ancient style as if it had been painted with a Chinese calligraphy brush with fading black ink that was merely a series of rudimentary peaks and curved lines for rivers. But without an edge to the landmass it was near impossible to distinguish which continent it was, let alone the country! And of course, there wasn't a single symbol or word written to give you a clue.

It reminded me of an old Exodus Route Map I had seen once which had been framed in an Antique shop by someone who had no clue as to what he really had. I had bought it and naturally donated it to the museum, because it was beautiful and needed to be shared with the world…or at least it was to me and probably people of a similar geekish nature.

But now this, well what it was supposed to tell me I had no clue. So, I turned my attention back to the box and looked inside only to find it was as useless as the phantom map to nowhere was. Because inside there was nothing but a series of grooves and carved lines that made about as much sense as the map did. Which was when panic started to hit me, *what if I had been wrong?*

What if this was simply a ruse for some mug to keep the

box open for longer? Longer for what I didn't quite know yet but what if it had held some kind of curse, one only catered for Vampires? What if I had been a complete idiot and listened to my heart, my gut or whatever other stupid body part I had inside me that I listened to over my head, like any intelligent person should have done!

"Shit!" What if right now Lucius was in danger or even worse...what if it was already happening to him? What that was or even could be I didn't know yet but the thought of it wouldn't leave me, as dread had replaced all earlier thoughts of opening that box being a good idea.

What if he needed me?!

I suddenly scrambled back from the counter as the full extent of what I had done started to seep into my conscious, now becoming fully aware of the ramifications of what I could have done.

"Gods!" I shouted before grabbing the map, folding it back up and then grabbing the box, before taking off running. Okay, so granted I only got to the living room before I stopped and I did this by looking down at myself still dressed in a bathrobe, holding two of the most wanted items on the planet right now. An open box that had been the cause of I didn't know how many deaths and one where collateral damage was probably written into every mercs contract in small print on the bottom.

"Okay, so new plan," I said aloud before racing back up to the bedroom, deciding clothes were a good idea. So, I stashed the box and the map, after first checking the walls again for any hidden safe and coming up empty. So naturally, I improvised before I grabbed a pair of stonewash jeans that had a bit of flare at the hem and frayed pockets and then the first shirt my hand touched, which unfortunately for me ended up having smears of blood on as trying to get dressed one-handed wasn't fun. But seeing as it was still bleeding a little, then I had no choice but to keep it covered.

And anyway, I didn't have time to worry about it, I just had to find Lucius and make sure he was okay and what I had done hadn't brought about my worst nightmare.

"Fuck! Fae, what the fuck were you thinking!" I shouted at myself as I ran out of the room, after kicking my feet into some sneakers, stretching my arms into some chunky knit cream cardigan and wishing I could beat my own ass!

Then I ran back to the living space knowing this was the only way that would get me back inside the main part of the castle where I had no doubt Lucius was to be found. Now where exactly he was, well that was where shit could get tricky seeing as he told me not to go exploring on my own. Something once again I was disobeying, but then again, I was claiming the 'when needs must' card on this one.

Besides, Lucius had mentioned something about the exits being guarded, so my plan was simply to demand that I was taken to wherever Lucius was. Doing so with the threat of getting lost if they didn't as I knew which was the worst of two evils and hoping they would too. So, hopefully, they would just show me the way being in fear of their master's wrath. For really which would be worse for them, turning up with me in tow where Lucius was or with news that I was now missing…*yet again.*

Something I think that at this juncture, I didn't think Lucius would be able to cope with, not considering the number of times I had gone missing on him in such a small period of time. I mean I was starting to think that the guy really needed a break, especially when even tying me to him as we slept hadn't worked out so well.

Maybe that private island home wasn't a bad idea after all, I thought as I took the steps up from the living space and towards the tunnel. But then my first hurdle faced me as I was now confronted with the bridge that, when looking at it now minus my wonderful winged boyfriend at my back well, let's just say I wasn't feeling half as confident as I once had. Which meant taking a more conscious effort not to be a clutz and go plummeting to my death. Because really, I think that would be the straw that broke the camel's back...as in, the permanent kind where that camel actually dies a horrible death by becoming a shish kebab.

So, needless to say, I took it slow and steady and, all but getting down on my belly and dragging myself across it like a slug, I did everything I could not to trip over and plummet to s shish kebab death. Meaning that after this was pretty smooth sailing in reaching the main entrance where the three arches looked over Lucius' personal domain. But once there I was quickly faced with two main differences from the first time I had been led here.

The first was the obvious difference to the room as it looked as though the Hulk himself had grown wolverines claws and suffered a massive man paddy! The black and white diamond floor was now cracked from what looked like a giants steps taken and there were crumbling holes in the walls from what was most likely a fist. But this wasn't the strangest part. No, it was the demonic-looking claw marks that had been slashed down one of the statues that had taken deep, long hollows out of the length of stone.

The second difference was the man I now found standing

guard there. He was cute and had kind of a Zac Efron thing going on, with startling blue eyes that gave him an eternally handsome babyface. He was also someone who, I must say, not only was faced with the shock of having me suddenly appear, but also who had me manhandling him. This was because the first second I saw him I grabbed the top of his arms and started shaking him when he didn't reply quickly enough after I fired my question at him,

"Are you a Vampire!?"

"What?"

"Are you a fucking Vampire!?" I shouted again making him frown down at me and then say,

"Uh…kinda obvious."

"No, obvious would be high collared cape, ass crack hair and a creepy sidekick named Renfield…now answer the fucking question!" I informed him making my demands quickly after. In turn he gave me a pointed look and one that said if I wasn't his boss' girlfriend then he would have proven it a different way, like when his fangs pierced my jugular.

"That's Vampirist," he informed me making me laugh before swallowing it as he was totally being serious here.

"Erh…sorry, look I am just asking you to prove it for my peace of mind, that's all, no biggy," I said folding my arms and waiting expectantly, oh and also making his baby features frown before he rolled his eyes as his fangs grew in length.

"Yeah, okay, so you remember who I am right, fangs aren't gonna cut it," I said knowing this was the same as demons and yes, that I was also going overkill on the questions.

"Gods, you're annoying," he said making me agree,

"Yeah, I get that a lot."

"The fact that I am inside the castle is proof enough, as only those he sired are granted entrance and those he invites...clearly," he informed me, adding this last part by looking down at me as if making his point. But I didn't care, as this knowledge had an instant effect. As now I could finally relax and take in a deep breath, as what he said was true, meaning that if he was alive then so was his Sire.

"Now, is there anything else I can help you with, human? Maybe I could slit a vein for your inspection, or would you like to ask my husband to come down here and you can question him too?" he asked making me grin before I said,

"Only if he is more polite."

"I doubt that, although he is slightly more impressed with you now he knows you're not completely hopeless with a knife," he said making my mouth drop open in shock,

"Your husband is Ruto!?" This time he granted me a knowing one-sided grin before leaning against the massive pillar that framed the large red doors, one that wasn't damaged.

"You're cute," was his strange response.

"Thanks…I think."

"You're also bleeding, and I am pretty sure our Sire is going to have fucking skinless kittens if he finds out." I pulled a face and said,

"Eww…jeez, what did the cute little furballs ever do to you?"

"I am more of a dog person," he said shrugging his shoulders in that nonchalant way.

"Anyway, moving swiftly on, that being away from our

favourite pets and the unspoken rule about caring for them *and their fur*…I need to find Lucius." His lips twitched as if he found what I said funny before pushing away from the pillar and saying,

"Yeah, I will agree with you, party girl, considering you will need healing…that or stitches seeing as you're still bleeding." I couldn't help but frown at the idea of stitches, that and his strange nickname for me.

"Well, come on then, let's get you to him before you start making a mess of the floor…I hate mess," he said and well, from one look at how immaculately he was dressed, then this wasn't surprising. What was surprising however, was that he looked like some cute high school jock with hair perfectly styled, fashionable clothes without so much as a wrinkle and muscles that looks sculptured ready for some designer clothing ad in some glossy magazine.

That or he was going to be in one these cologne ads where they basically just walked through a stylish and modern room full of beautiful people who seemed to swarm towards him. One with club lighting, a view of some cosmopolitan city, before getting into some expensive car at the end of the night with some gold-digging beauty on his arm. This all as if trying to fool the consumer into believing this lifestyle was within reach for even plumber Billy, who is sporting a beer gut, and just wanted to smell okay for the pub before getting shitfaced on eight pints of lager.

"You need to add more pressure," he said bringing me from my thoughts about make-believe Billy.

"Um?"

"That's why it's still bleeding, add more pressure," he

told me nodding down to my hand and he was right, the tea towel wasn't exactly cutting it.

"Thanks," I muttered as I started to follow him through the maze of tunnels and basically now going a new way I hadn't been before, telling me that it was a bloody good thing I'd convinced him to take me to Lucius as getting lost would have been my next drama. But then again, with my blood dripping on the floor, it was like dropping bread crumbs and would make me easy to find for a Vampire.

"I'm Keto by the way," he said making me need to suppress a giggle seeing as he was married to Ruto.

"You mean like the diet?" I asked before thinking, making him frown down at me as he informed me,

"I don't know what that is."

"Erm never mind…so pressure, eh?" I said making him once again grin down at me.

"Well, only if you want to stop the bleeding before lover boy finds himself a Bloody Mary served by a party girl."

"Why do you keep calling me that?" I asked with a frown and pushing my glasses up.

"No reason," he replied with a smirk, one that showed the hint of a fang. It was a look that made me shiver and quickly do as I was told by applying pressure. Doing so now without answering him because let's face it, I was going to be in trouble either way.

Because when Lucius had found out what I had done, then one thing was for sure…

The Party was over.

CHAPTER TWO

LUCIUS

MY LITTLE NERD

Gods give me patience but that private island was getting closer to becoming reality by the fucking day!

Because waking up and finding the cord that bound us together cut in two was all it took for me to welcome my demon to consume me. I had slashed the bedding to shreds as I roared out my wrath to the damn Gods who seemed dead set on allowing the Fates to continue down this fucking path! A roar in utter astonishment and fucking disbelief that she had been taken from me, yet *a'fuckin'gain!*

So yeah, putting it mildly, I had lost my shit and in a way that, at the time, I wasn't sure I would ever come back from. Because it was as if my entire soul had been swallowed up by the darkest part of me, one that ruled with the hand of a fucking Titan!

Pure fucking evil wasn't just a title, it was walking reality with every step I took after that moment, for all I needed to sate my need for death was seeing those responsible for taking her from me writhing in fucking agony at my feet, before I then stepped on their fucking hearts!

As expected, furious wasn't a strong enough word to describe what I had been at the time, but with this being said, I also knew the best way in finding her was by using my council to their fullest capabilities. Of course, they knew the second the Demonic side of their King had emerged, for every being I had sired would have felt my wrath humming within their very veins!

Which was why, by the time I had released my wings and flown to the entrance of my personal quarters, my people were already there waiting. I had bellowed my orders, barely even getting the words past making sense over the roar of rage. I hammered my fist into the walls, and the second anyone spoke, I ended up answering them with my talons raking down the nearest statue. This was just for something to take my fury out on as I remembered the irrational jealousy I felt seeing Amelia when trailing her fingertips down the sculptured form.

Even the black and white floor had cracked with every footstep my demon took, demanding Hakan retrace her steps and to do so fucking quickly. I had then ordered every single being within the castle to look for her, search behind every door, every stone wall, every fucking inch of my home! I just couldn't understand at the time how she could have left the castle without being seen…it just wasn't possible! Which was why I had been convinced that she was still here and just needed to be found.

So, I had torn through my domain searching for the other half of my soul with my Demon side questioning me as to why it felt so hard to breathe. Because even through my blind fury I could still feel that foreign emotion my Demon struggled to understand and that was out of my fucking mind with worry. I had even found myself stopping as I stormed through my castle, crashing into the walls as if my mind was screaming at me. I would take pause with my forehead to the stone, before hitting myself over and over again as I tried to regain some shred of control that would allow me to focus. Gods, but I was glad none of my people were there to witness my twisted demonic fallout, a title given and one named 'my hellish turmoil'.

I felt as though there was some ticking clock, echoing every second it counted down telling me I was losing her with every minute stolen from me. In the end I had found myself fucking running through my home until I came to the first fucking door that would get me the fuck out of there!

I just couldn't breathe!

I felt as if I was fucking drowning in carved bedrock and couldn't take a fucking breath. So, I had launched myself up in the air high above my mountain just with the hope of silence. Just to stop the screaming in my mind long enough to concentrate and cease the roaring panic of my Demon who didn't yet understand what I did.

For this was what love did to you.

Dom had said it best once, something I had foolishly mocked at the time, but the stronger and more powerful we are the harder we fall at the feet of our Chosen. I had never believed it at the time, believing myself immune to such sentiments. Believing in my own strength to rise above such weakness. Gods, but how fucking wrong I had been! I had naively once thought Keira to be at the core of my only weakness but since Amelia came into my life I knew just how wrong I had been. My ties to Keira had been one the Fates had forged purely because of what destiny would grant me if I formed that bond. That overwhelming sense and need to keep her safe all those years ago and now I knew why.

My gift from the Fates had been entirely in her hands.

But then I had needed to fucking focus because in that moment that gift was in danger of being taken from me! I had known this. So, I took to the skies and bathed in the moonlight, taking a moment to absorb its essence and repaying it back with my rage as it was being drawn from me. This gave me clarity and finally stole the sound of my own agony, doing so just long enough for me to hear her.

For me to hear her screaming my name.

After that I had dropped from the skies like some Hellish, avenging Angel ready to wreak havoc and destruction upon the Earth. And oh yeah, there had been destruction alright, that and much more.

Revenge cast in blood and snow.

This was what the night held the second I saw the first hellhound leap for my girl, ready to tear into the perfection I owned. Needless to say, it took no time at all before I tore into them, in what may have appeared to Amelia, with startling ease. And it had been for my demon and I, taking these dogs apart was as easy as fucking breathing!

Now trying to keep it together long enough so as not to terrify my girl was the real battle I fought. Which had been the reason I had told her to run, knowing that I would simply catch her once it was over. Also knowing that I would do so with as much ease as ripping apart Hell's summoned scum from fur, down to flesh, to shattered bone, painting the snow crimson. It was quite beautiful and once finished I took a few calming breaths to quench my thirst for revenge and extinguish my rage by taking in the sinister beauty I had created.

But then it wasn't enough, for there was only one beauty this beast had wanted, and I looked back at her seeing her now lying amongst the snow. She looked like some fallen angel, and I swear in that moment had I seen blood pooled at her back, I would have not been surprised to find a pair of wings torn from her gifted vessel. I winced at the notion, tensing and cursing myself for the fucking thought, because I knew exactly what she was.

"My little mortal." My demon had growled before we took our first steps towards her. I had hoped that by the time I had reached her my demon would have released his claim on me, but this hadn't happened. This meant I had no choice but to force her to endure this side of me.

I swear walking to her at that time wondering which side of her would welcome me, meant that each determined step was also one shrouded in fear…another emotion that was solely foreign to my demon and one it struggled with enduring.

But her strength had astounded me, for even after seeing all the darkness in me, her trust in my demon to take care of her was like a fucking gift. Something I had informed her of after she made it clear she hadn't wanted me to leave her in the bathroom. Fuck! But it had been nearly too tempting to take her in my other form, and one I nearly gave myself the freedom to indulge in. But I knew in that moment the dangerous side of me was too close to the surface and I wasn't exaggerating when I warned her how I couldn't afford for my demon to get too comfortable with the control I had momentarily allowed.

And he would.

Of course he fucking would!

Because Amelia was my only fucking weakness in life and that wasn't just a man in love, or an angel consumed… it was also as a demon obsessed. Gods, but it made me wonder how I'd ever managed it in the past. How had I managed to keep her at arm's length for so fucking long? Looking back on it now and it seemed like an impossible task and one I would never be strong enough to accomplish again.

Once again, it made me think back to what Dom had been through with his own Chosen and all the impossible decisions he had been forced to make. Decisions I knew at the very core of me that there was no way I would have been able to make as he had once done!

No, I was too selfish for that and his daughter was rooted far too deeply into my soul that there was no chance at ever carving her out again and it was the only way I ever fucking wanted it!

So, I had carried her from the crimson snow after feeding her the way my demon craved to do. An act I was completely unashamed to say had been done whilst I found my release without her knowledge. Wasteful, as spilling my seed was beneath the confines of denim, it couldn't be helped, for it was just the sight of her consuming a piece of that Hellish side of me, one straight from the source, that did it. It filled my mind with images of taking her back to my home in Hell as my prisoner, my claimed victory and one I would chain to me... *her new master.*

Lucifer's blood, but images of her on her knees taking my cock into her mouth, not as she had earlier but instead doing so with me in my demon form. Then with her own blood dripping down her naked form from my latest feed, well, it was no fucking wonder I had found my release.

But then I was also forced to think back to the way she had protected the box. Seeing the way it had rolled from her cradled form, tumbling in the snow from her frozen fingers as if the moment she saw me, she knew she no longer had to take on that burden. By the Gods, she had made me so proud! So, so fucking proud, it was near bursting from me. The strength she held inside her heart and soul was unlike anything I had ever thought possible, let alone witnessed from a human. I had once believed her mother had been the strongest mortal I had known. But then I knew that this had been something that had grown inside her through years of experience and endurance that had no choice but to strengthen with greater time spent in Dom's world.

But with Amelia, this hadn't grown, this had simply been a quality she had been born with and it angered me that Dom was too fucking blind to see it! That he'd missed that side of his daughter, being too shortsighted by the mortal cloud that tainted the sight of it shining from her. Gods, but she was the bravest fucking being I'd ever known, and similar to her mother in the sense that she would risk everything for what she believed in or everyone she cared for.

I knew this the moment her main concern after she had been saved, had been mistaking my thoughts, thinking that she had been trying to escape me by being on that rooftop garden. And I hadn't lied in my response when I had told her that it had warmed my heart to hear her say this. For keeping her by my side of her own free will had been my main goal since making her mine.

Which meant I was finally at ease with the knowledge that she would no longer try and run from me. Knowledge that managed to simmer down the rage I felt at the latest attempt at having her taken from me.

Which was why the second I walked into my office after forcing myself to leave her, I did so on the fucking warpath, slamming the door behind me, doing so with enough force that Ruto wisely healed the broken hinges and cracked frame behind me so I didn't have to.

Naturally, my whole council was there, after I had summoned them all to do so after leaving Amelia in the hot springs pool so I could get a handle on myself and my demon. A handle I only managed to grasp when I had been facing our bed, with my head lowered and my horns butted against the support pillars. I hit out against them, seeing that the tips of my horns surpassed the width of the bed, as I tried to get my head back in fucking gear. Of course, it was also a chosen state of mind that I kept my wings in place, for walking through the doorway they had evaporated to enter the room with ease before remerging.

But hitting out against the pillars was something I did every time my demon got the urge to turn back around and join her in the pool in this form. Needless to say, I ended up needing to fix them from the cracked grooves my horns had created by doing this more than once.

Strangely enough what had the strength to bring me back

in the end was the sight of my girl's humour now fixed to the wall and something I had missed up until that point. But then again, with her in the room with me, then it was of little wonder how I had missed it, for she captured my attention like no other.

"Fuck me, my little nerd," I had muttered on an amused growl the moment I saw the framed poster of a man in a blue uniform. He was a strange-looking being, with a harsh black haircut, hard slanted eyebrows and pointed ears. But it wasn't the man himself that did it, it was the words written beneath that made for a startling reminder as to my own role in life.

Words that were more than enough to drag me from the Hell that I had allowed to consume me for a short while. And what exactly were those words a man named Spock had spoken…

'The needs of the many, outweigh the needs of the few.'

CHAPTER THREE

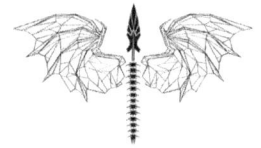

BLOODY REGRET

I took one look at my council and knew, despite my anger, that each of them had felt this latest hit. They each felt responsible for having someone who would one day soon become their queen nearly stolen from them yet again, as the failure settled deep in their eyes was easy to see.

However, this did nothing to diminish the fury I still felt clinging on, clutching at my Demon and near begging him to take back control.

"Now would someone like to explain to me how the FUCK that bitch infiltrated Castle Blutfelsen!" I roared the second I made it to my desk and forced myself to resist the urge to destroy it. To say that I was pissed wasn't just an understatement but at this rate it seemed to be a permanent state of fucking mind!

"Simply put...*she's fucking hardcore,*" Ruto answered and like I said, looking just as pissed off as the rest of my council did. They each hated weakness of any kind and this personality trait was a requirement in all of those chosen to sit at my table.

"Not helpful." Liessa muttered side on to my second, receiving a shrug of his shoulders in return.

"Did you get a track on her at least?" I asked Clay this time, who had been the one to receive my call ordering him to call off the search for I had found my girl. My next demand had been for him to hunt her ass down for she had disappeared into the dead forest beyond the silent garden. Named as such, for nothing with a heartbeat ever survived in it for long as it had been cursed with my own witch's wards years ago. And since then only two had ever infiltrated such power and those two events had been thirty years apart. The first time belonging to Amelia's mother when Malphas had tried to claim her in his attempt to use her as a sacrifice during the Triple Goddess ritual. The Mother and the Crone had tried to lure her away from my protection and thankfully had failed to do so at the time. However, it seemed as if history was fucking destined to repeat itself!

"Fucking vanished, seriously it was as though the bitch had never even stepped foot there…even Hakan couldn't get a trace of her essence." Clay replied surprising me, making me turn to the powerful being in question.

"Is this true?" Hakan nodded his head respectfully, before speaking,

"It is true, my Chieftain, I have never seen such power to be able to ghost her essence from one such as I," he said, unable to help that spark of annoyance from darkening his eyes, making the strip across them vibrate with anger. A rare sight to see on my tracker, that was for sure. Even in battle he would wield his deadly barbs with calm and collected precision. But then his greatest weakness was that of casting his gifts into the shadows of others that were immune. A master of his craft stumbling backwards to nothing more than mortal abilities. It was a hard blow for any of my people, let alone that of my council who were the strongest of the strong.

"When does Nesteemia arrive?" I asked enquiring about my own witch who needed to be the fuck here already!

"Her flight lands within the hour," Clay replied and then when he opened his mouth to speak again, I warned,

"Fucking save it, Clay, tomorrow night is still fucking happening and that is that…I will not appear weak in front of my people, is that understood?" I snapped, with half of me hoping he wouldn't get the hint for I needed a good fight right then, and Clay was one hard mother fucker!

But then luck was not on my side, for he obviously would not chance igniting my wrath once more, for he answered quickly,

"Yes, my Lord." But of course I didn't let my disappointment show and instead continued on with running my Kingdom and doing so whilst trying to ensure its queen was actually fucking safe for once!

"Now what is being done to ensure that this shit doesn't happen again, and my FUCKING CHOSEN ONE IS SAFE?!" I roared the last part of this as I hammered down a fist on my desk. Each of my council members looked awkwardly around the room for I knew that not a single fucking one of them had a plan and unfortunately this also included myself. Which was why I forced myself to take a deep and hopefully calming breath before taking a seat and getting down to all the shit this new attempt had caused.

"Let's run through it all again," I said knowing that with these words said it was going to be a long fucking night.

Too long without my girl...*or so I thought.*

Because a little time later suddenly the door was being opened in a way that Amelia literally burst through it in nothing short of blind panic. Naturally I stood, my whole being turning to fucking ice and stone the second I saw her, asking the fucking Gods what now!

But in her face, I could see that it held something more, something at that moment I couldn't comprehend or give it greater time to try to. Not as another importance quickly overtook the first, now taking priority. One that started with the quick scan of her body as I was trying to detect the reason she had desperately sought me out. And the second I saw her hand behind her back I breathed deep, taking in the scents of the room, and coming back with one very distinct smell...

Her blood.

Blood now mixed with the very scent of my own. This was after having shared more of it each day, and something that was stronger now she had done so when feeding straight from my demon. Blood, that I could now scent wasn't entirely inside her body like it fucking should be!

"Oops, so sorry to interrupt with your...uh meeting and stuff, I just...well, I just had to...erm...*see you.*" She added this last part with that delicious blush invading her cheeks and I had to say that both the admission and sight of her here now helped to at least ease the rage I could feel mounting at the scent of her blood. But I knew that it would only last so long. So, without taking my eyes from her I snapped,

"Everyone, get the fuck out, *now!"*

"Oh…erm, that's okay I can just…*wai…t,*" she started to say but this last word whispered was in response to the pointed look I gave her telling her without words to be silent. Something she thankfully took seriously enough to do so. Along with each of my council, as one by one they all rose and started to walk towards her. And each of them all couldn't help but smirk down at her quirky choice of shirt, one that given her confused gaze in return told me that she had been in a hurry and no doubt simply grabbed hold of the first thing her hand touched.

Which had me questioning again as to the reasons why?

I waited until my council left, which wasn't easy when I could smell her blood and was already close to the fucking edge, something I constantly seemed to be around her. Then I allowed myself a quick glance beyond her and saw Ruto's husband Keto who had been placed at the main entrance of what was known to my people as my Herz des Berges. This translated meant 'heart of the mountain' in German as that was precisely what it was. I was in effect the heart and life source of my people so having my personal space at the very core of the mountain had my people giving it the adopted name.

But one look at Keto and at the very least I could account for him being a good choice to lead her to me. For he was as trustworthy as any on my council and right now, that was my main priority. As until all rogues were taken out and sent back to Hell, then I was taking no chances.

The door closed behind her, yet she still remained by the

door, hiding what I knew was a bloody hand behind her back.

"I must say, for someone who desperately wished to see me, now that we are alone you seem far from certain of the reasons you came here," I told her seeing that she was still yet to come forward. So, instead I rose from my chair and went to stand in front of my desk before leaning casually back against it, which of course was a front for how I really wanted to react to her suddenly being here, bleeding. But then I knew what she had been through tonight and the last thing she needed was any added stress or just one more reason to find herself beyond her limit.

So, with this in mind I swallowed my demon's instincts and buried the impulse to grab her, hauling her over my shoulder and taking her on my desk just to remind myself what it felt like being connected to her body and dominating that perfection.

Which was why I gestured her forward with a jerk of two fingers. However, when I saw her gulp, I knew the reason she was here now was due to her own instincts and impulses, which now begged the question as to the cause.

"It's not wise to keep me waiting, pet, not with the scent of your blood dripping on the floor," I said knowing in that moment she would turn to look, thus giving me a chance to see for myself what she hid behind her. Of course, the second I saw the blood-soaked towel wrapped around her palm I knew it wasn't just bad, but it was worse than I first thought. Meaning that my plan to take it easy evaporated in a single heartbeat of hers and instinct and impulse was back to being my action.

Which meant that I had her in my arms before she even

knew that I had moved, only instead of tossing her over my shoulder, I swept her legs from under her with an arm around her back. Then I carried her to my desk, placing her down just as the first surprised yelp had finished passing through her delectable lips.

"Lucius I was…"

"…Taking too long," I finished off for her and at the same time I tried to reach for her injured hand. But this was met with resistance, now finding her holding it back from me. Something naturally that pissed me off. Which was why I growled her name in warning,

"Amelia."

"It's nothing okay, I just cut myself by accident," she said lying badly and continuing to do so when I raised a disbelieving brow at her, combining it with the blatant sound of my scepticism,

"Is that so?"

"Yeah, it's…hey, I said it was…" she snapped yanking her hand back and giving me but a glimpse of the deep laceration in her palm, one I knew was only achievable by that of a blade. After all, I had seen enough of them in my time and couldn't count any injury I couldn't recognise after so many years inflicting them upon others on the battlefield.

"…fine," she finished off stubbornly.

"And that happened how exactly?" I tested as I really was hoping it wasn't the reason I feared it looked to be. Because if it was then I wouldn't just be pissed, I would be blinding fucking mad!

"It's nothing, I was just cutting something in the kitchen and slipped is all," she said lying once again, so I leaned forward getting in her space and whispered in what I knew was a dangerous tone, one that if she were as smart as I knew she could be, she would choose to take seriously,

"Bullshit." Her eyes grew wide and also, *fearful.*

Now why would they do that I wondered?

"I am sorry, I shouldn't have come," she stammered as she slipped off the desk, something in the height of my surprise, I momentarily allowed before I snapped back into action. *For why would she say that?*

"Oh no you don't, sweetheart," I said as I banded an arm around her waist before picking her up once more and putting her right back on the desk. Then, as I took in the worry in her eyes, I thought back to the other look she had held when she first burst inside my office…

Fear.

She had run inside with fear on her face before it had morphed quickly into…

Relief.

Gods, but how did I miss that or the fucking importance of it? Because now I was starting to fit all the puzzle pieces together and it was unfortunately painting a picture that chilled me to the fucking stone cold core!

This was confirmed when she had tears rise in her beautiful eyes, morphing them into a sight I believed far beyond spectacular. I knew of the depravity in such a thought, for witnessing her tears should not have been a sight I found half as beautiful as I did. But just because it was what convention would class as being wrong didn't make my thoughts mute, or the sight any less profound.

But those tears, the ones that glittered in her eyes like moonlight caressing the forbidden depths of a lake, the ones that threatened to fall any moment...*those were the tears of guilt.*

The knowledge of such making me now having no other choice but to question,

"Amelia...*what have you done now?"*

And my answer ended by being confirmation it wasn't just bad... no, *it was a potential killer.* For it had been a risk she had been willing to take.

As she now opened up her hand, unwrapped the bloody towel to show the self-inflicted injury and said,

"Lucius...I'm so sorry."

CHAPTER FOUR

AMELIA

THE GENTLE HAND OF HELL

I could tell with that one look alone that this was a big 'oh shit' moment for me. I knew it the second he took one look at my hand and he just knew what it was. Sure, I had tried to pass it off as an accident at first, but he wasn't stupid, as he knew…*he knew what I had done.*

Which was why I had broken the second he had asked me what it was I had done now. Giving me no other option but to unwrap the crimson soaked towel that had been masking my guilt and say the only words I had left.

"Lucius…I'm so sorry."

And I was.

I was sorry for doing something so rash without considering all of the risks. I had allowed my heart to rule over logic, letting the words of a witch manipulate me into making that decision. I mean, yeah sure it seemed as though it hadn't brought on my worst nightmare by taking those I cared for from me, including the only man I had given my heart to. Because, even though Keto was alive, something he wouldn't have been had the one that sired him been dead, I had found myself running the rest of the way because I was desperate to see for myself that Lucius was fine. Caring little at the time on how I would explain my interruption.

Okay, so sure, I knew that I would have had to admit to him at some point the reasons behind my sudden panicked appearance, along with letting him know what I had found inside the box. Because I wasn't stupid or foolish enough to believe I could deal with it on my own. For starters, I didn't even know what the map held seeing as it looked as if it could have been a million and one places on Earth!

But right then, looking at the caged fury he was keeping on lockdown the best he could, I was wishing I could have just texted him what I had done and then gone and found some closet to hide in.

However, there was no escaping him, not when Lucius looked down at my hand and took it into his own to hold. He hadn't said anything and I was starting to worry, feeling a stray tear escape, rolling down my cheek.

"Please, say something," I pleaded making him raise his eyes to mine for a moment before he said in a stern tone, one that was laced with nothing but disappointment,

"You did this to yourself." It wasn't so much a question as it was a need for confirmation and I lowered my gaze, no longer with the strength to withstand that look of regret.

He suddenly dropped my hand and turned his back to me,

taking what I knew must have been needed space between us. Then his next question near crushed me.

"And was it worth the risk... *was I worth the risk, my Šemšā?*" I swallowed hard as even more tears overflowed this time, and I tried in vain to wipe them away in an angry effort to rid myself of my guilt, one I felt myself drowning in. A river I couldn't swim through and one made even worse with the sound of him calling me his sun. But yet I still tried,

"I...Lucius I...I didn't think that..."

"No, you fucking didn't!" he snapped suddenly making me jump.

"I'm sorry, I..."

"Yes, you said that already!" he barked in a dark tone that hurt, but again, could I really blame him? As far as he was concerned, I had opened the box that could have destroyed him and truly, I wanted to hate myself for it! But then how could I now describe the overwhelming feeling I'd had at the time, believing that it wouldn't happen, that opening that box had been the right thing to do? How could I describe, in that moment when looking at him, looking beyond furious as he did, why I had been so sure, when even I didn't fully understand it myself? How could I make him understand? To understand that my panic had only set in after it was opened, and not before I was slitting my own hand and actually doing it.

Yes, I was drowning in a river of 'hows' with each one seemingly more hopeless than the one before it. For there was no explaining. There were no words to express a reason beyond all doubt, for there hadn't been any. As those feelings had been a lie. A witch's trick in making me believe in nothing else but the opening of what could have had the power to destroy not only an entire race of demons, but more importantly…*the man I loved.*

Which was why I didn't deserve his forgiveness and was why I felt I had no other choice but to choose my only option left.

"I should just go," I said in a small voice as once more I was about to slide from the desk, which was when he whipped back around to face me and warned dangerously,

"Oh, but you are not going anywhere, Princess!"

I would have snapped back at that one, knowing that he only called me this to tell me how pissed off he was at me, something I didn't need as it was already blindingly obvious with his tone alone. So, I flinched, scooting further back on his desk, something for a single moment he softened his harsh gaze at.

"So now what?" I asked quietly.

"Now I am going to fucking heal you, that is what!" At this I frowned and clutched my hand to my chest, thankful that the bleeding had calmed before this point. But then with that movement alone, I had spoken too soon in my mind, as I hissed through my teeth and cursed the fresh blood that started to drip down the side of my wrist.

But despite this I was appalled at the idea, snapping back,

"No, you most certainly are not!" A reaction that caused him to growl at me,

"The fuck I am not!"

"Lucius, I can't let you do that, not now…*not with us like this,"* I said hoping he would finally get my point, something he obviously didn't, not when he folded his arms across his chest before demanding,

"And pray tell me why the fuck not?!"

"Because we are not doing…well, that…" I said, trying again and failing when he snapped,

"That?!"

"Yes *that*…you're angry at me," I said adding this last part when he still looked confused.

"Oh, sweetheart, I am not just angry, *I am fucking furious!*" he snarled leaning forward and making my back go rigid.

"Yeah well, I am not going to have an orgasm while you're 'fucking furious' at me!" I said making quotation marks with my fingers and going red with both embarrassment and anger, as was anyone's natural response when being shouted at, even though I was still fully aware that this was my fault.

"Oh yes you fucking will! Now all that is up for debate is if I can wait until after I have put you over my fucking knee or not!" he threw back at me literally making my mouth drop.

"You have got to be kidding me," I muttered in disbelief, shaking my head as if he had lost his ever-loving mind! But then he was suddenly at me, his hands on the desk either side of my hips and leaning his large frame into me, consuming my space as he whispered down at me,

"Do I look as though I am joking, beautiful?" Then, without waiting for my reply, he was lowering his face to my neck after first brushing the loose hair away, placing its length down my back. He started to slide the chunky knitted cardigan from my shoulder so his lips could replace it, making me suck in a startled breath the second I felt his gentle kiss against my skin. The feeling of his gentle action,

even though knowing that he was furious with me, was almost making my head spin. Especially as now he started to rid me of my cardigan altogether, taking care when slipping the sleeve over my injured hand. Then he threw the item to the floor, discarding it as if it never should have been there to begin with.

But, as amazing as his touch felt, I still couldn't allow him to heal me, for I refused to let him do that to me until we were past our argument.

"Are you at least willing to listen to my reasons first?" I asked, admittedly in a tone that didn't come out as forceful as I had hoped. He pulled back a little, and then took possession of my hand, prying my own fingers from it. Then he lifted it up, taking care not to hurt me with the movement.

"There is no reason in this world to ever take a fucking blade to this skin," he said before licking up my skin, starting at the bottom of where the blood had dripped down my wrist and forearm, now making a show of it. Making a show by not once breaking eye contact with me as his tongue travelled the tempting line of blood that I knew he craved. I could see it all written there in his eyes…eyes that darkened with his desire.

A desire to suck, fuck and feed from me.

I could see it all.

"No reason to spill blood I own, unless I deem it by my own doing, for nothing more than to feast on for my pleasure. To drink from you, binding you to me and tying you to my life. *No other reason my Šemšā…do you understand?"* he said whispering this last part against the inside of my blood-stained wrist after he had licked it clean.

"But I…"

"Say the fucking words, Amelia, *say them now,*" Lucius said interrupting me on a growl telling me he was on the edge, especially when I saw his eyes flash dark crimson. So, I gave him what he wanted and told him in a small voice,

"I understand." At this he seemed to relax a little, now taking in a deep breath, still with my arm captured in his hold, as if he was not yet prepared to let it go.

"Good girl…now I will listen," he said once there was nothing left but a crimson smear along my arm from where he had licked the length back up to my wound. Of course, just because he said that he would listen, I knew it didn't mean that he was going to make it easy for me. I knew this when he grabbed my hips and slid me closer to him before his lips once more went to my neck. Now leaving my hand in sight of my pulse point, one that had quickened thanks to where his lips were, along with his fangs. Yet he didn't bite me, he simply decided to tease me with them. Running the length across my tender and sensitive flesh like a warning of what was to come.

"Speak!" he demanded on a throaty growl that vibrated against my skin. Oh yeah, cause this was going to be easy…*not!*

"Can't we just take a minute to…"

"Lose my patience? Yeah, you take those minutes, sweetheart, and see where it gets you," was his response, one that made me hurry the hell up after he proved this by finishing his warning with my neck held at his mercy. This was in the form of a bite, one that stung even if he hadn't yet pierced the flesh.

So naturally, I took the warning seriously and hurried the hell up.

"Something the witch said to me made me realise that I had translated it all wrong," I told him.

"And you truly believed this...*yes?*" he asked after releasing my bitten flesh but still with his lips held against my skin. For he didn't let up and was now kissing up the column of my throat, making me melt into him. This was despite wishing I had the power to resist him, as I didn't want to be like this together, not until we had sorted through this latest fuck up of mine. Lucius however, obviously felt differently about that and had other ideas. Ideas that included manipulation and using my body to get what he wanted.

It was a cruel game.

A cruel game that a Vampire King played so well.

But it was also a game I had no other choice but to allow him to continue to play, despite knowing it was one I would never win.

"I do, I mean I did at the time, strongly enough to want to open the damn thing!" I told him making him tense a hand at my waist.

"And now?" he asked, wanting to know that if that was the case, then why was I there in his office? I also knew it was an important question for him to ask, as he ceased all movement and simply held himself still, with his lips hovering over my neck.

So, I told him,

"Well, after I opened it I panicked, *obviously*, which is why I ran straight here needing to see proof that you were... well, you know...still..."

"Still hungry for you?" he teased by nipping at my flesh, which I took as good sign as at least it was obvious I had passed some sort of test. Yet despite this, there was still more I needed to say.

"But I swear to you, Lucius, I would never have taken that chance if I hadn't felt it was the right thing to do...*down to my core,*" I told him and doing so in a tone that spoke of every word being said in earnest. And he heard it...*heard the heart of it*. That was why he finally raised his head from my neck and this time looked down at me.

"Your blood was the key?" he asked nodding down at my hand, one he still held in his grip.

"Actually, it was yours." He raised a brow at me, so I elaborated.

"The witch, she said something about the blood of kings was in me and it made the box shake in my hold when my blood touched it...she also seemed freaked out by me after that." Lucius pulled back a little so he could raise my hand between us and then he ran a finger around the wound making sure not to touch the torn flesh.

"My blood in you," he murmured to himself and I nodded.

"And what did you find?" was the question he finally asked and one I would have thought would have taken precedence over everything else...*Evidently not.*

"Well, obviously not the destruction of all Vampire kind, but it may be something that leads to it," I said making him grant me a look of curiosity.

"A map?" he guessed.

"Yes, although a pretty useless one at that, as it tells you nothing...I mean a bloody child with a crayon playing pirates could have done better!" I complained making him grant me a warm grin.

"So, this feeling you had, the one that compelled you to open it, do you believe this was something the witch intended or was it something potentially fated?" he asked and it would have been a total cop-out to tell him with utter certainty that yes, I believed it was. But at the very least I knew she had planted the seed. So instead, I went with diplomacy.

"I think so, I mean I don't know for sure other than the feeling I had at the time. But either way, her words stuck with me and festered until I believed no harm would come from opening the box. Now had that been her plan all along, I don't know because let's face it, if she had taken that box, where would she have got your blood from? Could she have got it from someone you sired?" I asked obviously giving him enough food for thought as he continued to stare down at my hand

"No, once my blood has been gifted and the change has taken hold, it will no longer hold the same strain, but becomes something new…it is not the same as when you feed from me." I listened to what he was saying and hated to ask my next question, already feeling a sickening emotion rise the moment I forced the words from my lips,

"And what about…erm…*past lovers?*"

"What of them?" he asked, obviously not understanding what I was getting at, which I found odd…well, at least until he explained it further, something he did after I asked,

"What about past lovers that have fed from you?" At this he grinned, and I swear I wanted to slap him, that was until he put me out of my misery,

"As adorable as this spark of jealousy is to witness, I have never gifted my blood to a lover before and no other but one has ever fed from me more than once," he said but then before I could ask, it dawned on me who that 'one person' would be.

"But of course," I muttered before I could stop myself as I turned my face away but then he didn't allow this for long before my chin was in his grasp and being used to force my face back to looking at him.

"My blood is yours. It belongs to you and no other...*do you understand?"* he demanded in a stern voice that vowed his words to be true. So, I nodded making him growl,

"The fucking words, Amelia!" This I knew was a big thing with him, as he always wanted my words. Words that obviously helped soothe his frayed soul that I had pulled at too much lately.

"Your blood is mine, Lucius," I told him making him release me after giving me a firm nod.

"Good...Now it is time to take in which belongs to me in return," he said before releasing his fangs, allowing them to grow in length. Then he raised his own palm and I winced when he sliced a line in the same place where the knife had sliced through my flesh. Then he grabbed my hand, interlocking his fingers with mine, yanking me forward the second I felt his blood mix with my own.

And the impact was instantaneous.

I cried out as the intensity struck me, a scream that ended being consumed by his kiss. This was as he fisted a hand in my hair and anchored me to him to ensure I couldn't escape, not that I would have wanted to...*ever.*

After this my world started to tilt as I felt myself falling with the strength of my orgasm building and ripping through me so fast, I wasn't prepared for it. But I was the only one who wasn't, as Lucius was prepared. Which was why I realised I wasn't falling after all... *I was being pushed.* I felt the pressure of his hand at the back of my head the moment it hit the desk as he began climbing up my body like some jungle cat crawling over his kill.

But at the same time this was happening so was my back arching up, pressing myself further into him as a silent scream shuddered through me before it ended by panting his name over and over again. I was so lost in my pleasure that I didn't realise what was happening until Lucius was no longer over me but instead was stood at the desk. And I realised this when he suddenly grabbed the back of my knees and was dragging me to the edge.

I started to sit up which ended quickly as he tutted back at me, before quickly collaring my throat and pushing me down until my back was again flat against the desk. Then with the full length of his arm held straight, he held me prisoner this way, free now to do as he obviously intended. And what he intended was to share me with a slice of his demon side.

"Now you're all healed...*do you know what comes next, my pet?*" He almost purred down at me and my eyes went wide, questioning if he could mean what I thought he might mean. But then he made a show of holding up his left hand, one gloved as it always was. However, with a click of his fingers it started to transform into what it had been earlier when I had been faced with his Demon.

Hellish armour seemed to come from nowhere, as if the air around him had started crackling as he drew in some unseen demonic essence from the air. A black mist, circling his hand before growing like giant scales overlapping in a wave against the leather until his entire hand was consumed. Then it started to harden and form the same demonic gauntlet as before. But this close up I could now see it in fine detail, and it was as equally beautiful as it was terrifying.

It was made up from layers of triangular interlocking plates that were framed by strips of smooth black metal with a rough centre. It looked more like volcanic rock forged with the only smooth piece being that of a thick band just below his elbow, one that held etched demonic symbols, one of which I could now see was his personal sigil. One I knew the meaning of thanks to the lesson he had given me when being faced with one of the doors that led into his personal quarters.

I moved away from the sigil of a Vampire King and along to the pointed plates that tapered down to his hand. They continued down until each finger was encased in metal knuckles, ones pinned and riveted for movement. But it was the gleaming black talons that tipped each finger which worried me the most, especially as they started to move towards my waistband.

He even grinned down at me when he felt the hard lump in my throat being pushed down past his hand at just the sight of them.

"But...but I explained and..." I mumbled quickly not knowing how I felt about what I thought he was going to do next.

"That you did my sweet, good girl," he agreed, pausing before telling me,

"But even a good girl can turn bad…" he told me, still holding me still as the back of his talons started to caress along the strip of bare skin between my top and the denim of my jeans. A dangerous action that made me shudder, as he watched himself do this.

Then his eyes found mine before he growled,

"...And in my world...

"Bad girls get punished."

CHAPTER FIVE

BAD GIRL FALLING

I sucked in a deep startled breath,
One named...*punishment.*
For this was my only warning before I felt the first tear in my clothes as his talons hooked my waistband and started cutting into the material as if it had been nothing but paper. And I was powerless to do anything more than lie there being torn between wanting to squirm away and being too fearful to move a single inch! However, with my decision taken away from me thanks to his hand still holding me down in my place, then there was little option left than to just lie there and let him continue.

Soon my jeans were cut open down the centre, so my panties were on show underneath the denim. Which meant that I could now feel the back of a single talon caress down the centre of my barely covered sex, something that had me shuddering in his hold. It was as if he was igniting some darker side of me, some deep taboo that was feeding from my fear and morphing it into something sexually addictive…*something alive.* And all the while he watched me, as if not just looking but actually absorbing every breath I took, every flinch of my body, every single reaction was being filed away and memorized, calculated and abused.

I didn't know whether this was what turned him on the most or whether he was simply watching me, making sure he would notice any signs that told him to stop. I really didn't know, but one thing I did know was that he got off on watching me squirm. Now how far he would take that I didn't yet know…

Well, not until he showed me.

But first he released my throat and plucked my glasses from my face, slowly folding them and placing them down on the desk, telling me,

"You won't be needing these." Then suddenly I was flipped over, making me shriek in surprise, a reaction he chuckled at and just as I started to push myself up from the desk, Lucius took the option from me. The hand that had once collared the front of my throat, switched so it now gripped the back of my neck, once more forcing me down flat. Then I felt those talons of his continue to tear through my clothes, only this time doing so up the line of my ass, tearing through denim until it cut through the waistband at the back. Then I felt my jeans start to roll down my legs without aid as there was nothing more to hold them in place. After this he released the back of my neck so I could move again now that it was safe to do so, making me realise that by holding me down was so he was assured I wouldn't make any sudden movements with his talons so close to me.

I had to say that the mixed feeling of both care and rough treatment in doing so was a heady mix I could barely quantify. I tried to make sense of it, and question why the two combined turned me on so much, but no answers were found. The dominance, the commanding and masterful way he controlled me was only driving me forward towards something that felt mythical. Something just there within my grasp if I was only brave enough to reach out and take it...or more like, allow him to push me into reaching it. It was like leaping without the safety net and trusting that he would be there to catch me before dropping me safely into his dark world.

And by the Gods, did I want to fucking fall!

I felt Lucius leaning down over me before his right hand curled back round to the front of my throat, doing so to raise up my face. I was lifted from the desk, with his thumb pressing my chin up, keeping my head from the desk. This allowed his gauntleted hand to palm my breast, making me suck in a shocked and fearful breath.

"Easy," he whispered as he stilled his dangerous hand, and then told me,

"Just close your eyes and allow yourself to feel it." So, I did as I was told, placing my trust in him and closing my eyes. It was only then that I started to feel what he wanted me to feel. The heavyweight of his demonic hand squeezing my breast felt amazing, and the fear of him hurting me unintentionally faded away. But I wanted more and wished the rest of my clothes had been taken from me so I could have felt the texture of his hand against bare skin.

To feel such strength, to feel the hand of destruction being so gentle was like being stroked by a weapon made to hurt, not one made to soothe. It was an arousal like no other and even when the very tip of his talon gently circled my nipple, pulling at the material that covered them, I only felt myself dripping even more with anticipation.

But then that weight was soon gone from my breast and was at my neckline, joined by his other hand so both could be used to suddenly tear my top in two. I jumped at both the sound and the feeling of having my clothes literally ripped from me, making my chest heave with eagerness and with only my bra in the way of giving him what he wanted, it was nothing more but a mere of a flick of his talon in the centre, making my breasts burst free.

After this his gauntleted hand went back to playing with me and any minute I was expecting him to enter me from behind, wishing it would happen soon for I was near out of my mind wanting it! I was so desperate for his cock. Which was why the word slipped out before I could stop it,

"Please." I heard him humming behind me before a talon tapped at the side of my breast making me shudder.

"Mmm, I must say, I do enjoy hearing you beg me for it," he told me, making me lower my head in shame, something he didn't like. I knew this when I felt my hair being twisted in his hold so he could yank my head back and growl in my ear,

"Don't you dare be fucking ashamed of that…now fucking own it and say it again!" he demanded. But when I didn't do his bidding right away, he bent over me to take my tender flesh in between his teeth, with his lips now at my neck causing a small nip of pain. This happened before his demon was now demanding it of me,

"Fucking say it again!"

"Please."

"Again!" he growled.

"Please...please, please," I whispered again and again, making him smile at my neck before telling me,

"Alright, my pet, *my good little human*...now, let's see how well you beg for your punishment." I froze in his hold and started to mutter,

"Uh, but I..." This was when I felt him pull back and the moment his hands left me, I nearly did beg for it. Well, that was before I felt the sting of a slap to my backside.

"Ah!" I shouted making him scoff in amusement.

"That wasn't you begging me, pet. Now let's try this again should we?" he said slapping me again, this time twice, with a swift one to each cheek.

"AH!" I shouted again, only this time a burn added to the sting. But now when he leaned down over me, getting close to my ear, there were no bites or kisses, only a whispered,

"I know you can do better than that." Then I braced myself for another slap, but it never came, instead he palmed my cheek before caressing around the palm mark it felt that he had made.

"Such a beautiful sight...*fucking stunning.*" He almost hissed this last part, and then just before I could speak, he slapped me again, making me scream and push up with my hands.

"Uh huh, no you don't," he told me and suddenly I found myself being pushed down flat to the desk and the ruined, torn top and bra being pulled back down my arms.

"I see I will have to do something to contain my willful

girl." This was my only warning as once my top was gone, I heard the tearing sound. I chanced a look over my shoulder and saw that he was tearing down the length of material, now gaining a thick strip from the middle.

"Eyes upfront, pet," he ordered making me do as I was told. But this wasn't all as the second he tapped the lowest part of my back, he ordered,

"Hands together here." I swallowed hard and did as he said for me to do but not before I needed something in return, so I whispered his name, the trepidation easy for him to detect,

"Lucius?"

In response to this I felt his bare hand run down the length of my spine, free to do so now that I was completely naked, all but the denim still caught at my knees and my soaked panties.

"Do you trust me to take care of you?" he asked me and I swallowed again before nodding.

"Words, beautiful," he said softly, reminding me of the rules.

"Yes."

"That's what I want to hear…now be good for me and do as you are told," he ordered, tapping my lower back again and this time I put my hands behind my back without hesitation, leaving me little choice but to allow more of my weight to press down against the desk.

"Mmm, but the Gods have blessed me with such rewards with a sight I will never forget, for you are simply exquisite, my Amelia," he told me as he wrapped the length of torn material around my hands making sure to tie it tight enough that I wouldn't be able to get away from him any time soon.

"Now where were we...ah yes," he said before another sting burned its way across my ass making me cry out again. Then came the soothing hand that I was starting to crave. But this was when things started to get confusing, for I didn't know which one I was starting to crave more, as I knew which one it should have been. However, with each crack on my cheek I found myself losing the will to try and dislike it, now switching to the opposite. I was actually holding myself still and actually pushing my ass back into it, to gain more of the powerful swing.

But of course it hurt, but nowhere near as much as I knew he was capable of. And I didn't even fully understand why or how or even when it had started to happen. When exactly the time switched, and the pain had started to merge into pleasure. Gods, but I wanted him to fuck me so badly that pretty soon I was doing as he said I would...

Begging him.

"Please...oh Gods, please...please Lucius!"

"And there it is...there is even more of my beauty...now shout it for me this time," he said with a controlled edge to his voice that told me he was as deep into it as I was.

"Please! Please...Please!"

"Ah, such pretty punishment, you take it so well...*so fucking well,*" he praised slapping me again, and this time his gauntleted hand went to my neck and raised up my head, taking care as he held me steady to take the last of his hits.

"Fuck! Please, Gods, please Lucius!"

"What do you want me to do to you, pretty girl, umm? Say it now, for I can see you dripping for me, soaked and ready for me...is it my cock? If it is, then say the words and I will give it to you," he told me softly... *so fucking softly*...so close to my ear as he had turned my head to one side in that rough hold, something that contradicted his gentle tone.

"Yes…oh please, yes!" I begged again but he growled low and reprimanded me,

"That is not what I asked of you…now give me the fucking words I demand!" I shivered in his hold and after one more powerful smack, one that made me burn and leak even more from my shuddering core, I told him,

"I want it! Please, please… GIVE ME YOUR COCK, SIR!" This came out on a shout of desperation the second the pain burned all the way to the junction of my thighs making my back bow into his hard torso leaning over me.

"There's my good girl," he praised again, turning my head, yanking it to the side and holding it there by my chin as he kissed me in a rough and demanding way. This was at the same time he suddenly ripped off my panties and reared up inside me. I screamed in his mouth as I quickly found myself impaled on his length as his cock thrust as deep as my body would allow. I cried out desperate for him to move, with him still kissing me. He grinned before biting my lip and making me whimper before he started to hammer into me, still with his lips to mine. I could barely move, with no other option to just take all he had to give, for his other arm was banded across my chest. I was anchored to him, completely imprisoned by muscle and flesh. His hold on me was one that was steady enough for his hard, punishing thrusts. And by the Gods it was out of this world amazing and as we both knew it would, had me coming in seconds!

"AAAHHH LUCIUS! Yes, yes, yes, yes!" I screamed again and again as he continued to drag the never-ending orgasm out of me. Only then did he leave my lips, licking at the cut he'd made to heal it before then moving back. Doing so, so he could take hold of my hips and really start to drive into me. Then, just as I flinched the second I felt a tiny prick at my skin, he moved his gauntleted hand to a safer spot. Now with it positioned at my lower back and fisted in the material around my bound hands, he used it to pull my body back into his, using it as leverage to pound into me.

This meant that once again I felt it building up, higher and higher. So high that I even feared the moment I was forced to the peak before being made to tumble back down to earth. For it felt like the force of it was powerful enough to completely shatter me!

But I obviously wasn't the only one who felt this way for Lucius was nearing his own limit, that much was clear the moment he started growling down at me. It was a mixture of his demon and the Vampire King that commanded him. I knew this when I felt another smack to my ass and I cried out as it only managed to drive me beyond that peak and the sound of my scream did something to Lucius. As just as I was about to come and come fucking hard, his demonic hand-hammered down against the top of the desk, landing by my head and his other hand yanked my head to the side before suddenly he sank his fangs into my neck.

And with that first pull of my blood leaving me and being sucked down by my King, I exploded.

"FUCK! YES, YES, YES, YES, AHHH!" I came harder than ever before as I went hurtling off that mountain top and shattered around the length of him buried deep within me.

But the last thing I heard, saw and felt was Lucius roaring his own release, feeling his seed coating the walls of my sex. This was as his taloned claws, ones so close to my head, started to curl deep, gouging into the wood. Dark, razor tips creating curls of wood, now being peeled back under gleaming talons of a demon that fucked me straight to Heaven.

For this time when I fell unconscious…

My winged demon was the one to catch me.

CHAPTER SIX

TICKLED PINK

The next time I woke I did so faced with Lucius' chest rising slowly and it took my confused mind a minute to piece together the moment. I was currently lying with my head rested against Lucius' pecs with my arm draped across his torso. His hand was curled around my forearm and the other was alternating between softly trailing his fingers up and down my side and squeezing my hip.

I was stuck debating whether or not just to go back to sleep seeing as I was so comfortable like this, it felt like I was going against my body by waking fully. But then again, I also wanted to know where I was and how I had got there. Because unless I had missed the massive bed in his office, then I doubted we were still there.

Of course, this decision was taken from me as Lucius must have known the moment I had started to come to, as his hand left my forearm and hooked under my chin before tipping my head back to look up at him.

"Hello, my little party girl," he said making me frown in question before asking,

"Why does everyone keep calling me a party girl?" At this Lucius chuckled and replied,

"Well, not anymore after I shredded the words and had no choice but to re-dress you in my own shirt so I wasn't carrying you back here naked."

"Sorry?" I asked not quite understanding and again he started laughing before surmising,

"I am going to take a predictable guess here and say you were in a hurry to get to my office…yes?" Again, I frowned still confused.

"Your shirt, before torn once said…*I like to party, and by party, I mean take naps.*" Hearing this and I couldn't help but moan, now understanding all the smirks and chuckles I had received from his council members as they each left the office.

"Great…I bet that was sexy," I commented on a grumble, as I loved my aunty Pip but sometimes her funny t-shirt tradition was best left for those private days inside and not when trying to look hot in front of your new boyfriend.

"Actually, it was very sexy, especially when it was in pieces and used to bind you whilst I fucked perfection," he said making me blush to my roots, to the point that I purposely face planted back onto his chest and groaned against his skin, making him chuckle as I murmured,

"Don't say that." Then I felt him force my gaze back to his and he told me with a throaty growl,

"Burned to my mind." Then he ran the backs of his

fingers down my heated cheek before leaning down to kiss me softly. It was a gentle gesture done before he could ask me,

"How do you feel?"

"Erm…a little sore," I admitted because I could still feel the heat across the skin on my ass and his hand left my hip and caressed my cheeks softly,

"Poor baby…*however*…" He paused so he could grip my ass cheek, making me suck in a breath at the bite of pain, one that was drowned out when he growled down at me,

"I am glad, for it will remind you how I feel about you hurting yourself and be a lesson never to do it again." I swallowed hard and nodded before telling him,

"I promise." He nodded once and then eased his hold before going back to caressing the new hurt.

"I really am sorry," I told him making him nod before telling me softly,

"I know you are, sweetheart." Then he lifted the newly healed hand to his lips so he could kiss my palm.

"I didn't like seeing it," he told me tenderly and I had to say, it was sweet the way he cared and wanted to protect me, even if strangely that also included slapping my ass as punishment.

"Along with that…" he said shifting his eyes to the side where I had put up my poster of Spock and one he had missed previously. But I knew why as unless you were at a certain angle in the room then it was easy to miss. Which was what I had been aiming for as it had all been part of the 'annoy my boyfriend with all my shit being around plan'. Something I knew I had finally accomplished when he told me,

"I am not sure how I feel about having homage to another man on my wall in the room where I fuck my girl."

At this I burst out laughing and ended up burying my head in his side as I continued to chuckle, but then as I did this I felt something from Lucius that I had never felt before...*he flinched.* This was when I froze and lifted my head slowly, pushing my hair back as I did.

"What?" Lucius asked and by the Gods it was one of the cutest things I had ever seen...*Lucius was squirming!*

I knew it when suddenly I blurted out,

"You're ticklish!"

"No...no, I...well, I am most certainly not ticklish... that's absurd...of course I am not," Lucius said and by the Heavens above, he was actually acting embarrassed by it. He was even talking quickly, the way people do when they are trying to lie...*badly.* My eyes widened and I raised myself up from his chest, getting almost giddy from both the thought and also how he was acting so...well, so bloody human about it.

"Oh, my Gods, you so are!" I shouted on a laugh making him frown, before getting close to my face and saying,

"I am not." I rolled my lips to hold back the laugh so I could then argue,

"Oh, you so are!" I then giggled making him growl and in return I laughed harder.

"Amelia, I am King of all Vampires, do you really think a being like me would be fucking ticklish?!" he snapped and again I burst out laughing making him suddenly flip me to my back so he could loom over me, no doubt trying to intimidate me. But it so wasn't happening, not after what I knew.

"I see my girl needs another lesson," he growled making me frown back before coming to a decision.

"Alright, I will make you a deal, you prove to me you're not ticklish and I will take any punishment you dish out, mister!" I said making him frown before sitting up, putting his back to me and saying a definitive,

"No." Again I couldn't help but bite a lip so as not to laugh.

But trying to stop myself from laughing wasn't easy, as he was clearly sulking. So, I allowed myself a silent giggle behind him before trying a different tactic. I got on my knees and plastered myself to his muscly back and wrapped my arms around him, smiling when a hand came up and held my arm across his chest, telling me he wanted me there. I then rested my chin on his bulging shoulder and looked down at the sexy, muscular sight before me. Lucius wearing nothing but a pair of jeans was utterly drool-worthy.

I also knew that had I not been wearing his T-shirt and been currently pressing my naked breasts to him that I would have had more chance at sweet manipulation.

"What if I say please?" I whispered getting closer to his ear before kissing his neck and making him moan and this time it was because he was cracking, not because he was getting annoyed.

"Amelia, I am not…"

"Then prove it, show me your skills, Vampy," I teased making him growl this time, but thankfully in a playful manner. Then, after releasing a deep sigh, he suddenly grabbed me tighter and pulled me so I had no option but to be dragged around him. I now ended up in his lap with his T-shirt twisted and tangled up near my breasts.

Once there I wrapped my arms around him and continued to kiss his neck, getting to his ear before I whispered,

"Be brave, my King." He scoffed at this before telling me once again.

"Fine woman, if it is the only way you will cease this ridiculous notion," he complained, making me grin against his skin before I came back to his face, kissed his nose and said,

"Thank you, honey." To which he rolled his eyes but even I could see the way my soft words had affected him. So, I shifted off him, back on to the bed as it was clear I wanted to get started.

"Lie back," I told him gently trying to coax him and it was the very first time I could see trepidation in his eyes. I don't know why but it gave me such a strange thrill. Maybe it was because I was usually the one he was pushing into new situations and now here I was, doing the same to him.

"This is ridiculous…I am not even sure what you're trying to achieve here," he argued making me hold in my laughter but not quite managing to prevent the smirk as I said,

"We will just see, won't we?"

He shrugged his shoulders, clearly acting as though I wouldn't be able to make him laugh by tickling him, yet despite the act, he still tensed his muscles. In fact, he lay down as if his back had been replaced by a wooden board. Seriously, he looked as though he was ready for me to attack him any minute!

"Wait, what are you doing?" he asked sounding panicked and I laughed, as I was just getting lower to his belly. So, I looked up at him and said,

"Relax, handsome," then smirked down at the tensed abs bunched at his stomach knowing that this was going to be way too easy. For starters, he flinched the second I first touched him, and I knew he was holding himself rigid, forcing himself from reacting the way he wanted to.

Gods, but it was fucking perfect!

So, I decided to build it slowly, instead of just going in for the easy kill…after all, I had received my punishment and now…*well, now it was time for his.*

And I intended to enjoy it.

Which was why I ran my fingertips featherlight across his belly, making him shudder underneath my touch, and I found him staring down at me. Combined with this uncertain look were his fists in the bedsheets, which I was only now realising were torn. I would have to remember to ask him about that later, but right now I had a mission to accomplish.

The expression on his face looked almost pained and for a moment, I nearly granted him mercy…*almost.*

"Raise your arms up above your head," I told him making him frown down at me before saying,

"Not happening." I laughed and said,

"Well, if you're not ticklish like you claim, then doing so won't be a problem for you, will it, Vampire?" I challenged and I swear I had never seen him looking so freakin' cute. He released a sigh before doing as he was told and the way his biceps hardened and bulged, made my mouth dry. Gods, he was utter perfection. The body of an Adonis!

"Close your eyes," I told him, making him frown down at me before complaining,

"Anything else, Princess?" I leant down and started

kissing near his belly button before looking up at him and murmuring softly,

"Play nice, baby." To which he released another sigh before doing as he was told and making me grin against his skin yet again at my first victory. Then I pulled back and enjoyed the moment at just being able to look down at all that perfection that was mine to explore. But he must have been getting impatient waiting for something to happen as he growled,

"Is there any reason nothing is happening?" I rolled my lips before breaking into a large grin. Then I placed both my hands on his chest and swung my leg over his body, holding myself above him on my knees so I could get closer to his face. I saw his muscles tense as I lowered myself to kiss down his jawline. Then I whispered,

"My rules this time, handsome...so shut up and let me play." I bit playfully at his lobe making him growl again and this time he was fisting the top of the pillow above his head, looking near pained. My reaction to this was a chuckle before licking at his neck.

"Word of warning, sweetheart, I have my limits here," he informed me as I started kissing down his chest and I stopped to look up at him, to see him cheating by watching me beneath hooded lids. So, I told him,

"Mmm, let's try and have fun finding them then, yeah… *now close your fucking eyes, Vampire,*" I demanded forcefully making his chest rumble again and his fists turn white-knuckled. But amazingly, he did as I ordered and closed his eyes. So, I sat back, lifting up the large T-shirt I wore enough that it put my bare sex to his crotch, and I grinned when I heard him suck in a breath.

Good, it was about time I was the one igniting these types of responses from him. Man, but I don't think I had ever felt so powerful in all my life. In fact, if anyone had ever told me a month ago that I would be here teasing this big bad Vampire King, then I would have told them to pop whatever bubble they were trying to put me in!

But then, as sexual as I was tempted to take this, I had a goal and I was sticking to it. So, I trailed my fingers down the centre of his defined pecs and in between the line of his abs watching as he tensed as I did so. I also looked to see the strain on his face as he was trying hard not to react the way I knew he really wanted to. Well, if he thought this was as hard as it was gonna get, then it was time to pop his own bubble.

It was time to drive my point home, I thought, which was why I went for the sweet spot and with his arms still raised above his head, it left his sides wide open. This naturally became my new target and the next destination for my featherlight fingertips to trail up. Now this was when I knew I was really hitting the mark, as the further I danced my fingers up the side of his torso, the harder he tried to fight it. I knew this when he suddenly crossed his legs and actually bit his lip!

Holy shit, he really was ticklish, I knew this the second he started squirming more beneath me, soon shaking his head as if this would help, but the closer I got to under his arms, was when he finally lost it. Suddenly I hit my mark and he burst out laughing hysterically!

Gods above, but I swear I had never heard anything like it!

Of course, I had heard Lucius laughing before but not

like this. Not so carefree and lighthearted. He sounded years younger and acted like someone so full of fun and full of life. The way he strained his neck, putting his head back to the pillows as he let it all go and I ended up half wrestling him just so I could keep it going. I pinned him down, in a way I knew would at least work for a short time, as his untamed laughter was preventing him from stopping me as he couldn't concentrate.

In the end we were both laughing so hard, that even I had tears in my eyes. But then finally he managed to get the upper hand by holding at least one of my hands at bay. Then, still laughing, he rolled me under him and with stunning grey/blue eyes gleaming with hilarity, smiling down at me, he cupped my cheek before telling me softly,

"So yes, I'm ticklish." But then the answer to this didn't come from either of us. No, instead it came from a scream of excitement at the doorway in the form of a high pitched screech.

One I knew well…

"Gods be damned bollocks hockey, I freakin donkey balls knew it!"

CHAPTER SEVEN

PEACE SHATTERED AT BLOOD ROCK

"Oh, my Gods, Aunty Pip!" I shouted on an excited squeal that matched her own, only I was now poking my head around my half-naked boyfriend.

"The one and only bitch from Down Under Hell without a BBQ!" she said and as usual not making much sense to anyone but herself. Lucius groaned and then lowered his head to my chest, muttering,

"And just like that, peace is but a thing of the past," making her giggle.

"Master boss man, how you rocking…or should I say *who* you be rocking, as it looks like my baby doll I see? I mean finally! Jeez, dude, but how long does it take a guy to ask the girl they love out on a date…?"

"Winifred!" Suddenly my Uncle Adam's voice came echoing from beyond the door, making Lucius mutter,

"Thank the Devil."

"I told you to wait, my love...*and for good reason, Winnie,*" Adam said, adding this last part the second he saw us both half-naked in bed together.

"Yeah, I know but I wanted to surprise them and just look at them about to have sex, don't they look sooo cute together...just darling really." I closed my eyes, and this time hid my face in Lucius' neck and groaned,

"Oh, by the Gods, kill me now." This made Lucius chuckle and say,

"Only if we make it a pact, call it a double suicide and end up in some bed in Hell together." I smirked up at him.

"Well, you do have the castle there...I'm sure it must have a bed in it somewhere," I commented making him grin before telling me firmly,

"It does indeed." Then without moving his eyes from mine he said,

"Adam, if you would be so kind."

"Sire, but of course," Adam said with a grin before suddenly flinging his colourful little wife over his shoulder and turning on his heel to walk out the door. All the while my Aunty was grinning at us but then said in a panic,

"You'd better not be long before setting loose those Vampy swimmers, Mister, as I brought gifts...toodles!" Then we heard her complaining from a distance,

"Oi, aren't you forgetting something, Mr Immortal... OWW...there you go, Tiger, GRRR!" she said after Adam had slapped her ass, something I was actually used to seeing considering it was a normal sight when growing up, or at least once I had become an adult.

To say that my Aunty was a little unusual was a planet-sized understatement and we were not talking about one of the small ones, we were talking a freakin' gas giant here. Hell, but she ate unusual for breakfast and I was pretty sure that if there was a possible way to shit out rainbows and belch glitter then Pip would have accomplished it!

In fact, I couldn't actually imagine a period of time in history where Pip would have been forced to live through before the invention of neon colours and glitter. But first, a few things to know about my Aunty Pip, who granted wasn't really my aunt, as she wasn't related. But she was my mum's best friend…this happening shortly after kidnapping mum first. But that was a can of worms while lying under a certain Vampire, I never wanted to open.

She was also hundreds of years old, looked a very young side of twenty, was short and skinny, had green hair with bright pink tips, that in Pip's words had been blue for a donkey's age. She had tattoos everywhere, piercings, and her dress sense could be described as Tank Girl dipped in a vat of sparkly rainbow paint. Oh, and it just so happened that she was married to the most powerful being in existence who only she could control if he ever went…well, *Hulk like*. Ironic really when his vessel looked more like a handsome GQ model who could have been, A, an accountant, B, an Architect, or C, a professor dressed in tweed.

But despite how different they were, one thing was blindingly obvious, Adam utterly adored his wife. Actually, besotted wasn't even a strong enough word to describe how they were with each other. It was cute and the older I got, it became apparent that Pip's quirks weren't restricted to just what she wore and how she spoke. So, this was why hearing him smacking her ass and her giggling like a loon, wasn't exactly a surprise.

"Der Frieden in Blutfelsen brach erneut zusammen," Lucius muttered in German, and I translated it as 'Peace shattered at... *something*... once more.' So I asked,

"What is Blutfelsen?" Lucius looked back at me as this grumble had been said in my neck.

"It means 'Blood Rock', it is the name of my castle here," he said making me smile before saying,

"But of course, it is. So, didn't fancy Castle Greyskull, huh?" I mocked which kind of failed seeing as he probably had no clue what I was talking about. But then he flipped me again, so now I was lying on top of him, and I felt his hand run up the back of my legs to my bare ass, before he said,

"I might be blonde but even I wouldn't look hot with that haircut and fur underpants, now what I can do with my sword is another matter." Then he squeezed my cheeks and pressed me into his very obvious erection.

"Holy shit, you know who He-Man is!?" Lucius laughed before saying,

"Are you joking, you might have had twenty-seven years with her but I've had hundreds, so trust me, there is shit I know thanks to that Imp that I couldn't forget even if I wanted to...oh, and trust me, sweetheart, *I want to.*" At this I burst out laughing before pushing back his blonde hair and kissing his stubbled jaw. But then his fingers brushed through my hair seconds before it made a fist, which became the start of him taking over, doing so by bringing my lips back to his own. So that this time he could kiss me deep, delicious and most importantly... *undisturbed.*

"Now, I like this one, it feels like an invitation," Lucius commented in my ear later, only it wasn't quiet enough for no-one else to hear as Pip started laughing like a madwoman.

This was in reference to the light blue T-shirt I was now holding up which had two yellow pots over the breasts and the childish lettering written underneath that said,

'Come Play with My Doh'

But let's rewind a little and explain where this all began in what was to become the latest addition to my funny shirt collection that Pip had heard needed replenishing. This had been because the majority of my others had become a patchwork comforter that Lucius had commissioned to be made for me after realising how upset I was at seeing them in pieces...*after the bastards has trashed my flat,* I thought with a clench of my teeth.

So, Pip being Pip, had brought gifts as she always did, with the theme being T-shirts. I had already opened one that was blue with white lettering across the chest that said,

'I do yoga because punching people
is frowned upon.

And in small print at the bottom...

Plus
Save the Pandas, because those lazy
Bastards won't save themselves'

Now, when I had informed her that I didn't do yoga, she nodded at the tight pants I was wearing and said, "No, only ten minutes ago it sounded like you did, without the trademark *Fae Fart.*"

Then she giggled when I placed my forehead to Lucius' shoulder and said, "Just how Hellish is that castle of yours, and could I get away with sunscreen without burning my skin?" He smirked down at me and said,

"I like you hot." I laughed which turned into a groan when Pip said,

"Oh, just look, honeypie bean baby, aren't they uber adorable and when I say uber, I mean the kind that knows where they are going." I looked to Adam and saw him mouth the words 'sorry, honey' at me making me hide my smile so as not to get him into trouble with his wife.

We were all currently sat down in the living space after I realised it was actually the next day and that Lucius had dressed me in his T-shirt after I had passed out in his office. Not that it was any wonder because if the crazy night of running from demonic wolves in the forest and crazy-ass witches wasn't going to do it, then amazing sex twice with Lucius certainly would. And that's not even mentioning stupid reckless mistakes like slitting my own hand open and unlocking stupid ass boxes!

Something else I had learned was that after Adam had taken his wife from the room, keeping her busy long enough to give his master time with his girlfriend, was that Lucius hadn't slept. No, instead he had stayed awake and spent the entire time watching over me to ensure nothing else could happen. This I had found out after getting out of the shower and finding Lucius getting dressed in what was now our shared dressing room.

Of course, this question only managed to make it past my lips after I had first spent time perving on him for a good few minutes. A show of watching him zipping up a pair of charcoal jeans, feeding a belt through the loops, buckling it up, and then adding a burgundy shirt that he folded to his forearms.

Unfortunately for me, he had known I had been there the whole time even though he had his back to me, for he said,

"Now, if you would like me to take it all off again only for you to enjoy seconds, I will happily oblige...*for a fee of course.*" This last part was said when looking over his shoulder at me and telling me with his leisurely gaze down the length of me in just my short towel, exactly what that fee would be. So, I smirked before telling him,

"You know what, I'm good thanks but hey, you can hold this for me if you like." Then I whipped off my wet towel and threw it at him before turning to my side of the room, smiling when he growled playfully. But of course, this wasn't the end of it as I shrieked the moment I felt myself being spun around and pressed up against my hanging clothes, which enveloped our bodies in material as we kissed.

Naturally, it took me a lot longer than Lucius to get ready, this was mainly down to him making me come with his fingers and his tongue in my mouth tasting my screams. And later also ended with me being smacked on the ass and being told to meet him down in the living room when I was...and I quote, *'finished hiding temptation from him'*.

And hiding that temptation resulted in me picking the tightest clothes I could find just to get a reaction out of him, something I accomplished in five seconds flat, as the moment he saw my black yoga pants that had cut out mesh-covered stripes across the thighs, ones I had matched with a baggy black mesh top that fell off my shoulder, his eyes grew heated. It was also a top that knotted high at my waist, so it showed off my belly and one that was definitely becoming more toned thanks to all the sex I was having.

Hell, maybe my Aunty Pip was right, maybe I could class it as yoga!

But his reaction to this was to look at me over his shoulder after I had shouted down to them that I was grabbing a drink. He slowly scanned the length of me before casually standing. Then he tugged down his shirt before excusing himself, releasing his phoenix wings and suddenly landing behind me in the thirty seconds quicker than it would have taken had he used the stairs. After this he had my hips in his hands and pushed me up against the counter I was stood facing. Then he growled in my ear in a rough tone,

"You do understand the meaning of temptation, don't you, pet?" I grinned down at the countertop and said,

"I do have some basic conception of it, yes...Helen of Troy comes to mind."

"Fuck Helen of Troy! For starters, she didn't have these fucking pants I now want to tear off you..." he said fervently.

"I think you did that already," I reminded him after pushing my glasses up my nose and swallowing hard.

"...with my fucking teeth," he whispered in my ear on a demonic growl that turned me on even more when at the same time he yanked me back hard against the proof of his words.

"Now don't keep me waiting, pet, for I want this ass in my lap in under a minute, for that is all my patience will allow," he said before parting ways with his demanding words. So, what did I do, I made the quickest tea, thanks to the boiling water tap next to the sink and was down there in forty-five seconds. Something I discovered the moment he reached up, took my hot mug from me, before yanking me down into his lap and telling me,

"Good girl…fifteen seconds to spare."

"Mmm, then I'd better use them wisely," I replied before quickly kissing him, something he deepened the moment I tried to take my mug off him. But he held it from my reach, plucked my glasses off and kissed me properly this time, despite our company. Something I was starting to get used to with Lucius as my boyfriend, as it was clear if he wanted something, then he just took it regardless of who was around to witness it. Then, once he had finished, he gave me back my glasses as he had done this morning. This was before I had grabbed a shower, doing so after first cleaning them for me. I don't know why, but I found the gesture both sweet and sexy in that charming and old fashioned gentlemanly way that seemed ingrained in Lucius.

Something I secretly adored.

But then there was very little about Lucius that I didn't adore. Like the way he seemed to always want to touch me and it made me question if this was down to all those years he watched me from afar and never allowed himself the temptation to do so. I mean, even Pip had commented,

'…but how long does it take a guy to ask the girl they love out on a date…?' which would suggest that even she knew how he felt about me all that time ago. Had he forbidden her from saying anything to me? It would seem so, along with forbidding a lot of Lucius' past to be discussed around me. I could even claim my mother as being someone who also kept things from me about his past, as it had been

many a time before my heart was broken that I had asked her about him. Obviously, she had told me very little and after that first night I set foot in Transfusion, I had always put it down to their past together. Now, however, I wasn't so sure. Could there be more to it? Could my mum have known how he felt about me or that I was always destined to be his Chosen One?

This only managed to bombard my mind with questions. One of which felt like the ultimate question when thinking about my family and that was one member's reaction to finding out who I was now dating,

What was my Dad going to say?

Or should I say…

What would he do to Lucius?

CHAPTER EIGHT

THE ONLY DAY THAT MATTERS

After this little internal freak out of mine, one that I was surprised I managed to get away with without the hawk eyes of Lucius suspecting anything was wrong with me, the afternoon continued. And it continued, but not without its hiccups. As there was one thing about Pip that you could have bet money on and that was her mouth getting her into trouble. In fact, the term should have been 'letting the Pip out of the bag'.

And this day was no different, other than the fact that what she let slip proved that... *yes, it was.*

This began when yet another gift was being thrust at me.

"Open, this one! This one is saucy awesomeballs!" Pip shouted excitedly as she passed me one wrapped in kid's dinosaur wrapping paper. I had also opened one gift where the T-shirt had been the wrapping and the inside was a ball of screwed up gift paper. Another had been wrapped in a blue wig of hair and tied with a bow by what would have been the fringe at the front.

But this unique way of wrapping wasn't new to me as growing up and being spoiled by Pip on a daily basis, then that came with some imaginative extras. Like the time she made me a Lego picture frame wrapped in printed paper covered with pictures of her pulling silly faces.

Of course, that was Pip, and she was utterly perfect! Because, as silly, funny and quirky as she was, she was equally kind, generous, sweet and one of the most loving people I had ever known. She never failed to make me smile, even during my darkest times. And this also meant that as the only person who knew exactly what I had been through after Lucius had broken my heart all that time ago, then she had been the only one there able to offer me comfort.

But then how anyone could not love Pip was beyond my comprehension, as just looking at her now she brought sunshine and rainbows into your life. She was currently wearing a pair of black tights that were covered in colourful graffiti underneath a pair of cut off frayed denim shorts that were spray-painted with arrows pointing to the crack of her bum and the words, 'Adam was here!' by the waistband.

But this wasn't all Pip was wearing as she combined this look with a set of jewellery made from plastic bread clips of different colours, graffiti makeup over her eyes that said 'love' over one eye and 'Adam' across the other. But I think overall the craziest accessory was the knitted beanie hat she wore over her curly pigtails, one that made it look as though she was wearing a green zombie brain. Sneakers covered in smiling sloths completed the look along with the green T-shirt she wore. One that was just begging for someone to ask the obvious question written on the front.

Of course, I had asked the question moments after being allowed to shift off Lucius' lap to sit next to him. Her T-shirt had the words,

'Ask me about my Tit Rex'

So, I did and my answer had been in true Pip fashion, as she had took hold of the hem and lifted it over her head to reveal her own laughing face printed on the underneath that now covered her actual face. Then, on her bra were two T Rex faces roaring at each other. Of course, I snorted in my tea, making Lucius laugh more at me than at Pip's funny dress sense.

"I would have got you one but didn't think Mr Macho el Fango would have been too pleased with you showing your tits to everyone…Lucky for me Adam's rule is no nipplet sniplets and we're all gravy on the dress front!" Pip informed us making Lucius shift the arm he had resting at the back of my shoulders so now he could band it across my breasts. This naturally ended up putting me snug into his chest, one that vibrated as he let his demon growl playfully,

"Mine."

"I most certainly understand that sentiment, my Lord… even if achieving its good behaviour is a constant battle," Adam commented making Pip suddenly throw herself in his lap as she raised a tipped toe in the air and dramatically threw the back of her hand to her forehead.

"Oh, but Heavens to Betsy, Mr Ambrogetti, just how do

you survive me?" Adam smirked down at his wife currently draped across him before growling down at her,

"With a firm hand, my dear." Then she patted his cheek and said,

"Hell yeah, you do, you sexy pussy slapping tease, you!" Naturally this ended with me twisting in Lucius' hold so I could face him and say,

"So, this castle in Hell, does it have running water so I can wash my hair?" Lucius smirked down at me and replied,

"I'll even pack the soap."

It had been after this that Pip had jumped up from my uncle's lap and grabbed the 'Dinosaur' present, telling me impatiently,

"Quick, quickie, quick...open it already." Clearly in true Pip fashion, she was getting so excited and doing what she normally did when she thought I was taking too long to open gifts. This was quickly coming over to help me, tearing into it with gusto. This revealed a tank top with a picture of a rhino covered in rainbow war paint stood over a pile of bones with the line written underneath,

'My Battle Unicorn eats dinosaurs for breakfast'

"Oh my Gods, Pip, I think this is my favourite one so far!" I shouted grabbing her to me and hugging her.

"Whoa, don't squash my Tit Rexes...ahh, who am I kidding, squash 'em all you want, Little Toot!" she said now purposely smushing her chest into mine and making me giggle. Little Toot was a nickname she'd had for me for as long as I could remember. This was because she called my mother Toots, or should I say, a catalogue sized variation of Toots. Anything from Tootsypop, to Tootie pants, Tootmaster, Tootanator, Big Titty Toots and the list went on. So, on this front I considered myself lucky I just got Little Toot and very few variations and thankfully none that included my tits.

However, I did get some nerdy nicknames instead, due to my cult sci-fi following.

"Now no ripping these, you feelin' me, mighty fang master?" Pip said sending a pointed and knowing look to Lucius who simply grinned at her and said,

"I promise nothing, little squeak." This was when I elbowed him in the ribs combining it with a pointed look. Then I said,

"Of course he will behave, Pip." And boy did this make her grin. Especially when Lucius made a show of rubbing his ribs and faking an 'Oww' down at me which made me roll my eyes. But all the while I couldn't help but notice the soft looks my Aunt and Uncle were giving us, as if they had been waiting just as long as we had for this moment to happen.

Pip handed me a pyramid of boxes, starting with a huge one on the bottom. It was even wrapped up like one, with limestone blocks printed on paper and used as wrapping. If the wrapping paper didn't exist in the world with what my aunt wanted on it, then she would simply make it herself.

I tore into them, with Pip's help, and squealed in delight the second I saw all the Lego boxes, with the biggest one being the Harry Potter Hogwarts Castle, complete with the light set so you could illuminate inside once it was made.

The other sets were a combination of things I loved, like the London skyline model set that included the London Eye, Big Ben, and Tower Bridge. This, Pip told me, was so I didn't miss home whilst I was here. I thanked her but didn't miss the look Lucius gave her, making me question what it had been about. Was it because she had reminded me of my flat back in London or because she had said, 'whilst here' implying that I wasn't going to stay?

I didn't know either way and at that moment, I didn't think it was the best time to ask, so I decided to just let it go. And in doing so I then found the next Lego box pyramid was all Star Wars themed. This included a Yoda, Obi-Wan's Hut, complete with a Princess Leia Hologram. And last was Anakin's Podracer which had a cute little Padmé Amidala included.

"Seriously, is it like my birthday and I forgot about it or something?" I asked after thanking them both for all my gifts.

"Well no, but funny you mention it as it is… *what?* Why are you both shaking your head at me…oh yeah, now I remember…it's err…my rabbit's birthday…yeah, that's it…" Pip said this after obviously taking some unspoken hint not to spill the beans which, like I said, Pip usually did…*and often.*

"You don't have a rabbit," I said giving her a pointed look.

"Yes, I do," she argued, making me put down all the boxes piled on my lap so I could fold my arms.

"Alright, so what its name?"

"Fresh Prince," she said making me scoff a laugh.

"You named your pet rabbit Fresh Prince?"

"Yeah, why not, he's black, cute and handsome." At this I burst out laughing and asked,

"Then why not just call him Will Smith?"

"Because that name is boring, now Fresh Prince, he should totally own that shit and change his name by deed poll, I think Mr Prince has a nice ring to it and my furry Fresh just loves it when I call him that, especially when I want him to eat his pizza and wear his little booties." I gave her a sceptical look side on before turning to Adam and saying,

"There is no rabbit is there?"

"Damn it! What gave me away?" she asked looking back at her husband who was dressed in brown slacks, white shirt, and red tie under a ribbed sweater the colour of oatmeal. His dark hair was perfectly groomed and his thick black glasses were currently being pushed up his nose as he answered,

"I believe it was the pizza and booties, Sweetpea."

"Bum chins, I knew I went too far," she said throwing her arms down and making me laugh before telling her,

"So come on, fess up." This time she shot a panicked look to Lucius. This was before I noted the subtle nod Lucius gave Adam prompting him to suddenly get up, lean down with no effort at all and pick his wife from the floor, where she was sitting cross-legged like a child. He hooked her around the waist with one arm letting her dangle there by his side like a limp log with four branches dangling. Then he said,

"It's time to unwrap my own present…My Lord, little Bean," he said, calling me the nickname he'd had for me since I was a kid. A comment that made his dangling wife's eyes go soft, as she framed her own face with her hands as if her elbows were now resting on an imaginary table.

"Aww, just look honey, she's all grown up and now sexing it up with Lordy man…oh wait, did you say unwrap me…does this mean I get to wear my big bow underwear first, cause you tore the last six sets and this one has cute little pink love hearts." Adam just groaned before swinging her around so she was now fully in his arms, before he said,

"Only if you promise not to chain me to the bed again."

"I promise nothing!" she said with an over-exaggerated evil laugh, which in turn made my own head fall into my palm and moan,

"Oh, Gods."

Lucius, on the other hand, was just chuckling next to me, well that was until Pip obviously had one thing left to say. As, despite Adam's effort to obviously save his master from his wife's outburst, Pip shouted,

"Enjoy the rest of your birthday, Luc but don't step on the Lego 'cause that shit hurts…Laters, Toodlepip!" I heard Adam and Lucius both groan and my head whipped around to turn accusing eyes on my boyfriend. Something I did to the sound of Pip sighing out a loud,

"Ooops, My Bad." Which was like Pip's personal catchphrase in life.

"And you were so close," she added as Adam walked away with her, referring to her husband nearly saving the moment and obviously that moment was Lucius not wanting me to know it was his birthday.

"That I was, my Pretty Pickle…that I was," Adam said and doing so in such a way that it sounded as if this was the story of his life and being married to Pip, then it so was.

I, on the other hand, naturally ignored Lucius' groan, as he looked up to the Gods and muttered a French curse. But despite how sexy he sounded when speaking French, I still folded my arms and said,

"So, it's your birthday, uh?" My tone spoke for itself and screamed how annoyed I was.

"Yes, and one that, thanks to that pissed off look you're now sporting, will be anything but *Happy.*" Oh, he wanted pissed off, then he would get pissed off alright! So, I got to my feet and snapped,

"Damn straight!" Then I stormed off in the direction of the bedroom, doing so now to the sound of him groaning behind me, muttering something about irrational women. Meanwhile, I was just about to reach the arched doorway leading into his bedroom when suddenly I was faced with Lucius landing in front of me. Doing so now with his massive flame-coloured wings stretched out to the sides causing me to come to a standstill.

Now this was the thing with wings, as no matter how many times I had seen them, they were always going to be an awe-inspiring sight to behold when they were shown to you. And despite growing up with seeing them regularly throughout my life, it was still the same as watching a sunrise over water…*it was a beauty that never faded.*

It was still a sight you stopped to stare at and appreciate its magnificence. My favourite pair of wings had always been my uncle Vincent's. As King of the Angels he had, without a doubt, the most stunning pair of blinding white wings. It was a sight that, even as a child, I used to suck in a quick breath the moment they appeared. But then he would see my reaction, smirk down at me and then he would swing me up onto his back. Once there I would be nestled between them as he took flight, giving me a wild ride, one I adored.

Oh, he might be an Angel, but he was most definitely the one who taught me about speed, and I swear my mother would have had a heart attack if she'd known half of the stuff we did together whenever her and dad weren't around. This naturally including teaching me to ride a bike with some skill. Obviously, I adored my uncle Vinnie.

But despite these fond memories, when seeing Lucius' fire wings, then I most definitely had a new favourite, as they were nothing short of incredible. Like Heaven and Hell merged into one, which was exactly how they came to be… well, if the stories were true. As like all things Lucius, I didn't have a fucking clue!

Including knowing that today was his birthday! Which was why I suddenly turned my back on him and was about to walk away. Something that ended in a scream of fright the moment I was suddenly surrounded by a cocoon of feathers.

"Ahh!" I shouted and I had no choice but to stop my escape as I felt Lucius step up to my back and wrap his arms around me so he could tell me his own thoughts.

"Listen to me now when I tell you that the only day that mattered to me…wasn't the day of my rebirth, but it was…" He paused before he put his lips to my ear and whispered the only words that seemed to matter,

"…was the day I first met you."

CHAPTER NINE

NOT LETTING GO OF EVERYTHING

"*Was the day I first met you.*"

Naturally hearing this and my heart melted despite the fold of my arms and holding my whole body tense.

"I still feel like I know nothing about you," I told him firmly, because it was true.

"The way I feel about you is all that should matter," he told me and I knew on some level this was true. But then again, was it fair that the same could be said about me when he knew everything already? Which was why I turned around to face him, and said,

"And what about me, can you say the same when you seem to know everything about me?" He looked thoughtful for a moment before admitting,

"I make it my business to know everything about you for a reason, pet," he admitted quickly.

"And that is?"

"Because you were mine long before you stepped through the doors of Transfusion," was his firm answer and again it had me frowning in question and the reason I then told him,

"That makes no sense."

"To you it may not do but to me, it makes all the sense in my world."

"But I…" I started to say but he interrupted me with his firm reply,

"But nothing. You are my Chosen One, which means it is my job to protect you and with protecting you also comes the responsibility to find out all there is to know about all aspects of your life," he said and I could tell with his tone that in his mind he believed this to be an absolute and brook no argument decision, even though this wasn't exactly a fair exchange.

"And in return, I get what exactly, to become the very last person here that knows it's your damn birthday?!" I snapped because shit yeah, I was angry. At this his gaze softened before he took hold of one of my folded arms and used it to pull me into him, something I tried to resist at first. But then resisting Lucius was easier said than done and not just because he was hotter than all of Hell. Not even because with his feathers on glorious view he looked even more masterful than usual. No, this time it was all down to those eyes of his. Those steel grey-blue eyes that seemed to pierce right through to my soul and command it with ease.

But to this he added gentle coaxing with that velvet tone of his and I knew I couldn't hold myself rigid any longer.

"Come here, sweetheart." Naturally I allowed my body to be pulled forward until he had his arms wrapped around

me and as if it was on instinct, he also wrapped his feathers tighter around us until they curled back behind him. So, with my cheek pressed to his chest, listening to his heart beating beneath the flesh, he placed his leather-clad hand to the back of my head to hold me there. Then he gave me something I knew was huge for a man like Lucius. For a being with his power and authority, well I knew the next three words to be uttered from his perfect lips weren't ones heard often.

"I am sorry." After hearing this I put pressure on his hand and looked up at him to find him looking down at me.

"You should have told me," I said, this time without the pissed off tone as he had just apologized. But I wanted it confirmed, what he was saying sorry for, something he did when he agreed,

"I should have told you."

"Does this mean you are willing to share more of yourself with me?" I asked and to make my point, I took his leather hand and held it between us, something he didn't allow for long as I already knew he didn't like it being touched. This was when he closed his eyes and looked pained for a moment before his wings retracted back fully and he walked away from me. I had to admit that it hurt, and I was suddenly regretting pushing, wishing I could have the moment back instead.

But it was too late, for I knew I had lost that side of him for the moment as he turned his back on me. I even closed my eyes, expecting to feel the brush of his feathers as he was so close, I was surprised when the force of them didn't knock me over. But when nothing happened, I opened my eyes to find them gone, disappearing before they could touch me.

"That is not something I wish to share," he told me and I

swallowed down the pain and said something stupid. Something I knew would only cause more of it, more that I would potentially choke on.

"But *she* knows…doesn't she?" At this he whipped back around to face me, the shock of my words plain to see.

"Really Amelia, you think it wise to throw the past in my face, one I cannot change, for yes, she knows as *she* was fucking there!" he snapped, emphasising the mention of her as I had done. Which was why I withdrew back a step and looked away, hating that there would forever be a void between us and hating even more so that it was one forged with my mother's name at its core.

"I don't understand why you fixate on the past when it is only the present that matters to me." he stated and I tried to swallow down the tears I could feel rising, but then the moment I braved a look back at him, there they were, warping my vision under a veil of pain.

Tears that were rising up, as this was when I knew I would have to admit the reason why.

"Because Lucius, it means that she will forever get a part of you that I never will…a part that you refuse to give me," I said as the first tear fell and so he couldn't see them anymore, I walked away, going to the kitchen, as right then it seemed like the only safe place to be. And even though I most definitely could have done with something stronger than a cup of tea, like a bottle of vodka, I started to make myself a cup. Of course, I got clumsy and ended up burning myself on the fancy hot tap, as I wasn't concentrating.

"Oww FUCK!" I screamed, throwing the cup in the sink and smashing it in my anger.

"Ah!"

"Easy." Lucius' voice soothed behind me after I yelled in surprise at suddenly finding him holding me. Then he took my hand in his and looked at the red blotch over my forefinger and knuckle. After this he turned me to face him and raised my hand to his lips. One that was held in his as a gentleman would before he could kiss the back of a hand in a welcoming gesture. This was so he could blow over the skin and I marvelled at the cold air that came from between his lips, near-freezing the skin instantly so it wouldn't blister. It also quickly took out the sting.

Then he picked me up, taking me in his arms and holding me close to his chest and doing it so quickly that we were halfway to the bedroom when I asked,

"What are you doing?"

"I am reminding you of the only part of me that no other has ever owned but you," he said firmly as he walked with purpose through the arched doorway into his room.

"And what part is that?" I asked as he placed me down on the bed, because right in that moment my vulnerable mind needed to hear his words. Words he soon gave me along with the proof of them.

"A heart you taught to beat once more," he whispered over my lips after following me down and kissing me. A move that made me start to melt beneath him. And just like that, my insecurities fled me and evaporated into nothing. Because he was right. Why shouldn't I trust in his words, for I was the one there in his bed and I was the one he confessed his love for.

Then what was holding me back?

A question that seemed to die the moment I felt his hands running up my body, taking one leg with him so he could hook it over his backside. Then he started to do something different and that was pull back from the kiss, now using his other hand to push my hair back from my face. After this he simply stared down at me, doing so for so long I started squirming.

"You really have no idea, do you?" he asked as he swiped a thumb across my recently kissed lips.

"I just want to know you," I replied in a quiet voice trying to keep the tremble from it. His reaction to this was to place his forehead to mine and whisper back,

"You know me...you know me unlike any other." After this he ran his nose down the length of my face until he was at my neck, then he breathed me in deeply before his lips at my ear whispered,

"When will you understand that?" I swallowed hard asking myself the same. When would I finally allow myself to trust it...*to trust all of this?*

"I want to, I really do but..."

"But?" he asked now pulling back and looking down at me, scanning the length of my face.

"But it's hard when I always feel as if there is something you're hiding from me," I told him and the second I saw that demonic glow flash in his eyes like a heartbeat, I had no choice but to question why yet again? Was it because there was something and I was right or was it because he was shocked that I would think so?

I would never know because suddenly I was in his arms and before he could crush his lips to mine, he growled down at me,

"I am yours!"

After this no more words were needed as he made love to

me, making me feel whole again the moment we were connected. But even feeling whole didn't mean that it wasn't surrounded by the only question that mattered…

How long would I feel whole before that secret he kept from me was revealed and tore away what was mine?

How long until this overflowing heart started to rupture and crack from the force of what it could be?

How long did I have of this perfection?

How long did I have of being his whole world before the real truth of it ripped us apart?

For something was coming, I could feel it. And the only question that remained was…

Would we both survive it?

Survive it with…

Our hearts intact?

CHAPTER TEN

JEALOUSY KNOWS EVERYTHING

"So come on, pet, time to show me what was in the box," Lucius said sometime later as making love to me wasn't something that a man like Lucius did quickly. Something that four orgasms later me and my body were more than grateful for.

"I hid it," I told him playfully as I walked my fingers up his chest and flicked his nose. We were both now back in the living space after we had showered together, a place I had received my last orgasm and he'd had his after I found myself on my knees before him. I was starting to learn quickly that Lucius wasn't the only one who liked receiving oral sex as I most definitely got off on giving it to him. I think this was because of the power switch that would always happen, for even with his fisted hand buried in my hair holding my mouth tight to his erection, I still felt that level of sexual control over him.

But I knew this was down to the reactions I had the

power to ignite from him. The strain in both his muscles and voice drove me on to needing more from him. It made me want to push his limits and see what happened when he finally snapped. The crack in the tiles and stone was usually a good indication of being able to achieve this. As whenever I heard the sound of destruction echoing in the space above my head, I would find myself smiling around his cock.

Needless to say, that it didn't take much effort from his side before I was crying out as my orgasm ripped through me, doing so to the taste of him still coating my tongue after swallowing as much of him down as I could manage. But it wasn't just the act itself or the control I felt, it was also the way he handled me. The rough way he would hold me down on his length, forcing me to take it, liking it when I gagged around him before he released me. Then would come a gentle, tender caress at my jaw, stroking and praising me for being his good girl.

Just like when I felt the sharp tug of my hair before he soothed it back, telling me just what it was that I did to him. Gifting me with his thoughts, how beautiful he thought I looked as I worked so hard to please him and please him I did. But above all, it was when I was finished cleaning every last drop that he would hook my chin and guide me back to my feet so he could then whisper passionately,

"No other...no other ever made me feel so fucking good!" Then he kissed me, tasting himself on my tongue as he took command of my mouth. Gods, but it was so unbelievably hot when he did that and it was his words that I came to. That and his fingers playing me like an instrument of his.

"My perfect little doll to play with and fuck!" He called me and that was when I screamed his name.

"Yes...Yes, yes... *Lucius!*"

My masterful lover.

And well, here we were on the other end of that hot, erotic spectrum being gentle and playful with each other, on the sofa acting like teenagers. Kissing, tickling, and tugging at each other's clothes as though we couldn't get enough of each other...and really, we couldn't. But then I guess years of wanting and waiting for each other would do that to you.

However, as usual, the reality bit into our dreams for I knew he had put it off for as long as he could. After all, he was obligated to his people. And to be honest, I had been surprised he hadn't demanded to see it the second I had confessed in his office what I had done the night before.

"I am not surprised. Now, as to where my cunning little mortal decided to hide it this time is the question I really want to know," he said after I told him what I had done with the box and the map I'd found. Which meant I replied with a great big grin and a teasing tone,

"Oh, that's easy, as I hid it where no one would dare to go." At this he raised a brow in question, combined with the twitch of his lips. So, I leaned further into him and whispered in his ear...

"Under your bed."

At this he burst out laughing and it was both a sight and sound I absolutely adored.

"But of course, you did, you brave girl, you," he teased back with a snap of his teeth at me, making me giggle. After this I quickly went to the bedroom and as I said, retrieved the box and map from under the bed.

At the time, when looking for a hiding place, I had found a recess on the underside of the frame that the mattress sat on. One that was just the right size to stash it and well, without a man-sized vault to throw it in, then it was the best I could come up with so quickly.

By the time I made it back to the living space I found Lucius holding up one of the funny t-shirts my aunt had given me, now shaking his head a little, clearly amused at the idea of me wearing it.

"You can borrow it whenever you want, no need to be shy, just ask," I said with a smirk, making his lips twitch as he fought a grin.

"I was just testing the material to see how easy it will tear, after all, I wouldn't want to get into trouble and receive another elbow to my ribs," he said rubbing his side, and making me scoff,

"Baby...hey!" This ended on a squeal as he suddenly grabbed me, fisting my top and yanking me hard into his lap, which I ungracefully fell into. Thankfully, he hadn't torn the clothes I'd had on earlier so I was back to wearing them again, as it wasn't as if they had lasted long since putting them on. Lucius, however, was in his usual jeans and T-shirt combo, complete with one hand concealed in a glove.

"Now these fucking pants of yours, now those I will happily tear from your skin…shit, but I will have to peel them off you… *near fucking indecent."* He muttered this last part to himself making me laugh before slapping the box to his chest and saying,

"Here, this should help in keeping your mind from my ass."

"Fucking apocalypse couldn't keep my mind from that

temptation, sweetheart." I swear this nearly had me melting at his feet. Gods, but the way he made me feel, it was addictive...*he was addictive.*

But instead of blushing like a schoolgirl, I kept myself composed and acted cool by replying,

"Well, it's close enough." This I said before unfolding the map and placing it on the coffee table for him to see.

"Right, well..." Lucius said with a frown and I agreed,

"Yep, can anyone say vague, I mean it tells us nothing!" He granted me a look and could see for himself the frustration I was feeling even without the dramatic tone.

"And you say your blood opened this?" he asked now picking up the box and examining its inside like I had done.

"Not exactly, like I said in your office, it was your blood that did it." He raised his eyes to mine for a second responding with a short,

"Right."

"So, what do we do with it, and I mean clearly whatever warning was carved to the front was either misread or was put there as a ruse to prevent the wrong person from getting that map," I told him to which he replied,

"And the right person would be?" he asked making a good point, so I threw my hands up in the air and said,

"Oh, I don't know! It beats me, but if I were to guess, then I would say anyone who doesn't want to inflict genocide by eliminating an entire race." Lucius' eyes glanced at me before he said,

"It will take more than this fucking box for me to go down, have no worry about that," he commented on a growl.

"Then do you think that whoever wants this box has no clue what's inside like we did, but are just hoping it holds a way to bring you down?" I asked obviously giving him food for thought.

"Well, unless this map leads to something that has that power, then I see little use as to what they could do with it. Even if it told us more than just some crudely painted mountains and little else." It was true, as unless the map was used for something else then, like Lucius, I failed to see what use it could be, even in the wrong hands.

"Well, my best guess is that no one knows what is inside or how to open it…unless…" I let the sentence trail off and Lucius dropped the box and turned now to face me.

"Unless?"

"Well, the witch, I was just thinking about what she had said, as though she knew about my blood, so maybe she always knew that it was the key." Okay, in hindsight saying this to Lucius and basically pointing out that I could again be in danger, giving them a new reason to want to kidnap me, wasn't the smartest thing to do.

"Fuck!" Lucius said getting to his feet and walking away dragging a hand through his hair after cursing venomously.

"But then I could be wrong," I said in an unsure voice making him snap back around to face me,

"And just how often does that happen, sweetheart?" he asked in a sarcastic tone.

"Okay, well not often no, but still, I was wrong about the warning."

"Yes, and you were also the only one smart enough to fucking open it in the first place, so I can't say that offers me much comfort here, Amelia." I released a deep sigh and then said,

"Well, surely being here I am safe…" He raised a brow at

me considering what had happened last night, which was why I quickly continued,

"...I mean unless the witch comes back, which can't happen again...*right?*" I said making him bark out another curse, only this time in a language I couldn't detect.

"Lucius?" I said his name again to try and get him to answer me.

"I have my own witch," he stated making me try for humour,

"Did you buy her on eBay?" Lucius obviously didn't appreciate my joking side as he just said my name in that, 'it's time to be serious now' sort of way.

"Amelia."

"Fine, so you were saying, you have a witch...*one you didn't get like a mail-order bride,*" I muttered this last part to myself, one he heard but instead chose not to comment on other than with a silent roll of his eyes.

"Nesteemia arrived early this morning and since her arrival I have had her casting wards against it happening again," he told me with the anger still lingering in his tone.

"Okay, so what about any rogues, can they get inside the castle without you knowing?" I asked trying to cover all bases and in doing so, hoping that with his answer it would end up reinforcing the fact that *I was safe*, despite the little setback last night.

"No, they cannot," he said in a stern voice as though he was seething and on the edge. So, I decided it was time to try and tame the beast. So, I got up from the sofa and walked over to him, wrapping my arms around him from behind, telling him softly,

"Then, honey, there is nothing to worry about."

"Where you are concerned there is always something to worry about," he replied and I had to say it hurt and I took the hit to my ego for sure.

"Gee, thanks," I said letting my arms fall as I stepped away from him, to the sound of his frustrated growl. But then as I turned, he grabbed the top of my arm and stopped me.

"Be reasonable, Amelia, and think back to why I would say this…"

"Lucius, don't…"

"Car chases, break ins, near beaten, a blade to your fucking throat, getting yourself kidnapped, shot at, jumping from fucking helicopters, attacked by hellhounds and now this latest attempt at trying to give me a fucking heart attack, you opened the box when I specifically asked you only to examine it and nothing more!" he shouted down at me and unfortunately ending this accurate account by pointing to the evidence on the table. Meaning that I had no choice but to look guilty because he was right, it had been one thing after another and each one could have easily gotten me killed. So, of course I could see his point. I could also understand why he was still furious with me. Because if it was the other way around and he had been the one continually putting himself in danger by making bad decisions, then yeah, I would be pissed too.

"Okay, so I know I haven't made good decisions," I admitted.

"No?" he questioned sarcastically, one I wisely ignored,

"But I am here and yes, as risky as they were, you also have to admit that it is thanks to some of those rash decisions I made that I am." At this he scoffed,

"Dumb fucking luck, honey!" To which I yanked myself

free and squared up to him, getting in his face and pointing at his chest now being up on my tiptoes, to gain a little more height.

"Now you listen to me, Mister, if it wasn't for some of those *foolish* decisions, then just imagine where I could be right now, as you could be receiving my body parts in the fucking mail!" I shouted, referring back to jumping out of the helicopter.

"I would never let that happen!" he roared and I roared back,

"Yeah, well neither did I! I made my choice and whether you like it or not, it was my fucking call to make and I made it!"

"And last night when opening that box, you think that too was your call to make, or maybe it was mine!?" he snapped back and I knew he was right with that one but right now there was no way I was going to back down, so I yelled,

"Yes, well seeing as it seems to keep being my ass that is getting targeted because of that bloody thing, then I would claim that I had a bloody big say on the matter!"

"Fuck me, Amelia, but I can see the appeal in how your father wanted to just lock your mother up in a fucking tower!" he said after turning away from me and raking an angry hand across his neck.

"Yeah and why is that?!" I questioned back sarcastically, hating the turn this argument had taken.

"Because both of you are fucking infuriatingly stubborn and seem to make it a fucking hobby of getting yourselves in danger!" he said now turning back to me in time to see me taking a step back as if I had been struck.

"Don't fucking compare me to my mother, Lucius. Don't

you fucking dare!" On his hearing this, I knew instantly I had gone too far, or should I say, he had for forcing me into shouting it. I knew this when he took a menacing step towards me and said,

"Have you even listened to a single word I have said to you?!" I looked away hating that once again we were back to this and I wanted to slap myself for not being able to just let it the fuck go!

"Oh no you don't, you don't get to say that to me and hide away from the consequences of it! Now fucking look at me!" he hissed angrily, so, I looked, quickly slapping his hand away when he went to hook my chin to force the issue.

"Is that really what you think I am doing here, spending my fucking time comparing you both and seeing which one of you I prefer?!" he snapped on a barely contained growl of anger and I had to say his words cut like the fucking blade to my palm all over again, only this time it would have been drawn across my heart.

"You were the one who said we were both stubborn!" I argued even though I knew it was weak.

"Yes, and you also share that trait with half my fucking council but if I had said Caspian's name then would it have made you related? No, it fucking wouldn't have, so I picked words that were relevant and you fucking know it!" This time when I looked away, he did grab my chin and force me back to see the rage burning in his eyes.

"I will not be made to feel guilty every time I mention the woman who brought you into this world, despite what you foolishly believe I feel for her..."

"Through your own doing!" I snapped interrupting him.

"Yes, and I have more than paid my dues for that fucking

RISE OF ASHES

mistake, only years of suffering obviously are not enough for you!"

"That's not true!" I shouted back at him.

"No? Then why is it you feel the need at every fucking chance you get to lash out at me with a jealous venom, when I am already forced to suffocate on my regret!? What do you want to hear from me, for clearly, being buried inside of you and telling you I fucking love you isn't enough, so what more is it you want from me, Amelia!?" he shouted and this time I couldn't help the tears from falling as his words tore me apart. So, I pulled myself from him and walked away standing there now with my back to him as I thought about what it was I wanted. All those years of being made to feel as though I was the only one left in the dark. The shadow of my own mother who knew everything there was to know about a man who was supposed to be destined for me!

About the man I was obsessed with, the one I loved and continued to love even through all the heartache I suffered. The man I had long ago declared to be my Chosen One, even if he had shunned the claim.

But here he was and yet it still felt as though I had no right to have him.

No right to his heart.

"Alright Lucius, do you know what I want?" I started, making him growl,

"What is it you want!?"

"I want to know what happened to you, the full story on how you became a Vampire…I want to know what happened that day you turned…I want to know how you turned my mother into a Vampire and tied her life to yours, when I wish only I could make that claim!" I said now going on to add each new demand with every step closer to him I took,

"I want to know why your hand is always covered and why you don't like me touching it. I want to know why you pushed me away for as long as you did. I want to know why you and my father became enemies all those years ago and why you kidnapped my mother... and I hate myself for it, Lucius, I really do but I can't stop myself from needing to know what happened between you and my mother that made you so close..." I finished, now with tears streaming down my face. But even as I swiped angrily at them, I continued for there was one last thing left to say,

"I want to know everything, Lucius...everything that I should know, but more importantly, I want to know..."

"Everything that she knows."

CHAPTER ELEVEN

INSANE

Everything she knew.

And there it was. The real root of my problem. The snake of jealousy that sickened me to my poisoned core because I loved her like no other. Because how could I do anything but love my mother. My wonderful dear mother, who was flawless in my eyes. Who loved me unconditionally and gave me everything I ever needed, both as a child and an adult. And yet, I continued to let the jealousy consume me. I let it eat away at me as it festered deep within my mind, always there trying to convince me that I wasn't good enough…

That I wasn't ever going to be as good as her.

And yet none of this was her fault. In fact, it was no-one's fault. It was just a triangle of mistrust with my mother innocently sat at the top with no clue that the two points underneath her were about to crumble. And really, it felt like just a case of when it would all start collapsing around me.

Because we were all joined and there was nothing any one of us could do about it but simply let go.

Lucius had let go.

My mother had let go.

I had not.

I was the only one clinging on to my doubts. I knew this. I knew I was the only one with the problem here and because of it, it was now Lucius' problem as well.

"Oh Amelia, is that what you think, that because she knows more of my past that it makes her more important to me?" he asked, all anger vanished from his tone but instead pity had taken its place. One I hated the sound of. Which was why I slumped down on the sofa and raised up my hands before slapping them to my knees, telling him,

"I don't know!"

"Amelia." Gods, but even the way he said my name, made my heart ache.

"I don't know, I just...Lucius, I just don't know anymore!" I said again, hating the tears that wouldn't stop. Hating myself for letting it get to me as deeply as it did. Hating that he didn't trust me enough with his past and hating the jealousy I felt that he trusted another with it.

I heard him sigh before coming over to kneel in front of me. Then he took hold of my face, wiping my tears with his thumbs and raising it to look up at him.

"Gods, so fucking beautiful," he whispered after sucking in a breath. It was a reaction I didn't need to question as I remembered him saying once that when I cried he found me beautiful and I didn't know if that was a good thing or not, as it felt more like the latter.

"You have it all wrong, my Khuba...*my heart,*" he told

me after a deep sigh, and I frowned back at him silently asking him how.

"I don't care what Keira knows about my past and the reason for this is because she is not the one I care about."

"What do you mean, I don't understand?" He took a deep breath at my question and told me,

"I care about what you know because I care about what you will think of me. The things I keep from you, I do for a reason, sweetheart, and it is far from why you think it is." At this my eyes got wide and I could barely speak. Had I really got this so wrong? All this time, had I believed it was because he was closer to my mother than he felt with me? That he trusted her with his past more than he did with me because of some sort of bond I foolishly believed them to have?

Which is why I asked, after first rubbing my nose,

"Because you don't trust me?"

"No and yes, but not in the way you think," he answered making me frown and just as I started to open my mouth to ask why, he got there first,

"I don't trust you not to run from me." At this I jerked my head back a little in surprise.

"You think if I knew your past then I would leave you?" I said in that accusing tone that said it all. He shook his head a little and then pushed his hair back in frustration before telling me,

"Parts of it yes, and right now, it is not a chance I am willing to take. As for Keira, she can know whatever the fuck she wants as she is not my Chosen One. Nor is she the woman I love and am trying to keep in my bed." Okay, so I had to say it felt amazing to hear the words I'd always longed to hear. But then, discovering the root of why he kept his past from me, I couldn't help but utter,

"You're afraid?" At this he suddenly stood up and turned his back

to me before he turned suddenly, slashing a hand to his side as he snapped,

"Of course, I fucking am!"

"Lucius, you shouldn't think that I would leave just because…"

"Shouldn't I?!" he snapped, interrupting me before continuing on,

"Let's turn back the clock should we, Amelia. You have spent more time trying to run from me than you have convincing me of all the reasons why you want to stay. *I, however,* have spent more of my time trying to convince you of why you should, and I doubt any stories of my past would have aided me in that goal," he said making his point, but he wasn't the only one with a point to make.

"Well, did you ever consider that had my own fears been laid to rest that I wouldn't have needed any convincing on whether or not to stay, seeing as my biggest fear here is waking up one day and finding you no longer want me around." At this he actually snarled at me.

"Are you fucking shitting me!?"

"No, of course I am not shitting you!" I snapped standing and putting my hands on my hips.

"Fucking Gods, you're insane if you think that would ever fucking happen!"

"Don't fucking shout at me!" I shouted.

"I will damn well shout at you when you are acting insane!" he yelled back, making me growl this time,

"Don't call me insane!" This is when his lips twitched and he stepped right up to me and said slowly, over pronouncing each syllable,

"IN fucking SANE!" So, I did the only thing that came naturally to me when we were fighting, I pulled my hand back and slapped him right across the face. This made it snap to the side with the force and I knew it was a good hit as my palm stung like a slap-happy bastard! But then as he slowly turned his face back to me, with eyes now glowing like the sun, I had no choice but to give in to my next impulse. A desperate one as I grabbed his face and frantically pulled him to me for a desperate kiss!

Lucius quickly took over and he started this by grabbing my ass and lifting me so my legs could wrap around his waist, holding me to him as though he never wanted to let me go! And the second he pulled back, he growled down at me,

"Fucking insane if you think I would ever let you go!" Then he kissed me again and the next time I broke away was to tell him,

"You make me fucking crazy!" Then I kissed him back, trying to take over the kiss by running my hands through his hair and yanking him hard back to me. He growled when I started nipping at his bottom lip before biting it, tempted to see what he would do if I bit it hard enough to make it bleed.

"You haven't fucking seen crazy yet, sweetheart!" he told me before suddenly letting his fangs grow and burying them into my neck making me cry out at the pain, sinking into a pleasure so great, I made it a mission for him to hold onto me as I shuddered in his hold, screaming out my orgasm in seconds, for it was one he hadn't let me build up to.

No, instead it just exploded from me in such a way that I felt as if I was being pushed off a cliff and barely caught in time before hitting the bottom. He only took enough blood from me for the time it took me to finish shaking from my release, as he was soon pulling his fangs from my flesh, licking the holes he had made to stop the bleed. Then, before I had time to question why, he let a demonic talon grow, still making me silently question what he was planning? Something I didn't have to question for long. No, not when he stabbed the tip into his own neck, letting the blood pour down his T-shirt, soaking the material so it stuck to his skin like black water.

Then he started to guide me to his neck and demanded,

"Then we fall into madness together."

It was all the prompting I needed, as I lowered my lips to his neck, licking up the dripping blood, whispering,

"Always together." I latched onto him and drank him down, sucking harder and harder the more he moaned out as his own pleasure built. And just like mine, it didn't take long before he was roaring out his own release, only when he did it, he actually began to fall. Something he did first on a stumbled step, getting us to the sofa just in time so we both landed on something soft. He also turned his body at the last second so I wasn't the one to take all his weight but instead, he took mine.

After this he turned his head to the side and closed his eyes as I finished sucking his blood, his essence he offered to me like a gift of life.

The gift of him.

For we were connected. We always would be and now it was time for me to trust in that. So, I pulled my lips back and watched as the moment I did he allowed his body to heal itself as the hole he made started to close. I licked around the wound, as it fused shut, cleaning him of his blood, making him hold me tighter to him with arms wrapped around my back.

I lifted my head and when I did, he turned back to face me, opening his eyes that had now shimmered back to blueish steel.

"So, I might have over-acted slightly," I admitted sheepishly making him burst out laughing before hugging me to him and holding me tighter still.

"And I am learning that when you do, it usually ends well," he replied making me roll my eyes, despite still grinning. Then I looked down at the very obvious wet patch between us and said,

"And messy," to which he grinned big and replied,

"Another plus." Then he sat us up and told me to wait for him whilst he left me to clean up and seeing as his T-shirt was covered in blood and his pants were now... well, sticky...then I couldn't help but smirk when he did. Of course, it also gave me the time I needed to go back over all the things he had said to me. And to be honest, even as explosive as the conversation was, it was one I would forever be thankful for. Obviously, the outcome had been a mind-blowing bonus but it actually came secondary to what I had learned.

Because now I knew that I had gotten it all wrong before. The reason he kept things from me wasn't what I feared. That my mother meant more to him on that level, or that he trusted her more. No, I had totally let my own insecurities infect that part of my mind, warping his reality into my dramatic fiction.

But no more.

This was to be my vow from now on. I was going to let go of the past, one he had proved to me time and time again didn't mean to him what I had let myself believe it did. What I had convinced myself it did.

No, now I would trust him and that meant also trusting him to tell me his past when he was ready to. Something I decided I would no longer try and push for. Because it was me he needed to learn to trust, not the other way round. Meaning, there were only two ways to do this. The first was to try and stop being insane and the second was just as simple…

To stop running.

By the time Lucius came back, after his second shower of the day, his hair was deliciously wet and curling at the edges, making me want to run my fingers through it. But then at the time I would have only ended up probably getting mayo on it as I was making us both a sandwich. Or at least I was ready to make him one as I didn't actually know what he liked.

So, whilst waving a knife in my hand, one I'd used to cut my own in half, I shouted,

"Any preference on your sandwich?" He paused, took in the sight of me and then continued to walk my way and only answered me after plucking the knife from my hand, telling me,

"Yes, one without my Chosen One's blood in it please." I smirked and replied,

"Ah, okay, so you've turned vegetarian then." This joke enticed a silent, 'Ha, Ha' from him whilst looking down at me, which made me giggle back.

"I will eat whatever you make me, so long as you do so without wielding a knife around in the air like a madman," he told my neck after brushing back the loose parts of my hair and kissing it. I pushed my glasses up and said in a haughty tone,

"Excuse me, but I think you have seen what I can do with a knife."

"Exactly my point, I fear for my life, pet," he replied, making me roll my eyes even if it was pretty funny. Then he patted me on my ass and walked away, after making a show of dropping the big knife I had been using, in the sink with a clatter.

"Party pooper!" I complained, making him chuckle as he made his way back down to the living room. Meanwhile, I finished making our turkey sandwiches and carried them down to the same level catching myself when I nearly stumbled. Of course, Lucius saw it and flinched, making an action as if he was going to try and catch me. Even though I would have been too far away. Then he started mumbling something about railings and getting them installed, throwing a few F words in there for good measure.

"You know, I am starting to think that is your favourite word."

"What can I say, since you stepped through my doors, it has become increasingly more popular in my vocabulary."

This time I mouthed the same mocking silent action back at him, 'Ha, Ha' making him grin.

"Well, it is German in its origin, meaning to strike, so it had its uses even then," he replied casually, leaning an arm along the back of the sofa.

"But of course, well here you go my bloodthirsty, slap-happy Vamp, get your cursing fangs around this," I said handing him the plate and making him scoff, before telling me,

"Carry on with that smart mouth, woman, and you will see what else I can wrap my cursing fangs around."

"I think you already did that, handsome," I said, taking a big bite of my sandwich, crunching the lettuce and making a show of it by moaning. But then I nearly ended up choking on it when I felt his gloved hand run up the inside of my leg the moment he added,

"Mmm, I remember the first time…maybe I will save your clit for dessert."

"Maybe I should go and swap this for a nice big T bone steak. You know, for all the extra iron I will need as it seems like I might need it." He laughed before biting into his own sandwich and saying,

"I think you're safe, my little Šemšā, at least for a while yet."

After this we ate our lunch and I braved asking him about his birthday, something I was kind of freaking out about seeing as I hadn't known anything about it. Which meant that naturally, I hadn't bought him anything.

But he told me that it was a tradition his people insisted on celebrating, as it was more about the rebirth of his kind. He went on to explain that before he was turned and declared

King of all Vampires that the race was more like wild, uncontrollable beasts, demons that roamed the Earth, bloodthirsty and without purpose. Mindless creatures that needed more than a king and leadership, they needed a whole new bloodline to purify them.

Lucius had been that new beginning.

This was something he called 'The Cleansing', a time he didn't want to go into as I guessed that it was basically how it sounded. Something that no doubt ended in a lot of bloodshed for those that didn't particularly want to be 'cleansed' and found themselves with a new ruler on a throne that never used to be there. But even as accurate as my assumption may be, I still made a mental note to ask Pip about it when I saw her next.

Yet, despite how gruesome this event was, it obviously wasn't a period in Vampire history that Lucius' race looked badly on. Not if it was a time they wished to celebrate every year, for I guess it marked the new chapter in the lives of those who gladly chose to kneel to their new master. Chose to accept his blood in exchange for tying their soul and pledging their loyalty to Lucius in a way that usually meant death if ever such a vow was broken.

Naturally, this led on to a question about the rogues, which he explained that usually it was only the weak that could pull away from his control as the strongest of his kind relied more heavily on his command. But now, with the aid of what would seem like the most powerful witch on Earth, then Lucius didn't know the full extent of who could break away from his rule.

Either way, the celebration was to continue as a show of strength among his kind, despite what had happened the night before or the attack on his club. As Lucius refused to let anything or anyone make him appear weak in front of his people.

And Lucius was anything but weak.

However, for me this was when I learned which part I was to play in this show of strength of his and it included one excitable Imp by the name of Pip. One who showed up with a long black garment bag in one hand, shopping bags in the other and screaming in excitement as the dreaded words, both myself and my mother always loathed to hear…

"It's human dress-up time!"

CHAPTER TWELVE

IT'S GONNA BE A BALL

"Holy shit, Pip, does it really need to be that tight!?" I complained the second she placed her small foot at the base of my spine and used it as leverage to tighten the corseted part of my dress.

"Just a little wiggle more," she said and I could see in the mirror in front of me that she had her tongue sticking out of her mouth on one side and was squinting at all the laces at my back as if she was trying to solve a maths equation.

But let's rewind a moment as of course, our afternoon didn't begin there. No, it began after Pip announced her presence by declaring me her doll for the next five torturous hours.

I had, of course, turned my accusing eyes to Lucius who merely grinned back at me and said,

"Will you be my date?"

Well, what else could I say to that? As of course, I would

be his date. How I felt about doing so dressed up in a massive ballgown, and in a room full of Vampires all celebrating immortal life, I didn't quite know. But how I felt about being brushed, pinned, pulled, yanked and painted, I did know and that was...*exhausted.*

However, at least I got to spend some quality time with my aunt, who I had missed, as in *a lot.* So, I had swallowed every complaint...well, almost all of them, and let her do her thing. I had at least been thankful to learn that Lucius had appointed Liessa with the job of buying my outfit. Which meant it wasn't a dress that was either edible, painted, growing, playing music or something that could melt, as these were all types of dresses I had witnessed Pip wearing at least one point in my life.

My dress, however, was a stunning blood-red gown that was a flowing skirt of satin, with lots of body thanks to the layers and layers of underskirts giving it shape. The top was corseted, so it pulled in tight at the waist and every inch was encrusted in sparkling red crystals. It also fell off the shoulders in a classic style, with a sweetheart neckline that gave my breasts a great shape, or should I say my ample looking cleavage a great shape.

The matching satin shoes had a wicked heel that could have been classed as a weapon as they were bone-thin and made from metal painted red. I was, however, a little worried about them and just hoped that I could walk in them without falling. It was a shame really as they were mainly hidden thanks to the bottom part of the dress that trailed along the floor and included a substantial train at the back of the skirt. One that I had to keep gathering up in my arms to walk anywhere.

But I had to say, where my Aunty Pip really excelled was when doing my hair, as it looked stunning and more importantly, in an understated way that didn't include fairy lights like she had originally wanted to add. No, instead it had been curled and put up in a loose style so the curls cascaded down my back at different lengths so it gave the style volume. At the front a few curls framed my face and at one side a large and beautiful blood-red velvet rose edged in black had been pinned to the body of curls.

As for my makeup, I had insisted on doing that myself, especially when I saw her box of makeup that looked like a melted down rainbow that had been coughed on by a glitter monster. Thankfully, she hadn't taken offence to this but instead just laughed it off and giggled when I kissed her cheek.

So, I had left her to do her own makeup and hair whilst I did my face. Well, that was one thing about having all my stuff here as it didn't take me long to find the box of makeup I had. Meaning I had no problems creating the smoky, sultry look I thought would go with the dress Pip had shown me.

Once I had finished, I faced myself in the mirror where I found a woman staring back at me that I barely recognised. My eyes were silver fading into black at the sides that brushed along the thick eyeliner flicks that Pip had been a master at helping me with. This managed to make my bright blue eyes look a few shades darker thanks to the darker shades chosen. Of course, it also helped with them being framed by thick curling lashes that I had inherited from my mother.

Combined with this were highlights at my cheekbones and dark red lipstick that was supposed to be kiss-proof, and pretty much stain my lips for at least twenty-four hours. Now, as for being kiss-proof, I had never put it to the test before but was hoping tonight was the night.

"Wowzers, that poor bastard won't know what has hit him!" Pip said making me blush and try to hide my smile.

"Aren't you getting in your dress yet?" I asked her, looking around for it but just at that moment my uncle walked in carrying what I assumed was her dress, even though it looked more like a giant birdcage. He was also dressed in a black and white suit in 1800's style that made him look like Jane Austin's Mr Darcy.

"Why kind sir, I be thanking you later with the many accomplishments my mouth doth claim," Pip said skipping up to her husband and kissing him on the cheek before snatching her dress from him and I didn't even bat an eyelid at her comment as I was far too used to it over the years. To say that Pip was a highly sexual being would have been a Great Pyramid of Giza sized understatement.

I walked over to my uncle and kissed him on the cheek, noting one point for the lipstick that stayed put.

"You're looking very dashing, Uncle." He gave me a warm grin and said,

"And you are looking very beautiful, my niece. My King is blessed and will indeed be most pleased." At this I blushed before the moment was added to when Pip smacked my ass and said,

"I know right! Isn't she just the sexiest biatch you ever saw?" I laughed, moving out of the way when Adam grabbed his wife, spun her around before pulling her firmly to his chest, then he whispered in her ear from behind,

"No, for I must claim that title for my wife, for it is a sin to lie... now hurry, my little Winnie, for I am hungry for the sight once more." Then he bit her neck playfully and let her go, winking at me before leaving us to continue getting ready in Lucius' bedroom. Something Pip continued to remind me was now mine too. This was after she basically swooned back on the bed dramatically after Adam's affectionate display before leaving.

"Pip, can I ask you about something?"

"Anything you want, sugar bumkins," she answered as she completely stripped naked with only her tattoos on show. The beautiful soft colours of the earth and sky covered her entire arm thanks to the tattooed sleeve. I remember as I child I used to sit on her lap and trace the clouds in the sky with my little fingertips, which used to make her giggle.

But this wasn't the only one as she also had Adam's name written in different languages on different parts of her body, some surrounded in hearts, some flowers, some rainbow thorns. They were different fonts, everything from calligraphy, graffiti, ornate script to that of a typewriter. It was cute the obvious love they had for each other and it made me wonder how Lucius would feel if I ever had a tattoo with his name on my body?

But this wasn't my question.

"Lucius mentioned something about the celebration, about how it was his rebirth and..."

"When he became Kingy almighty...yeah, those were some fun days to hear about," she said as she started to shimmy the large dress type thing up her waist.

"You remember it?"

"Well, yeah, I mean I wasn't topside then or one of his turned, but I heard it was a freakin' bloody riot!" she answered with a grin.

"So, you know all about the cleansing?" I asked making her grin fade as she turned from the mirror to look at me.

"Alright Faebear, I guess this is the part where Luc mentioned some stuff to you, told you only half of it and kept anything grizzly out of it. Which basically means the cleansing was the big bad end of days for any smuckadoodle who didn't want to kneel to Lucius when he was declared as King. Which didn't end so great for them as they, Queen of Heartsed it...did that make sense?"

"Erh...all but the last word, which doesn't exist," I replied making her tap a pointed fingernail to her painted lips. Nails that were painted as chess pieces, with her thumbs covered in a tower of rings that covered her whole digit. Her lips were also painted black with a white liner to match the black and white theme she was going within her strange outfit.

"What I am saying is, it was an 'Off with their heads' moment and Loverboy was the one swinging the axe."

"Oh, Gods."

"Yup and let's just say a lot of heads rolled that day, but that's the thing with rogues, mindless little buggers who didn't exactly welcome change and those pesky little rules Luc was throwing their way. But then, I guess standing at a small mountain of heads covered in blood with a fecking big sword was one way to make a statement to all who crossed him."

"Tell me you are exaggerating here?" I asked after my mouth had finished its fish impression.

"Nope, if anything I am probably underestimating it to save your delicate human mind, but I kept telling him that he needed to get that shit painted as a portrait to hang in the main hall, then no biatches would say shit to him! Those bastard rogues need reminding of that day, that's for damn surely bob!" Pip said after finally twisting and jumping her little body into the strange dress. One that made her tight corkscrew curls bounce. Her hair had been plaited tight to her head all on one side with the rest of it all flicked over to the other side. A large blackbird skull was fixed at the point the curls were at their thickest.

"I can't imagine him like that," I muttered as I walked over to her to help her zip up the back after she first lifted up her small breasts, doing this so what she did have was now mainly on show, minus the nipples, which we had learned recently was an Adam 'no, no' rule.

"Watcha think?" she said, stepping back and twirling in the contraption as that was the best way to describe it. If I was even to try and describe it, I would have said it was a cross between demonic armour and a leather birdcage. The top part was made up from strips of leather crisscrossed over her torso wrapping around to shoulder sections that looked like two black horns rising up to the height of the top of her head.

The skirt, however, completely exposed her legs beneath as it was just connected straps of leather that looked like a giant spider's web. One that was stiff at the top by her waist so it was moulded outwards in the shape of a bell ballgown, with a giant black bow at the front. The ribbon also reached the floor along with the rest of the skirt.

"Wowzers, I think Holy Hole in a Doughnut, Batman,

you look amazing!" I said in 'Pipspeak' making her jump up and down clapping at herself.

"YEY! It's Piptastic isn't it, but wait, I forgot the light-up dead birds, now where did I put them...tada, here they are!" She grabbed a clear bag full of bones from a holdall and raised them above her head in one of those, 'Tada, I found them, aren't I great!' poses.

"Erm...please tell me they aren't what I think they are?"

"You mean plastic bird skeletons painted with glitter and with little battery-powered disco balls glued inside their ribcages...yeah?" she asked, making me rub my forehead as my mind tried to process all she'd just said.

"Erm, no, that wasn't going to be my first guess." Alright, so even on the Pip scale this wasn't exactly the explanation I was expecting her to say.

"You didn't think they were real, did you...? 'Cause eww, Faemymunchkin, that's gross and crazy ass!" she replied looking horrified at the idea and making me want to burst out laughing with the way she scrunched her nose up. But this might have something to do with the black and white feathers she had glued to her face in the shape of a mask, obviously continuing with the bird theme. But also it was the gold beak she had stuck to her nose that made it funny whenever she pulled a face.

She had even framed her lips with tiny little feathers to match. But it was the two gold commando stripes on her cheeks I didn't get, but then again, this was Pip, so getting her choice wasn't a requirement, just accepting her for her, was.

"Okay, so where are they going?" I asked because with Pip nothing was obvious. Then she looked down at her skirt and pointed to the inside. I released a deep sigh and then said to her,

"Any ideas how that is going to happen?" She shrugged her shoulders and said,

"You don't happen to know any Jedis do you?"

"Sweetie, I don't think even Yoda could help with this one," I replied, to which she shrugged her shoulders and said,

"I am good at cocking my leg if that helps." I laughed once, looked down at my big ass dress and said,

"Yeah, it helps."

Ten minutes later and if someone had told me how this evening would start with me sitting under Pip's 'cage spiderweb' skirt just wearing my sexy underwear, tying illusion wire to the wired scaffolding by her hips, that was attached to bird skeleton disco balls, then I wouldn't have called bullshit, no I would have said,

'Why, where is Pip?'

"Erm…I don't think you thought this out, Pip," I said after having no choice but get myself back out of my dress just so I could fit underneath her skirt as no matter how talented she was at 'cocking her leg' even a Russian ballerina wouldn't have managed it.

"Umm, maybe not, but hey, look on the bright side, at least the beastie boys aren't here to see…Uh-oh!" Suddenly I pressed my face in between one of the large sections in her skirt and looked up at her through it and said,

"Uh-oh what?!"

"Three, two, one...*that,*" she said counting down, as in that moment both Adam and Lucius decided now was the time to walk inside the bedroom and what faced them was a sight that would no doubt be burned to their brains and not for any of the right reasons.

"ARGG, DON'T LOOK!"

"CLOSE YOUR EYES!"

Me and Pip both shouted as this was down to a number of reasons. The main one being that neither of us wanted the first time they saw us dressed nice and ready for the ball ruined by the sight that met them now. Mainly me being half-naked, sat under my aunty's cage, hanging stuff with my head next to the crotch of her disco hot pants, which was the underwear she'd chosen to wear.

Lucius' eyes widened at the same time Adam's did as it was obvious this had been the very last sight they'd expected to see. And this shock would have been right along with finding us both dressed as astronauts jumping on the bed and pretending we were on the moon!

But then Lucius must have taken one look at me in my underwear and after allowing three seconds for his eyes to glow heated, he must have then realised another male was in the room as he reacted quickly. And he did this by grabbing the lapel of Adam's jacket, and dragging him out the door, mumbling about how they would meet us down in the hall. This I found shocking and completely irrational seeing as it was Adam, who was pretty much an uncle to me and also madly in love with his wife, who I was currently sat under.

In the end, me and Pip just ended up nearly falling over laughing so hard, which needless to say, also ended with me needing to re-attach half the birds.

And something that was totally worth it!

Sometime later Pip led me down a series of hallways that were all carved cold stone that dripped with damp in some places. All the while I could hear a faint rushing of water that sounded as though I was on the other side of a waterfall. We were also both being escorted to what I was told was the main hall. But seeing as I was yet to be shown around the rest of Lucius' castle, one I'd learned was named Blutfelsen, meaning Blood Rock, then I really had no clue where I was.

Our escort was the growing familiar face of Keto, who Pip told me was actually named Ken Tobias. Which was therefore shortened by taking the first two letters of his names. Something that was his husband Ruto's idea. Apparently, they hadn't known each other long, less than thirty years, which to Pip was like a shake of two lamb's tails at a shindig...*whatever that meant.*

"You know I can hear everything you are saying...right." he said in front of us making me giggle.

"I don't know him that well as he was added to the party after I left for a Tootie sabbatical...although he fills out a suit nicely, don't you think?" she said even though he'd just said that he could hear her, which made me wonder if it was a test, one he passed when he turned around and said,

"Yeah and I heard all about you, missy. Ruto said you're nuts and that we will get on well because I am the gay side of gay, whatever the fuck that is supposed to mean. But now, meeting you and I am digging your style and freaky dress, so I guess now I know why I like you already." At this she swallowed hard, then popped the bubblegum she was chewing and said,

"I think I just had a mini orgasm."

"Pip!" I screeched making Keto chuckle.

"What! It's not like I don't flick the bean just 'cause I am married, besides, just look at him, he looks like freakin Zac Efron for the Gods eat and must like noodles sake!" she said fanning herself and looking down over her neon pink glasses at the length of him. Glasses, I should mention that were minus the lenses being that they were made from a giant curly straw. One she was currently sipping, thanks to the free end being poked into a whisky flask that she told me held a cocktail called Adios Motherfucker.

I had also made the mistake of asking her what was in it, which was rum, vodka, tequila, gin, blue Curacao, sweet and sour mix and 7-Up. Then she had asked me if I wanted any, which I declined, telling her that I didn't fancy spending the night with my head in the toilet, discovering whether or not Lucius was any good at holding my hair back.

Keto winked at her, before continuing on and I rolled my eyes at her antics, knowing that she was just a big flirt and mostly acted this way to get a rise out of my poor uncle. This was because, in her words, 'a naughty world is a fun world that equals getting punished in said world of mine'. I can't say it was going to rival the likes of philosophers Aristotle or Plato of Ancient Greece any time soon but hey, it worked for her. Especially seeing as she had been teasing my poor uncle since the 17th century.

"Hey, are you not putting your lights on yet?" I asked nodding down to her skirt, wondering how she could even walk in it, let alone the crazy heels she wore to match. They were knee-high boots which were made up of leather bones that looked like a rib cage was wrapped around each leg. The heel was a bone spine, with the section over her foot, being what looked like a pelvic bone.

"Nah, I am waiting for just the right time, boo yeah, can't wait to show those bitches!"

"Erm, what bitches?"

"Oh, just the other Vamps that don't like me...but then they are just jelly bellies as they are sour they aren't in the Lucius fold, you know." Keto scoffed at this and held out his fist for her to bump with her own saying,

"Hail fucking Mary up the ass, sister!"

"Oh great, I am so not getting the warm and fuzzies about this night, Pip," I complained making her pop her gum again and then hold out another hand to me and say,

"Wanna suck on my pop ring...it's cherry?" I looked down at the edible jewellery on her finger which was a lollypop shaped like a giant red diamond.

"I'll pass, but thanks."

"You will be fine, I mean those jelly peeps probably won't see you anyways as they will be lost in the crowd somewhere." Keto again scoffed a laugh at this making me frown as if I was missing something and knowing Pip, it would be Ghostbusters Stay Puff man-sized. I also translated that jelly peeps was a nickname for jealous girls. It was that or there was some demon I didn't know about that expelled a jelly-like substance and if this was the case, then no wonder they weren't in the 'Lucius fold' as... *eww*.

"Master wanted to remind you of his orders," Keto said, passing Pip a box as we neared a large pair of double doors.

"Oh panties, I almost forgot!" Pip squealed in excitement before pulling me off to one side and telling me,

"I have to put this on you."

"Why? What is it?" She opened a white box that looked like a standard jewellery box you would get at the store and grabbed something black and lacy before throwing the now empty box over her shoulder.

"Luc got you this, as he didn't want anything that covered…oh, what were the exact words he used…that's it, 'a perfection he owned'…romantic eh?" she said showing me a cut of black lace that was roses, thorns and had holes cut out for the eyes. It was also one that stuck to your skin so it lay completely flat, after she removed the backing. And this was the moment I realised why Pip looked like a bird wearing glasses…

It was a masked ball.

Which was why I let her put it on me, hoping this was the only surprise of the night. I looked to Keto, who was dressed in an embroidered white and gold suit, one gleaming with a double row of gilt buttons making him look very regal. However, he wasn't carrying a mask, so it made me wonder if Ruto had his waiting for him. Aww, maybe they would be matching, as that would be cute, I thought without expressing as much.

"Ready, ladies?" he asked as he stood at the double doors ready to open them both.

"We twin titties were born ready, right mini Toot?" I laughed, somewhat a little nervously before running my hands down my crimson dress, taking a deep breath and nodding. This was Keto's cue to push the doors wide open allowing us to see for ourselves the entire room below.

And what did I find.

Every single inch of it was decorated in black and white. This, of course, also included every single person in it.

Everyone but…

Blood red me.

CHAPTER THIRTEEN

A KING'S CRIMSON CLAIM

"*P*ip!" I whispered her name making her pause and turn to look back at me to ask innocently,

"What?"

"*Erm, don't you think you forgot to mention something kind of big here!*" I hissed, looking around to find everyone on the surrounding balcony that framed the upper level staring at me. Oh, and one that currently had a few hundred people all situated along it.

"Nilly nope, I don't think so," she said with a knowing wink making me growl and her giggle. Of course she bloody knew! She knew that I would be standing there, sticking out in the crowd like a bleeding severed thumb, that's what!

This was because everyone in the room was wearing black and white as it was clearly the theme of the freakin' party, and I was the only one in the whole colossal space wearing red! And speaking of colossal spaces, the great hall was exactly that, nothing short of greatness. In fact, it reminded me of some gothic church, not so dissimilar to Afterlife in that way. Only Afterlife looked more like the night club it was and this looked like some mighty King's hall.

The stone walls were covered in layers of black material that looked like demonic waterfalls thanks to the uplighters focused against them and at each centre a beacon of blood red. One that was the only colour decorating the room…well, other than muggins here who was staring at the sigil, one that I recognised as belonging to Lucius.

But it was in this grand hall that it finally felt like the castle it had been declared to be and right then, I was stood at its entrance, looking down into the belly of Lucius' masterful domain. To be honest, I was astounded by the sight, as you couldn't have found anywhere more different from inside the walls of Transfusion. A club where its interior could be described as gothic, grunge and industrial.

But as for this place, well, this was pure gothic opulence and royal grandeur and it spoke only of the dark Vampire King who owned it. Even the dual staircase warned you of its true nature, with its ornate railings of twisted iron that rose up from the steps like the flames of Hell were trying to reach the Earth.

Even touching them could put you in danger of bleeding before you even made it to the main floor, for massive shards pierced through the smooth parts of the railings making it anything but safe to use. The rest of the room had obviously been decorated for the ball, in what looked to be bleached white thorns, making it look like some deadly fairy-tale was trying to take over the entire room. They were entwined around the massive wrought-iron candelabras, with flames flickering on top of black candles. The thorns also trailed over archways, framing the edge of the room, dance floor and around the stage, as though it was a living creature trying to branch out with deadly fingers.

The whole room was a statement of strength and power, but to me there was also something hauntingly beautiful about it. Like the rustic beauty of its natural stone walls that had been carved smooth in some areas and left deadly and jagged in others. Or the imposing, yet elaborate, chandeliers that hung down from the cathedral ceilings on thick black chains. Each chandelier was the size of a small car, and the round frame held ten winged griffons. All of which were sat with lanterns held in their beaks and with skulls piled at their feet.

It was breath-taking.

And it was freaking me out. Especially seeing as I had no chance of blending in and hoping to find Lucius without the fuss of making an entrance.

"Everyone is wearing black and white, and I look like a bloody steak amongst the wolves!" I snapped after grabbing her arm in a serious way that was needed to keep me from turning around and running. Something I wanted to do in that moment more than anything considering all the people looking at me from the top level.

No one was wearing one particular fashion, as there seemed to be outfits from every era. There were dresses in every style, from A line, to sheath, empire waist, mermaid and ones named the trumpet cut for good reason. This was because the skirts bunched out in lots of ruffles low at the thighs and was a little like the mermaid design but with a lot more umpf. And of course, there was the classic ballgown style that I wore, which most opted for.

But every single one was either black, white or a combination of the two and even if a hint of anything more was added, then it was either gold or silver, nothing more.

The same could also be said for the men, as there were styles of suits that spanned the ages. Even military-style suits were worn, some of which were embellished with weapons. In fact, I think I could see costumes as far back as the 14th century, although most did prefer this side of the 1800's. I also think it was fair to say that nearly all guests were beautiful, or at least they would have been had it not been for the masks they wore.

Many of which were horrifying, or at least might have been. That was if I had not been born a Draven but been the type of person who was frightened of monsters. However, the monsters under my bed were the type that would have been there playing hide and seek with me, before reading me a bedtime story and tucking me in at night.

Demons didn't scare me. Not when you grew up with them being the type that welcomed you with a hug or snuck you handfuls of candy when your parents weren't looking. How could I have been frightened of that? But then, I wasn't claiming that none of them ever affected me and let's just say that I stayed well clear of my father's prison for good reason.

But just like those demons, not every mask worn was gruesome or shocking, as there were also those that were as beautiful as the faces I knew were hidden behind them. Masks made in every material you could think of... leather, lace, metal, ceramic, paper, even glass and all of them handcrafted and moulded to fit their owners perfectly. There were faces of smiles, snarls and sadness, with crowns of feathers, beads, animal ears or horns. And like the costumes worn, not a speck of colour could be found on them.

"You do remember that I am a mortal right, did we really think it wise to dress me like a giant blood bag in a room full of Vamps?" Pip chuckled and said

"Chillax dudette, you're like the safest person in here right now."

"Oh yeah, how do you figure?"

"You're Luc's bed buddy girlfriend of course, so don't sweat it...besides most of them haven't even noticed you yet so you're all...Ooops, spoke too soon!" At this I shot her a panicked look the moment the music suddenly stopped, a song that had been playing from the stage in front of us. It was one that faced the staircase and reminded me of one where you were more likely to be watching some gothic opera. It was framed by great lengths of the same black material that was against the walls, only it was one that had been draped over a massive stone beam above the stage. One that had been carved at the end so it looked over the whole room. It was a massive black and gold gargoyle of a horned demon, with wings that resembled those of Lucius' in his Hellish form. In fact, the similarities between the carving and his demon were a little more than a coincidence.

And speaking of the demonic king in question, suddenly the sea of people below started to part, making a clear path for their master as he came into view. And boy what a masterful sight he was, as even Pip sucked in a breath and muttered,

"Holy wet panties, Batman."

A sentiment I had to agree with.

Lucius, I quickly noted, was the only other one wearing red as it soon became obvious the statement he was making. Telling me he was the reason I was now wearing the same colour choice. And unlike anyone else, he was wearing a typical suit of the 1800's only with a Gothic and royal twist. Basically, if Mr Darcy had been a demon sent to retrieve you for Hell, then the image of Lucius currently walking down the centre of his people towards you would have been it.

He most definitely stood out, that was for sure and by the Gods, I could barely breathe at just the sight of him!

He was wearing a black pair of trousers tucked into high boots, a black shirt with cravat tucked in the high folded neck of a gorgeous double-breasted, tailored jacket. One that was crimson in colour, with black filigree embroidered at the double collar, and down the centre where the jacket was buttoned in parallel lines.

The same design was on the large cuffs that rested at the wrists of black leather gloves, this time covering both hands. At his waist lay multiple belts, holding two black sabres that were slightly different in size, and a dagger at the other, all sheathed and what I was hoping would end up staying that way for the duration of the night.

But despite all of this, it wasn't the most menacing part of his outfit, for that claim was made by the mask he wore. As, unlike like the rest, his was the most intimidating of them all. It was a dark red colour, smattered with a rough black patina, making it look more like a demon's skin. And if words could fully describe it, then I would say it resembled the skull of the devil, with its over-pronounced bone structure of angry features, frowning brows and a pair of horns that rose up towards the ceiling above. These were there to mirror the ones I knew were on his back, only seen when his demon had consumed every ounce of his Angel.

The mask covered his nose and arched down, either side of his jaw, framing his lips and stopping with wicked points. And through this mask I watched as he took in the sight of me, a pair of steel-blue eyes scanning the length of my body, looking sinister with the black paint on his skin, beneath the dark demonic mask he wore. This too, along with his outfit, made it clear who the ruler of this dark world was, for he stood out amongst a sea of black and white, like some crimson soaked God, the blood of life, with the sight of him being nothing short of symbolic. It reminded all around him the very reason they breathed life, one connected to him from the gift of blood he gave them. It was a show of the strength and power he represented…

His powerful rule.

And now there was me.

I knew this the moment he nodded to the band on the stage as its singer suddenly stepped up to the mic and covered it with his hands as he started to sing. It turned out to be a dark, slower rock cover of the song, 'Every breath you take,' by the Police.

And as the lyrics sang out, echoing through the hall to the haunting beat, the words penetrated my very soul, for I knew why Lucius had silently demanded it be played the moment I arrived. For it wasn't only a message, it was a vow singing out as he walked towards me…

'Every breath you take and every move you make

Every bond you break, every step you take, I'll be watching you.

Every single day and every word you say,

Every game you play, every night you stay, I'll be watching you.

Oh, can't you see you belong to me,

How my poor heart aches with every step you take,

Every move you make, and every vow you break,

Every smile you fake, every claim you stake, I'll be watching you.'"

And it was because of this intimidation that I hadn't yet moved a muscle, still stuck at the top of the staircase unable to take my eyes from the sight of him. Like some handsome nightmare who was now raising his hand to me, beckoning me to come to him with the barest flicker of his fingers.

"Go to him, Fae." I heard Pip whisper as obviously this was when I needed to make my move and in all honesty, I was beyond terrified. And just like the words in the song being played said, he watched every single move I made. Every shuddered breath I took. Every unsure single step I took down towards him. He watched me as though he was burning the sight to memory. But despite the way he made me feel, I continued on, knowing that I needed to reach the bottom by the time he reached the last step. As for a man like Lucius, well... *he waited for no-one.*

Not when there was something he wanted.

And this Vampire King had clearly claimed me.

I swear that for the whole descent I couldn't breathe for fear that if I did, I would end up screaming. Because the way the moment was affecting me may have seemed irrational but at the heart of it, I knew why it did. Because it was taking me back to the first time I had ever set foot inside his domain.

Back to when he had been cruel and unfeeling. Back to when I was nothing but a silly little virgin he toyed with. Gods, but he had been intimidating, it was little wonder why I had been scared out of my mind.

But at that moment, then I didn't know why I was so afraid, for I knew at heart that behind that mask was the man I loved. It was the man I knew could be soft and gentle and tender with me. He was the one who could be funny, witty and caring.

But then he was also the man who spoke of my ownership. He was the hand that brought me unspeakable amounts of pleasure, some inflicted by a rough hand at my throat, and the other at my core. He was the masterful figure stood at my back that dished out punishment he deemed I needed. He was the hand that fisted in my hair as he lowered me to my knees before him, ready to swallow all he wanted me to. He was all of those things.

But right then, there was only one of them that stood before me now and that was…

My Master.

And he didn't want to be kept waiting. So, I finally ignored the parted sea of people that, like him, watched every step I took, and finally I made it to the last step before I found myself on the same level as him. And at the same time, he took the very last step needed before bringing him right up to me. This was when the music changed to one far less sinister and instead spoke of what he looked to be feeling. Because now his eyes were no longer eyeing me up like prey but instead as if he was simply in awe of me, scanning down the length of my body and finding himself taking in a sharp breath.

He even lifted a hand to his chest, placing a fist there for a second before that same hand came to my cheek, doing so slowly and above all, lovingly. It was as if he didn't care about the hundreds of people all staring at us, witnessing this moment between us. As no one in that moment would dare try and take it away from him by making a sound. So, even though we were surrounded by life, it was as if not a single person took breath and time stood still for his entire world,

Stood still until finally…*he touched me.*

This was what broke the spell for the moment he did, he was awakened to me being there, as if I suddenly became a reality he could claim. One he wasted no time in doing. Because a second later I was in his arms, taken in his dominant, possessive hold as he kissed me so passionately that I knew I would find myself surprised when it ever ended.

It was by far one of the most profound moments in my entire life, for it was the first time I ever felt the life I had been born into.

The first time I had ever been made to feel like a Princess.

His Princess.

CHAPTER FOURTEEN

A ROSE AMONGST THE THORNS

That kiss.

The one that was nothing short of a statement made to his people, letting them all know who I was to him. It was one that told the entire room that he had claimed me and dared anyone who was suicidal enough to touch what was his. It spoke of ownership, possession, and belonging solely to him and him alone.

It was that type of kiss.

Which was why it was also one that I almost felt myself getting drunk from. His gloved hands were a contrast as one was held tenderly cupping my cheek and the other a firm and unyielding grip at my waist. And what was the rest of the room doing during this blatant display of ownership, they were completely and utterly silent…that's what!

But then his kiss ended, and he silently looked down the length of me, not giving a damn that the entire room was obviously waiting for their King to allow the evening to continue. I watched as he took in every inch of me, taking his time to do so and the moment his eyes became a heated crimson beneath the mask, I blushed. Then, with his hand still to my face, he slid it back so his palm was positioned under my ear against my neck. Then he caressed his thumb along the apple of my cheek over the lace at my face, before telling me,

"Your beauty far surpasses any other the world has to offer, as tonight, you are the only rose amongst the thorns." I sucked in a quick breath as his words seeped into my very soul and took root. His words, along with every inch of him, was beautiful and utterly perfect.

"Lucius…I…you…" This was as far as I got in response to such a compliment and he smirked because of it. So, I swallowed down the lump in my throat and tried again,

"Thank you, you look…*are,* very handsome," I told him making him bow his head to me at the compliment and before I could try and get him to move us from being the centre of attention in the room, he took a step back. Then, after bending at the waist slightly he held out one hand to me and asked,

"May I have this first dance, my Princess?" I ended up rolling my lips inwards and fisting my hand to stop myself from biting my fingertips. As for once it wasn't a nickname spoken in a mocking tone but one of sincerity and for the first time in my life, it was a title I started to feel as being my own. For my hopes of one day being asked to dance by Lucius at a ball was finally happening and my dreams were coming true.

"I would be honoured to," I told him and he granted me a grin before turning back to the stage where I noticed that the singer had gone and instead four men were all sat in a line at the front of the stage. Then Lucius raised up a hand and circled two fingers signalling for them to start. That was when each swung around a black cello from the back of their chairs and dug the end pins into the stage, making an echoing sound around the large open space.

And then they began to play and instantly I knew the song, as most would.

"Phantom of the Opera?" I questioned the moment he had led me into the centre of the dance floor, one framed by a crowd of masked people all staring at us.

"I thought it fitting," he told me with a grin, one that looked handsome and demonic at the same time thanks to his mask.

"And speaking of fitting…" he said before suddenly tugging me closer to him and doing exactly as he said he would, which was fitting me tight to his tall, muscular frame. Then, just as the song started to play out, Lucius started to move me around the dance floor in a waltz with such ease it made me question just how many others had been given the gift of a dance with Lucius.

"Many, but none as precious to me as you, nor half as beautiful," he told me and I couldn't help but ask in shock,

"Are you reading my mind."

"No, I am reading the question in your eyes as, unfortunately for me, my gifts do not extend to a mind such as yours," he answered as he continued to hold me close and swiftly propel us gracefully around the room, which I was only barely keeping up with and was thankful that he had hold of my waist and my hand clasped tightly in his own.

"Trust me when I say that it is a blessing. Oops, sorry." I

said the moment I stepped on his foot, missing my step. However, this just made him grin and the longer I went without speaking, the more it seemed to amuse him.

"You're very quiet, *my Khuba...any reason for that?*" he whispered this last part down at me after first calling me his Love in what I now knew was Sumerian.

"I am trying to concentrate and remember the steps," I told him on a whispered hiss, at the same time looking around the room and seeing every single person following our every move. I wished in that moment that we weren't the only couple dancing so my mistakes wouldn't have been so easy to detect.

"Been a while has it?" he asked with a smirk and laughed when I clenched my teeth and replied with a short,

"Something like that."

"Then hold on, sweetheart, and enjoy the ride," he said suddenly before taking me by the waist and at the crescendo, lifting me up and spinning us both around, making my full skirt flare out majestically around us. I had no other option than to hold onto his shoulders as he did this before he lowered me back to my feet, doing it slowly down the length of his body, his eyes never moving an inch away from mine as he drank in my reaction.

And suddenly, in that moment, it was as if we were the only two people in the room, and as the music continued to echo around us our steps had frozen with our bodies becoming captured and entranced by each other. We were both breathing heavily as we continued to take in the heat of the moment, one that spoke only of each other and our ignited passion that felt sexually charged between us.

Then suddenly the room seeped into darkness and all I

felt was Lucius crush his lips to mine in what this time was a kiss of burning desire. It was one he didn't want to share with the world, and he made it so he didn't have to. As the music still played on, our kiss continued like some hidden love painted in sight of every eye I still knew could see us in the dark. For we weren't surrounded by those of mortals, but those of the Vampires he had sired.

But it didn't matter, for my heart was lost and consumed by this man and in just that one kiss alone, it spoke of our future, our eternity together. As a man like Lucius would never let me go...and I prayed to every God out there that he would never want to.

"La perfection," he uttered down at me in French after first placing his forehead to mine the moment the song ended and all we could hear was our heavy breathing and the beating of our hearts. Then, before I could say anything in return, the lights suddenly came back on and at the same time he swept up my legs and with an arm around my back he picked me up. Doing so now to the sound of the whole room erupting into applause.

He walked over towards the right side of the hall where a raised dais, higher than all the rest, stood waiting for us. It held a large U-shaped seating area, that looked fit for a King. It was black to match the rest of the room's décor, but unlike the rest of the seating in the room, which looked to be Gothic style Chesterfield booths, this was a work of art. It almost looked like a giant throne, as at the centre were three tall arches that reminded me of a church window without the glass. They even resembled highly decorative church benches, that were heavily carved wood and painted with glossy black lacquer. The side sections were designed like the lower backed pews you usually found lining each side of a church, ones that were covered in white thorns, as was most of the hall.

But this wasn't the only reason it stood out as the main part of the room. No, this was down to the fact that the whole piece looked to be consumed by hammered iron flames, as if Hell itself was trying to swallow it whole into a blazing inferno. To say that it was an intimidating sight was an understatement, but then again, it was utterly fitting for the king who was now about to take his place at its centre.

Thankfully, the closer we got the more I could see that, at the very least, it still managed to look comfortable with its black velvet cushioned seat and back. And even the tall metal flames were cleverly incorporated into the design so as those deadly spikes at the back didn't touch its occupants. But the whole effect was made to look as though the people sat there had the power to command Hell itself, and one look at Lucius and I truly believed it was possible.

Lucius took the last few steps up to where he was clearly about to sit and let my legs go, lowering me back to my heels. Then he playfully tapped me under the chin before he turned back to the room, ready to address his people. So naturally, I took a step back to give him this moment without me by his side, but the second I went to move, he snatched my hand and pulled me back to his side.

"You are exactly where you need to be, my Šemšā." Then he raised my hand to his lips to kiss before letting me go, now assured that I wouldn't try to move again.

Then he removed the glove from his right hand with his teeth and with a dramatic draw of his sword, he raised it in the air before sliding his hand down its length slowly. I sucked in air between my teeth, knowing first-hand how painful that was. Yet, looking at Lucius and well, he hadn't even flinched.

But then he slid his sword back into the sheath hanging at his thigh before he raised his bloody hand to the room, fisting it and letting the crimson rivulets travel down his clenched fingers until they dripped onto the pale stone floor.

"This day we celebrate the lifeblood of our people, a rebirth and a day known to us all as the Cleansing and Rise of Ashes!" Lucius' voice boomed across the room as a powerful and masterful presence and each of them respectfully lowered to one knee as a wave of bodies moving as one. It was so profound that even I felt myself about to lower, following them all, but then Lucius snatched my hand once more and tugged on it the second he felt the movement. This was before he glanced down at me over his shoulder,

"You don't ever kneel to me, not unless I command it of you," he whispered before going back to address those now all on the floor, which even included my Aunty Pip and Uncle Adam, even though she was helped to do this by her husband's hand at her waist. This was thanks to the crazy dress that she could barely move in. And they weren't the only ones, as even his council who stood nearby all did the same. Which meant the only ones who weren't currently down on one knee were the only two people wearing red.

Oh yeah, this was Lucius making a statement alright!

"Now all rise and let's get this fucking party started!" Lucius bellowed making everyone do his bidding, as they rose to their feet and started clapping, shouting and basically celebrating the start of the night. Then he tightened his hold on my hand and turned us both around so we could take our seat. Or should I say, I was about to take a seat next to him, when Lucius had other ideas. He tugged on my hand to stop me, meaning that I was left facing him with a questioning look.

Then, without taking his eyes off me, he unbuckled his sword, as obviously it was about to get in the way of his comfort. Something I knew he was going for as he also undid his jacket, revealing a tight fitted waistcoat matching the jacket underneath. Gods almighty, he looked so unbelievably sexy, that I swear my mouth went dry and made it difficult to swallow.

He threw both jacket and sword off to one side before he was ready, making me wonder why I had to wait for him and if it was some kind of proper decorum or something.

However, I wasn't left wondering for long as the second he sat down, he grabbed my hips and pulled me down, so I had no choice but to sit in between his legs. Luckily the seating was huge and wide enough to accommodate both of us. But just to be more comfortable he raised a foot up on the seat, resting an outstretched arm on his knee and lounged back, taking me with him.

"Erm, this doesn't look very Kinglike," I commented, knowing I was tense in his hold making him scoff behind me,

"That show you just witnessed is about as 'Kinglike' as I get, sweetheart...*now relax,*" he said, lifting his mask up his face so it rested on top of his head, showing the slashes of black makeup beneath that reminded me of two thick brush strokes.

"I'm wearing a corset, Lucius, this is about as relaxed as you can get in one," I commented on a laugh. But then it died in my throat the second I felt his gloved hand rise to my pronounced cleavage as he ran his fingers over the curves.

"Mmm, then I thank you for the sacrifice for the sight definitely outweighs the discomfort," he told me with a knowing purr to his voice.

"Ha, for you maybe," I commented dryly.

"Indeed," he agreed in a sexual growl at my ear, before he left my breasts alone. As for the rest of the room, they had started the celebration which meant that half of them were now dancing. I even saw Pip and Adam dancing and the sight melted my heart. They were utterly adorable together and the love between them was near blinding.

But then a cover of Conquistador by Thirty Seconds to Mars started to play and Pip plucked a little control unit out from between her breasts and just as she was about to press the button I muttered,

"Oh, here we go." Lucius then burst out laughing behind me as the second she did all the hanging dead birds inside of her skirt burst into a rainbow of colour, all spinning like mini disco balls.

"But of course," Lucius commented making me look back at him over my shoulder to see him grinning.

"Come on, did you really expect Pip to stick to a black and white theme…speaking of which…" I then nodded down to myself pointing out the obvious and silently asking him why.

"My people needed to know that I had claimed you," was his self-assured answer.

"Well, mission accomplished, as I think other than tattooing your name across my forehead, then it's safe to say I think everyone got the message loud and clear, bucko."

"Bucko, is it?" he whispered in my ear before capturing my chin and bringing my face back around to look at him. Then he ran his leather-clad thumb across my forehead and said,

"I would never taint this beauty with my name, but now on your ass, well then that could be easily arranged, sweetcheeks." I scoffed a laugh and said,

"Yeah, keep dreaming there, Vampy." Then I turned to look back at the crowd as he chuckled. This was before he brought his right hand around to my front, one that was still bloody but no longer bleeding thanks to the slash in his flesh being healed.

"Living with you *is* a dream…now, open that pretty mouth for me and suck," he said surprising me twice. The first with how incredibly sweet that statement was and the second for the sexual demand that had me near squirming in between his legs.

"I can't do that here!" I hissed, unknowingly prompting him to start kissing his way up my neck, with his gloved hand going to the front of my throat, dancing gently along the skin.

"Nothing in this world will stop me from tasting that which I own, as nothing will ever stop me from feeding my girl…now be good and open up for me," he said, raising his hand to cup my jaw from behind and using his thumb to pry open my mouth. Then, once this was achieved, he inserted one of his bloody fingers, commanding me on a demanding whisper,

"Now suck." I did as I was told, having no choice but to close my eyes as I tried to shut out his world during what I considered nothing short of a dominant display and masterful

ownership over me. One where I could feel every eye watching me and, needless to say, it was a sexual act I wasn't used to displaying in front of others. Hell, up until recently I was a bloody virgin for Gods' sake!

"Hell's damnation, woman, but this delectable mouth of yours will be my ruin, one chosen gladly, if an eternity of its gift is my reward," he told me after I had finished being 'fed' his bloody fingers one by one. I curled my tongue around the last finger before licking up to the tip only letting him go once it was clean.

As it turned out, the act was one I soon got used to and my shame was quickly replaced by the heat in my belly and the arousal I could now feel seeping from the ache in between my thighs. But then he must have sensed this because he inhaled deeply at my neck, as if he was catching the scent of my sexual heat rising up my body. Lucius released a knowing growl against my skin and suddenly he grabbed the tops of my arms at the front of me and pulled me back tight against his chest.

"Gods, but I can't wait to fuck you again…you make me burn for you, ache to be inside you…my good, bad girl," he whispered making me blush at the strength of his words, as I swear my heart felt as though it would soon burst. In fact, this night was quickly becoming one of the best nights of my life.

It had always been a dream of mine to be included in a ball, one filled with who I should have regarded as my own people, for I had been born into this life. I had always been called Princess, yet I had been made to feel segregated for most of it until eventually the childish title had felt more like a lie.

But tonight, well it was the first time in my life that I had truly been made to feel like the Princess I was.

And it was all because of Lucius.

Lucius, who didn't treat me as if I should be sheltered from his world. Sure, he wanted to keep me protected, but in his mind that didn't mean keeping me from his people or the way of his world. It meant entwining me in it and nurturing the roots he wanted to see growing around me, forging me here right by his side. It was why he had made the decisions he had, by moving me in when he knew I would have argued against it. Because that was what I was used to. Being overly cautious when something was new and unsure. To take a step back and over analyse everything and all that could go wrong.

When really, I should have just done what Lucius had wanted me to all along, his words when dancing had been simply, *to hold on, sweetheart, and enjoy the ride.* And life with Lucius was most definitely that, and one I never wanted to get off!

"I know I am just guessing here but I am gonna say that I think people might notice if we went missing," I told him making him growl,

"Like I fucking care if they did."

"Well, I am sure your council would, and speaking of which, they are still waiting to come up here and…" Lucius cut me off with an animalistic snarl and tightened his hold on me as he said,

"Let them fucking wait, I will summon them when I am ready and right now what I am not ready for is sharing you with anyone!" This made me melt further back into him before telling him teasingly,

"Play nice, honey."

"With you in my arms, not a fucking chance of that, sweetheart!" I laughed before turning around in his arms, waiting for him to relax enough to allow me the movement. And when he did, I pulled my skirt around to give me more space to bring up a knee, resting it against his own. This was before I placed my hands on his cheeks, framing his face so I could tell him,

"You know what, handsome?" He smirked down at me with soft eyes despite the intimidating darkness around them.

"What's that, beautiful?" he asked in a tender tone and with a gentle caress on my back.

"I love you, Lucius." Then I kissed him, feeling my heart overflowing with the emotion and putting it into every second of the kiss. Also proving yet again the marvel that was my smudge-proof lipstick and naughtily wondering just how far I could take that test. Especially seeing as he enjoyed my mouth so much.

Lucius kissed me back, holding a hand to the back of my head, and being careful with my hair, even though I could tell he wanted to clench a fist there.

"Not that I am complaining but I have to ask, what was that for?" he asked obviously curious once I had finished the kiss by peppering gentle ones across his smoothly shaven jawline.

"Because it may be your birthday we are celebrating, but you have no idea the gift you have given me tonight." He raised a brow in a questioning way after first granting me a look of surprise.

"And what would that gift be?" So, I leaned in and told him exactly what gift he had given me, this time being the one to say the same words that his demon had not long ago said to me.

Because it was the truth of my heart and one whispered over lips I wanted to kiss forever...

"The gift of you."

CHAPTER FIFTEEN

MASKED FLIRTING

"*The gift of you.*"

The moment I said this he hooked me at the back of my neck and kissed me again, no longer giving a damn about my hair, or my dress or anything else for that matter as he practically dragged me up his body, his bare hand fisting the material of my skirt. A rough and primal action that told me exactly what he wanted to do to me and I had to admit, a large part of me wished that he would.

"Now that is the only birthday gift I could ever wish for," he told me, once he had finished kissing me in the most thorough way a person could be kissed. But he had said this whilst holding his forehead to mine, which was something he always did when trying to express the intensity of his feelings.

"You big softy, you," I teased making him smirk before telling me,

"Not all of me, no… especially with you pressed against my body and with the scent of your cream soaking that scrap of lace barely concealing that sweet, tight little pussy of yours I own," he told me making my mouth drop, a reaction he smirked at before tapping my open lips telling me,

"I didn't just pick the colour of your dress."

"You picked out my underwear?" I hissed out the question making him laugh before informing me,

"I like to think of it as the right of any Birthday Boy to get to pick the wrapping he wishes to tear off his gift…*one I cannot wait to open and play with later,"* Lucius told me with a sexual depth to his voice that made me shudder in his hold.

"Well then, you'd better behave, or I will just make you wait," I said as I didn't know what else to do but tease him… well, it was that or throw a dramatic hand to my forehead and release a breathy sigh, Scarlett O'Hara style. But then this just managed to invoke images of Lucius kissing me passionately before picking me up and running up the staircase with me in his arms.

"Behave? Um now, that's a novel notion, yet not one that is ever possible around you and the constant temptation you force me to endure," he replied making me smirk, as it seemed I wasn't the only one with romantic thoughts running through my mind. Although, I could imagine that his included something a little more X-rated than just being passionately kissed and carried up a staircase. Oh, but who was I kiddin', *a lot more X-rated!*

And speaking of X-rated, it was hard not to notice the glaringly obvious section of the room that catered for those who wanted to indulge in the sexual act without caring who watched.

It looked as though someone had picked up entire rooms from a high-class sex club and dropped them either side of the staircase. Everything from Saint Andrews Crosses, to sex swings, cages and spanking benches were situated on their own personal platforms. Meaning that the space was raised so its occupants could easily be seen by a gathered crowd. There was even a large metal frame that was the size of a bed hanging down from the ceiling, that I gathered was for strapping a body to whilst people below got to play, as the cuffs and spreader bars kind of gave it away.

But at least for the moment these items remained unused, although looking around the room and I didn't hold out much hope for it remaining like this for long. I mean people weren't exactly dancing as Lucius and I had. No, now the music had changed to a heavier rock that gave people the excuse to screw decorum and this included very near screwing each other on the dance floor! Something I could see was already close to happening in the booths on the opposite side of the room.

"Do most of your parties end in sex?" I asked curiously. Lucius chuckled behind me and at the same time he raised a hand to motion for his council to come forward, which was what they were all waiting for.

"Only the best kind," was his reply, making me turn to raise a brow at him before snapping,

"Actually, I don't want to know!" I said folding my arms and facing the rest of the room again. But this snippy response of mine obviously amused him as by the time his council joined us, they found their master with his head thrown back laughing. Of course, this only managed to piss me off even more and I huffed in annoyance.

"My past sexual exploits ended long before you entered my bed, sweetheart," he told me softly and suddenly my head whipped around to see if he was being as serious as he sounded.

"But what about the two blondes, the ones…the ones you had…well, that night…you know." I asked losing my bravery the moment that night came back to my mind, now making me want to curse my thoughts for going back there. However, Lucius gave me a soft look and hooked my chin with his thumb and forefinger the moment I tried to hide my shame.

"That night was nothing but an act, one with the sole purpose of pushing you away," he told me making me take in a deep breath before asking,

"But why? Why would you need to, I mean I was right there and what were the words you used…*ripe for the picking.*" Hearing this Lucius had the good grace to look regretful.

"I was a fool, but a cautious one at that, for I knew the time wasn't right," he told me choosing his words carefully.

"Yes well, I didn't exactly get a say in that decision, did I?" I snapped making his chest rumble before he ran a thumb across my lips, doing so gently, unlike he had done that night where he had smeared my lipstick down my chin.

"When it is your safety in question, then I will always be the one making those decisions, my Khuba, and you did not yet know the dangerous ways of my world. But trust me now when I say that you were not the only one whose soul suffered that night," he told me with such sincerity that I could do little but believe him.

"Now, no more of talk of the past, for this night is to mark our future and that is all that matters," he told me and I had to say, I agreed that it was best we moved past it, as I would have been lying if I hadn't said that the memory was still, and no doubt would continue to be, a sore spot with me.

"That, and no more blondes on tap," I commented making him laugh before squeezing me to him and telling me,

"They were gone the moment you were out of sight, Pet, and sat there merely for show…for there has only ever been one beauty I want *on tap,* and she is exactly where she should be…*finally."* I looked down and grinned, feeling the heat of his words in not just my blushing cheeks but also in between the juncture of my thighs. But instead of telling him what his words meant to me, I poked him in the chest and said,

"Yeah, well it took you long enough, Mister." At this he chuckled, before framing my face so he could tip my head down and place a sweet kiss on my forehead, doing so over the lace of my mask, telling me,

"That it did, Princess, that it did."

After this our moment was disturbed by the obvious presence of his council as they each took their seats either side of us. And it had to be said that even without all the theatrics surrounding them, they were a diverse bunch to say the least. But now in all their masquerade glory, well now they each looked incredible.

First to take his seat was Clay who was dressed like a Roman Gladiator, complete with spiked helmet that was also the face of a roaring demon, with Clay's face positioned in between the open jaws. Large fangs that looked as if from a sabre tooth tiger, came down past his forehead. The whole thing was matt black with a brushed white effect, with only the fangs being gleaming white. He also wore typical body armour to match what he obviously classed as a mask, instead of a suit like most of the other men did.

Next in line to take his seat was Ruto, doing so on the other side of Lucius, however I did notice he left a large space in between and I wondered if this was because Adam was back. After all, Ruto was only filling in Adam's place whilst he had been situated at my father's table, doing so on loan for the last twenty plus years. Basically, since I had been born because Pip had said many a time, there was no way she was missing out on me growing up. So they had basically lived at Afterlife with us all, after my father gave them their old quarters back.

Because according to what little I had heard about the past, Pip and Adam, although loyal to Lucius, had once been a part of my father's world back when Lucius was my father's right hand. But many of Lucius' council had been away on missions or whatever else Lucius had deemed they should be doing at the time. After all, there was only so many people needed on a King's council and my father already had his seats filled.

Which meant that Lucius' current table of the powerfully turned had only been seated at his side since world war 2, which was rumoured to be when the fight between the Two Kings first began. A fight, according to Pip, that had only ended thanks to my mother…or in Pip's words, (along with a shit donkey's load of other reasons too')

But again, being the only person not exactly privy to this information, it was all just pieces of things I had heard over the years and ones filled with more blanks than actual facts. And seeing as I was all about the facts, then needless to say, this didn't help me much.

However, getting back to Ruto and his obvious stepping down from the rank, I would have been concerned at some show of bitterness on his part. But by allowing that space to be filled told me he wasn't bitter at all, but perhaps welcomed the reprieve of being Lucius' right hand, as he didn't exactly look bothered about it.

Then again, he did have his husband sitting down next to him, who surprisingly, he looked utterly besotted with as he couldn't keep his hands off him. In fact, it was the first and only time I had seen Ruto look genuinely happy and not like some angsty teenager who had been told to pick up his dirty pants. For starters, he wasn't even playing with one of the many blades attached to his black 'Assassin Creed' style outfit. It was also difficult to see with the large hood up hiding most of his face, but I think his mask was like a jagged piece of metal following no particular style or shape.

Keto however, like before when guiding us here, still looked like some dashing fairytale prince in an embroidered white and gold suit, one gleaming with a double row of gilt buttons. But unlike before, he also had on a mask, which matched his style as it was typical of a Venetian Mask. One with a full painted face, including the perfect heart-shaped lips of gold against pearlescent white skin and black glittering swirls around the eyes. Gold edged curls of stiff black material tipped with bells completed the elaborate mask. Of course, the bells served a purpose as Ruto was in the mood for a drink and he started flicking the one closest to him, making Keto lower the mask and roll his gold painted eyes dramatically.

"I am sure our King is in need of a drink!" Ruto shouted loudly, getting the attention of a passing waiter, one naked apart from what looked like a clay soaked loin cloth. Of course, matching the black and white theme his entire body had been painted in a layered white, hard substance that resembled thick chalk. The only black on him was the large handprint that looked as if someone had slapped him head-on and then pushed his face back.

Lucius, on hearing Ruto's comment, spanned a hand on my stomach, one concealed by steel bones in my corset and pulled me back a little, before brushing the stray hair off my neck so he could whisper seductively in my ear,

"The King needs a drink indeed." I coughed to clear my throat before putting up my hand and saying,

"A bottle of beer is needed over here." To which he started laughing against my neck at the little joke I made.

"Mmm, not what I had in mind, Pet."

"Erm, sorry make that a strawberry milkshake!" I shouted in jest, this time making him throw his head back and laugh even louder,

"Little minx, behave now... A beer and a champagne for the lady," Lucius ordered still with a huge grin in place after playfully reprimanding me for my joke. However, the rest of his council seemed to enjoy the show. Liessa granted me a wink through her stunning mask that was clearly a mermaid theme. It was encrusted in different sized pearls and shells and it was also topped with long narrow shells that were coiled tight in a twist, with the larger one at the

centre of her forehead pointing up at the ceiling like a crown.

Her outfit had been chosen for the white mermaid idea also. A theme she had picked that naturally went perfectly with her living hair that was currently coiled around twists of curls, with each tentacle having been brushed with a gold dust making them shimmer. Her dress was a long, white fishtail design that not only looked hard to walk in but it also looked hard to move in the way she wished as she couldn't exactly do her usual trick of crawling up her husband. Not unless she first pulled up the dress-up to the top of her thighs, as it was that tight.

Speaking of her husband, Caspian, whose soul I now apparently owned, something I was going to have to have words with Lucius about as soon as I found the right time to do so, was also dressed for the occasion. However, his outfit, like the others, reflected his menacing appearance and he was wearing a black armoured biker suit with white piping. Lines of white that outlined what would most definitely have been a muscular torso underneath, including an eight pack set of abs. Added to this was a bone-white demonic skull mask, complete with horns and spiked cheeks. It was a full face one with his eyes painted black underneath like most of the males had done for added effect.

Which, I had to say, looked odd as he was currently playing the perfect gentleman to his wife as he held her hand and kissed its back after he had seated her next to Clay, and had been sure to lower her down slowly, as looking at her towering heels tonight, then I wasn't surprised by his caution.

After this he took his own seat, getting comfortable by

draping a heavy-looking arm at the back of Liessa's seat, now caressing a tattooed hand along her bare shoulder and toying playfully with one of the suckers there. I saw the drips of ink seeping from this and he would coat the tip of his finger before raising it back to his lips to suck on.

Talk about a match made in Hell...jeez.

"And once again, where is that little fucker, Puck?" Ruto asked as two waiters, who were all dressed the same, started handing out drinks. This of course, started with Lucius' and mine first. But then once more Lucius had to be the one to hand me my drink, taking it first from the waiter before doing so. It was an action that took me back to London and how he was the same even then. How he wouldn't let his driver open the door for me or even his friend in the restaurant pull out my seat for me. Making me now question if this too wasn't a sign of possessiveness.

"I ttthink he isth with a girl again," Percy said coming to join the group. He was wearing a black cloak with a hood that framed the full square mask he wore, that was jutted at the chin and looked like cracked white marble riddled with black veins.

"Oh, don't mind that little crackerjack titty lover, I saw him under some earth Imp's skirt licking her out, and I wasn't sure why but she was licking the spoon that sticks out of his head...I mean, why would a bitch do that...brain juice is just wrong," Pip said as she was now dancing up the steps and everyone naturally reached for their drinks off the low table in front, to save them from Pip's radical skirt knocking them everywhere.

"Squeak!" Liessa squealed in delight before they embraced, as clearly, they were close. Adam followed and as always showed respect to his King as he bowed and commented,

"Sire."

Lucius nodded in return and then after Adam had finally coaxed Pip into sitting down, after she first fist-bumped Clay and growled playfully at Caspian, Lucius then turned to his second and said,

"It is good to have you back, my friend."

"It is good to…" Adam started to reply but was quickly interrupted.

"OMGeeBees, it is soooo good to be back, like we must have spent three hours in bed screwing, as tying my Cockbear to the bed when it's surrounded by a giant cage is so much more fun than our other beds…oooh, waiter, can I have 'sex on my face' please!" Needless to say, half of the council groaned, and the other half chuckled, Adam being on the groaning side of that group and me being on the chuckling side.

The poor waiter nearly dropped his tray as he instantly shot fearful eyes to Adam who was literally the most powerful being alive, so it was no wonder. Naturally, I had never seen my uncle in his other form and from all accounts, never wanted to either. As let's just say he was the only monster in existence that had even Lucifer shaking in his boots.

But thankfully, it was that same unassuming badass uncle of mine that came to the poor Vamps aid.

"It's a cocktail, and the lady will have an Amaretto, cherry liqueur and pink champagne instead," Adam said making Pip clap and say,

"Oh yes, a cherry Bakewell fizz, I haven't had one in

donkey's...Good call, honey beaver!" Pip said and it also went without saying that my aunty liked donkeys and actually owned a sanctuary for them. Now as for the nickname honey beaver, that was one mystery I didn't want to discover.

"My Chieftain, it has been done," Hakan said, suddenly appearing from nowhere, after which he took his seat as the last of the council members to do so. He was wearing pretty much what he usually wore, meaning he was bare from the waist up and wore a pair of wide black pants that were tied at one side with a flap of material, appearing like a half skirt.

He didn't wear a mask, as he always had one painted across his face anyway. However, he did now wear a headpiece that was a crown of raven feathers and a twist of the same barbed wire that was wrapped around the upper part of his body.

"Chieftain?" I questioned silently.

"Don't ask," Lucius said with a roll of his eyes, telling me he seemed embarrassed by the title.

"Okay, but what does he mean by 'it has been done'?" This time I asked the question, not just mouthing it.

"My witch, Nesteemia, has been shown where I wish her to cast the first of her wards, so a certain someone won't slip past my clutches and is able to escape me again." I ignored that comment in favour of the first part, wondering now what Lucius was up to.

"And that is where exactly?" I asked, making Lucius smirk down at me before saying with a wink,

"Our bed."

CHAPTER SIXTEEN

DANCING WITH JEALOUSY

A little time later when the night was in full swing and after six glasses of champagne, then let's just say I was feeling pretty warm and fuzzy. Enough, so that when Pip suddenly unclasped her massive cage skirt and declared,

"Time for this Pip to make the floor squeak! Come on, sugar tits, let's boogie!" Then she reached for my hand and tried to pry me away from Lucius who growled at her, making her fold her arms and pout.

"She is happy where she is," Lucius exclaimed making me turn back and frown at him,

"Oh, is she now?" I said crossing my arms copying Pip.

"Oops, looks like you've gone and done it now!" Pip said laughing.

"You wish to dance, then so be it, but you can do so with me," Lucius declared stubbornly.

"Are you saying I am not safe to dance with my aunt not

twenty feet away from you?" I challenged making him frown as he clearly knew which answer he wanted to give me. Yet it was one that would have been controlling and domineering, and although I adored how possessive he could be, there were definitely times he needed to give me space and trust that I would always come back to him...or Gods forbid, that I would be safe for once.

"Very well, you wish to dance, then I give you leave to do so..." he said making a show of releasing me by holding his arms stretched out at his sides. But then, as I started to shift off the seat, he quickly leaned forward and whispered in my ear,

"I look forward to the entertainment, pet."

"Yey! Time to get our titties in a twist!" Pip said grabbing my hand and pulling me up the rest of the way as after what Lucius had just said, it had made my whole body pause. I was suddenly questioning whether or not this was a good idea, because I had overlooked the main factor in all this, and well, let's just say, I wasn't exactly like a graceful gazelle on the dancefloor. And with Lucius watching me like a hungry tiger, well it wasn't like it was going to help matters.

Oh yeah, this was going to be fun...*not*...but hey, at least my aunt was excited.

"No titty twisting, my Winnie," Adam warned making me laugh when, with her back to him, she just made a 'yap, yap' expression with her hands like a quacking duck but to him, she blew a kiss over her shoulder and said,

"Sure thing, my mad monster cock!" At this I groaned and like earlier, so did Adam. But she didn't care as she now led me down to the dancefloor and to a spot that unfortunately was directly in front of where Lucius sat, so he could be…*entertained.*

"So, earlier when I was sat under your dress in nothing but my underwear, did you not think to mention that your skirt opens up?" I asked, seeing her minus the skirt, with only her rainbow hot pants and the top part of her dress left.

"Ooops, my bad…Woohoo, I love this song!" she shouted as the music had changed from heavy rock to a dance track. So, I listened to the words, and started to recognise it.

"Is this a dance cover of…"

"Losing my Religion, yeah ironic right!" Pip answered laughing as we both started to move to the beat as it was just one of those songs you couldn't help but move to. So, as I finally let myself relax, I also allowed my body to get lost to the beat, starting with swinging my hips as the song started to build up. Then once it did I raised my arms up in the air, closed my eyes and let my whole body sway to the music, at the same time singing the lyrics I knew…and the words, well they were right, this whole night…*it did feel like just a dream.*

"Damn girly, you got yourself some moves!" Pip shouted before smirking over at Lucius and adding,

"And I am obviously not the only one who thinks so." I then looked for myself and saw that Lucius was indeed looking at me. And he was not just staring, but he actually looked transfixed. He was even leaning forward before he nodded his head, motioning silently to Clay. At first, I thought Lucius was asking Clay to come and tell me that he wanted me back but it wasn't the case. No, Clay was coming down the steps to stand guard, as he folded his massive arms and watched the rest of the crowd like a hawk. One ready to rain down terror and pain at the slightest sign of anyone getting too close to me. Which was when I turned around to see that others had in fact started to move closer, something that stopped instantly the moment Clay made his appearance.

I looked back at Lucius to see his eyes glowing and making a show of licking his lips before winking at me. I smirked back at him and then continued to dance, now doing it in what I hoped was a slightly more provocative way. Pip, on the other hand, was swinging her arms wide and moving in such a way it was as though she was creating a non-existent wave. The lights in her hair flashed to the beat, one we were both getting lost in.

But then, as the next song came on, I noticed three girls all dressed like Greek goddesses coming closer to the raised dais where Lucius was sat. Each of them was in a low-cut flowing dress of white with gold rope twisted around their bodies. They each held a mask painted in the same style. However, I couldn't see the details of them, seeing as one by one they lowered the sticks holding them to their faces as they each made a show when walking past Lucius. I couldn't help but frown as all three bowed, no doubt giving him more than an eyeful. But of course, they were beautiful, with glittering hair, each a different colour, black, blonde and red, but each face held the same beauty, for they were obviously triplets.

"Who are they?" I couldn't help but ask as I instantly took a hit to my confidence, especially when Lucius nodded back in return. Alright, so it's not like he invited them up to take a seat with him but still, he didn't exactly tell them to piss off either.

"Eww yuck, just the wicked witches of Eastwick that's all," Pip snarled pulling a disgusted face.

"They are witches?" I asked before Pip admitted,

"Nah, I just call them that, along with Ticks."

"Ticks?" I questioned as they each started to try and entice Lucius to dance with them in a teasing way that made me want to grow fangs and snarl at them.

"Yeah, it stands for Triple Idiotic Cocksucking King's Sluts…Ooops…"

"Don't say it!" I snapped after realising what she had just told me and I didn't have the patience for her, 'my bad'. So, Pip took my arm and turned me away from the sight and, having to shout over the music, told me,

"Okay, so yes, technically, they used to be his bitch fest of choice but that was a donkey's balls ago… now they are just sad mad fang hangers on."

"How long have they been around?" I asked folding my arms. Pip release a deep sigh making me snap,

"Pip!"

"Alright, so they are some of the first Angels he turned and yes, he used to fuck 'em, being as back then he obviously wasn't picky and clearly…he was a dick…but just look at them, they are as bitter as a dead man's pruney bollock," she replied making me pull a face and not just at the dead man's pruney bollock comment.

"Why, because he's not given it to them in the few weeks I have been on the picture!?" I snapped.

"No, try since the day he first laid his besotted eyes on you." I gave her a sceptical look that said I didn't believe it.

"Look, pretty girl, why else do you think they are currently trying to fry your pretty noggin with non-existent laser eyes?" Pip replied making me glance as they went past to see that she was right, each of them now looked as though they wanted to gouge my eyes out with a toothpick.

"You're the only one wearing red for a reason, so if I were you, noodle, I would own that shit and wear it like a fucking badge of Starfleet!" Pip added making me take her advice and I started to do this by looking down my nose at them as they openly sneered at me. So, I did something totally out of character, one because I was the right side of drunk and second, because I was fucking pissed off.

So, I slapped the back of my hand to my palm in warning, making them look totally shocked that a mortal would dare threaten to backhand them if they continued with their shit. But someone else who noticed was Clay as he burst out laughing, winking at me as a well done.

"Whoohoo, that's called being owned, bitches! Boo yeah, my Fae girl is in de house!" Pip said before throwing her head back and pretending to howl at the missing moon. But then I couldn't help but look over my shoulder to see that Lucius had been watching the whole scene play out. Meaning that when he raised a brow at me in question, I whispered only one word,

"Trouble."

Then I went back to ignoring him as the next act started to come onto the stage. It was a girl with a violin in the shape of a coffin, making me scoff a laugh. But she was dressed in a torn and ragged white wedding dress, complete with shredded veil. She also came with six backup dancers that stood either side of her. Each of the girls were dressed in black tux suits and had masks that resembled demonic white wolves. The girl with the violin wore a black mask of a rabbit with red tears flowing down her cheeks.

"Oooh, she is going to play Artemis," Pip told me as people stopped to watch the show, one that quickly started to resemble the demise of a woman, thanks to the wolf of a 'man' who breaks her heart and tries to tear her apart. This was shown by them trying to chase her throughout the dance, all flowing as one reaching for her and as she moved one way they moved the other. They would try and lash out at her dress as she continued to dance, all the time playing the violin with such perfection and beauty, it was incredible to watch.

But then, not long into the song, I watched as everyone around me started to give me a wide berth, taking large steps backwards until whoever, it was deemed it far enough. I turned around in the circle, looking for the cause and finding Lucius now walking down the steps in that masterful way of his, motioning with his gloved hand for people to move back.

I even took note of Pip who was giving me the thumbs-up behind him as she skipped back to Adam, now leaving me to his mercy. Then he came to me, only dressed as he had been without a jacket and a waistcoat that framed such a powerful looking torso. The way he prowled towards me now was like a sleek beast ready to strike at its prey.

I knew this when, instead of just grabbing me to him, he continued to circle me slowly. When he deemed it so, he clasped my waist just at the crescendo and yanked me hard to his frame. Then he started to pull me into a dance, only this time it was one far from classic. As now we started to tell our own story and it was one based on lust, addiction and burning passion. I knew this when he wouldn't allow an inch between us but stepped with me around the space in a dance I didn't know. It was hard to keep up with him but with his hands on me, I had little choice but to follow his lead. Thankfully, this time there was no stepping on his feet as the second it looked as if I might, he simply spun me out on an outstretched arm before tugging me back into his chest.

But the last time he did this I ended up so close I practically fell into him. At the same time the music slowed and in response he simply looked down at me as I slowly looked up at him. It just seemed in that slow moment as if nothing else mattered but the two of us. That singular heartbeat in time, one that slowed only for us to nothing but the sound of beauty in the background going at our own pace…it was beautifully profound. A stunning moment and one etched to my very heart and sealed with the most gentle kiss I had ever received as he lowered his lips to mine.

Then the moment the music continued, the spell was broken, and he spun me away from him again, only to bring me right back to continue the steps of our dance. By the Gods, but where had this man learned how to dance this way…talk about sexually aroused!

I swear by the time the dance had come to an end, I was panting and it had nothing to do with the steps he had taken me through.

"My Amelia," Lucius hummed down at me and I was so out of my mind with need for him that I suddenly blurted out the first thought that came to mind,

"I need the toilet!" He frowned down at me, the obvious question easy to see but instead he simply said,

"Okay…I will have Liessa escort…"

"No!" I shouted and before he could say anything more I said,

"Come with me." Then I started to pull him to where the obvious choice for them to be found was, as there were doors either side of the stage I had seen people going into and coming back out again. So, through the still beautiful notes by the girl on stage as she had started to play her next song, I made my way through the crowd with his hand in mine. Thankfully, this was easy to do seeing as Lucius' people parted for him quickly. But by the time we reached the doors Lucius nodded to the ladies one and I pulled him in that direction. Then once we were by the door, he started to tell me,

"I will wait here for…Amelia, what are you…?" he began to say when I started to pull him inside, walking backwards with my hands locked around his wrist, telling him with a wink,

"Ssshh, just go with it, handsome…" Then I leaned into him, knowing that it was time for a little demanding of my own, and whispered,

"…Trust me."

CHAPTER SEVENTEEN

A SINKING SEXUAL ENCOUNTER

Then I pulled him inside with me and to any of the women that were still in there primping themselves at the sinks, I circled a hand in the air and said,

"Alright ladies, everyone out…gehen, partir, idti, andare!" They all turned to us both in astonishment before quickly doing as I said. After Lucius jerked his head to the door, of course, telling them to do my bidding.

"Mmm, I think that covers all bases, love," he said in reference to my multilingual words for 'go' in German, French, Russian and Italian.

"Not yet it doesn't," I said slapping a hand to his chest and walking him backwards until he was against the wall. Then I grabbed the back of his neck in one hand and fisted a hand in his hair with the other so I could yank him down to me for a desperate kiss. Of course, this was Lucius I was kissing, so naturally he got the hint pretty quickly. And that meant him taking over the kiss, turning it from passionate to possessive in a second.

He wrapped his arms around me and held me so tight I could only just manage to breathe, and I felt his fingers at my ribs pulling at the metal spines he could feel in the corset. I knew then that he was close to tearing my dress in two, so I pulled my mouth from his, ignoring his growl, telling him in between kisses

"No ripping…room…full…of…people." He snarled but this must have sunk in as he eased his hold on me, instead going to my cleavage and deciding that was his next target. Because one second he was being gentle, caressing across my breasts and then he was snarling down at me,

"I can't fucking wait!" Then he yanked the corset part of my dress down what little it would go, so he could free a breast. Then he took it in his hand and lifted it to his mouth so he could bite my nipple. I threw my head back and released an echoing moan in the room. One that someone was about to walk into as the sound of the door opening could only just be heard over the sound of my pleasure.

"OUT!" Lucius roared and threw out an arm so the door slammed shut, and I watched as the door handle bent back against the door frame like a lock as it melted to it.

"Well, that solves that problem," I told him making him grin back at me before telling me,

"Now for my next one," he said tearing open the front of his trousers before raising up my massive skirt by walking his fingers up the material by my thighs and gathering it at the same time, Then once my legs were free, he bent, ripped off my panties and grabbed the backs of my thighs. I was quickly hiked up at the same time he turned with me so now I was the one against the wall.

"Yes!" I cried out the second he started kissing me, switching between my lips and down my neck before finding my needy mouth again. The heavy beat pounding through the walls was creating a sexual baseline for our actions and only managed to turn me on even more. But then he pulled back a moment and looked down into my eyes, ones I knew were glazed with lust.

"Mine...all fucking mine!" he said before suddenly thrusting up inside of me and making me cry out, this time screaming the word,

"YES, YES, YES...Gods Lucius, yes!"

"Look at us...look at how we fit...look at how fucking perfect you are for me...*LOOK!*" Lucius said after looking over his shoulder at the two of us reflected back in the mirror that filled the wall. So, I did, and as he pounded into me, he snarled the moment I looked away,

"NO! Keep looking, keep your eyes to the mirror and do not move them! I want you to see what I see every time I fuck perfection." I sucked in a quick breath at his heated words and let them wash over me, doing as he told me to. And I had to say, that watching the two of us connected in such a way, well he was right, it had my pulse racing as I felt it build like a fuse inside me. One that travelled the length of my body until it ignited every single part of me as I exploded, now doing so to the sight of our love, lust and passion coming alive.

Naturally, I came screaming and did so with my head arched back against the wall. But Lucius didn't stop. He was merciless, commanding more and more in every delectable way, as with each thrust of his cock I could feel the walls of my sex pulsating around him. The way I sucked him back inside the moment he tried to leave me, if only for a millisecond of time. I wanted him there inside me for what felt like forever.

"Gods yes, more…give me more!" I shouted, demanding it of him as I clawed at the shirt on his back, wishing it was flesh beneath my fingernails. But then he walked me over to the sinks and placed me down on the countertop in between two sink bowls. Then he hammered into me with such speed, I had no other choice but to cling onto him and let him use my body to its fullest, crying out for a second time and coming hard from it. I heard the sound of cracking and saw the mirror above my head branch out around the fist that had been suddenly embedded into it. Then he started to come inside me, and I knew this the second his hand left the mirror and instead found the edge of the basin. He fisted the edge so hard it rattled in his hold, but I quickly shifted my gaze to a far more pleasurable sight and that was my own perfection that was Lucius.

"FUCK! RAWWWR" he roared throwing his head back and bellowing his release at the ceiling, captivating me by the sight. Gods, but it was so raw and beautiful at the same time, I couldn't help but raise a hand to his cheek, even as his orgasm continued as he thrust inside me a few more times as he emptied himself. But then as he started to come down from his high, he lowered his head to my chest as he breathed in deep, kissing my exposed breast tenderly.

"Insatiable girl," he whispered against my skin before looking up at me, as he raised his head slowly.

"Perhaps...or maybe I just wanted to remind you who *you belong to,*" I told him, making him smirk before saying,

"Ah, the troublesome three...but of course," he said making me growl at him, which of course, amused him greatly.

"They mean nothing, but you know this, for there is only one who is currently caressing my cock, which will continue to be so until the day I turn to ash once more," he said making me frown at the strange end to that statement. And just as he could see me about to ask him about it, he tapped me under my chin and said,

"Now, I believe we still have a party to attend." Which I knew was his way of saying we had to get back. So, I looked down to where we were still connected and stated,

"I believe there is only one of us currently preventing that." His roguish grin said it all. Then he bucked his hips forward making me moan once more before he pulled out of me, chuckling at my reaction. Then after he righted himself, he took me by the waist and lifted me down from the counter. Then he began tucking my breast back inside my dress making me laugh before teasing,

"I think this dress is so tight that it might need punching back in there." To which he smirked down at me before saying,

"Take a deep breath." I did as I was told and the second I did, he yanked my top up, doing the job of covering me. Then I looked towards the wall at the scrap of torn lace on the floor and then back at him with my hands on my hips.

"Right, well, got any ideas about how to fix them while you're on a roll re-dressing me?" He shrugged his shoulders and said,

"My birthday, my wrapping." To which I smacked him on the arm making him laugh. Then he looked down the length of me as my skirt once more touched the floor and said,

"I think your modesty is safe under there, sweetheart." I held back my smile and got up on my tiptoes closer to his face and hissed,

"Yes, but now I feel naked." Then he leant down closer to my face and replied,

"And I wish you were." Then he clasped my chin and held me there whilst he quickly kissed me. After that he released me and said in a cocky way,

"I will give you a moment to...*compose yourself.*" I growled again at this last part making him chuckle and tell me,

"I will send Liessa to escort you back to me...so be quick, my pretty ravished princess." Another swift kiss later and he was fixing the door handle about to leave, but not before first making a show of bending down to the floor and retrieving my panties. Then, when I made a strangled sound in the back of my throat, he looked at me over his shoulder and said,

"Spoils of war." Then with a wink he left me to 'compose myself', which he was right, I most definitely needed the time to do so. Meaning, I quickly used the toilet, which wasn't as easy as it sounded with such a big skirt on. I swear, but I felt like an upside-down mushroom by the time I had managed to get my skirt up around my waist. And then there was the ungraceful monkey arm as I tried to wipe myself. Well, I was just thankful Lucius had left, as 'composing yourself' was about as sexy as dressing up as a turtle and dragging yourself across the floor to the bed.

Once finished, I found myself at the sinks, seeing now the damage Lucius had done to the mirror and I looked down at the now loose, wobbly sink which was a carved piece of white marble. Well, at least he hadn't burst any pipes or that would have been a double whammy on things exploding. I moved away from the damage with a smirk and focused on myself, now trying to re-pin my loose hair back in place and rubbing at the smudges under my eyes and around my lips, seeing that it hadn't passed the Lucius test.

Well, I didn't care, as it had been more than worth it. In fact, I was so deep into thinking about Lucius kissing me that I only realised I was no longer alone when I could see the three masked faces staring back at me in the mirror. Great, just what I needed, it was the troublesome three, AKA, the TICKS!

Each had their masks in place, held there by the sticks they grasped. Masks that were similar to Keto's as they were the typical Venetian style. Only the blonde's was an angelic glossy white face, with gold around the eye holes and lips. The redhead's was the demon, with horns and reddish-gold around the eyes and lips. The one with black hair like my own had the mask of a human, and the only face that was screaming in terror, with black around the eyes as if looking hollow to represent the death about to befall her. I knew in that instant what the three sisters were trying to achieve with their choice, no doubt trying to intimidate me. Yeah, well they didn't know who they were fucking messing with!

"Human…Gods, but how does he tolerate the stench of mortality?" The Angel said, as she lowered her mask before stepping up to the cracked mirror admiring herself. I rolled my eyes and said,

"The only stench is the rolling wave of desperation you three keep giving off." I said now turning to face them and putting my back to the mirror, folding my arms and showing them that their shit wasn't going to work.

"Ha desperate, please but we have thousands of years of the King's..." this was where I'd had enough and held my hand up in the 'human' one's face as now all masks were off so to speak.

"Let me just stop you there and fill in the blanks for you as it's clear you're all lacking enough of an IQ between you to grasp this for yourselves...but I don't give a damn what you did with Lucius in the past, so you can save your, 'I had his cock' and 'we will get it again' and your 'mortal stink shit' for... I. Am. A. Fucking. *Draven!*" I shouted this last part before getting in their faces after they each took a step back from my obvious rage.

"And that means that I am the only one here that was fucking born to be his! So, unless you want me to go back in there and ask your King to gift me the three of your heads as a reminder to everyone else never to fuck with me, then I suggest you shut the fuck up! And word of warning girls, I would piss off quickly before I decide which one of you will be nailed to my fucking wall as the monkeys see no evil, hear no evil and speak no evil!" I snapped, making the redhead and ebony-haired one both take another step back, before muttering something about me being crazy as they quickly walked to the door.

But then they stopped, looking back and the confusion on

their faces now told me something was wrong and most definitely not for what they intended.

So, I followed their gaze to find the blonde was currently leaning against the countertop with her palms flat and her head hung down, the mask now discarded to the floor by her feet.

"Sister?"

"What is wrong?" They both asked one after the other. But then this was when she started shaking, as if something beneath her skin was vibrating trying to get out. I knew something was wrong even if her own sisters hadn't yet guessed it. So, I started to take a few steps back, and the second I did, it became a real 'oh shit' moment for the blonde's head quickly snapped to the side, in my direction. And the second she did, it was easy to see that something was very, very wrong. Because gone was the angelic face of beauty but instead the pure bloodlust of a rogue Vampire gone insane staring back at me.

I knew this the second her eyes seeped with blood, veins turned to black and skin to a faint reddish ash. Her fangs dripped with saliva and deadly looking claws grew from under her fingernails, flicking the once perfectly manicured ones off to the floor in a splat of blood.

Then she snarled at me, and I was once again faced with a deadly moment, only this time I wasn't facing a mortal man I knew how to fight. No, this time I was facing the strength and speed of a vampire I had never fought before.

This time, I was facing death.

And death...

Lunged for me.

CHAPTER EIGHTEEN

SINKING SHOE FEELING

And here we go.

The moment she lunged for me I quickly sidestepped, making the crazed bitch run into the wall as I had slipped into the end cubicle. Then I saw her push off the wall with a snarl, coming back at me, so I kicked the door as hard as I could, making it slam into her, knocking her back against the wall, this time next to the sinks. She roared like a wild cat and just as she was about to lunge again, her sisters were quickly there, holding her back.

"Cleo, what is wrong with you!?" The redhead said struggling to keep a hold of the clawing sister.

"Why do you..." The one with black hair started to say but the second I saw her suddenly tear her head to one side, I knew some serious shit was going down. Because it wasn't just affecting one sister. No, it was starting to affect the other two. I knew this the moment I saw her start to vibrate just like her sister had done before turning into what I could only assume was back into a savage rogue. Only this wasn't like the two I had come across back in Munich, but more like the stories of the mindless rogues Lucius had eradicated during the Cleansing.

"Oh no," I said the second the blonde broke free of the redhead's hold who, for the moment, wasn't a raving lunatic like her sisters were. Which was why I let her deal with the black-haired one as I once more had to fend off the crazed blonde bitch coming at me again. So, I did the only thing that I could think to do, and that was to kick out at her the second she came at me, lifting my skirt at the same time.

Thankfully, my metal heel did a pretty good job at stabbing her in the belly, something that at least gave me enough time to turn and grab my next weapon. While she was howling in pain, looking down at the bleeding hole in her gut, I was busy trying my hand at a bit of plumbing. I reached for the back of the toilet and with a quick tug I pulled off the toilet's system lid just in time as she was once again coming at me. So, I swung it upwards just before those claws of hers reached me, making it connect hard with her jaw, that ended up snapping her head right back. It was like watching it in slow motion as I swear that was how focused my mind was.

Zombie blonde staggered back from the force, allowing me enough space to get out of the cubicle. The second that I did, I spun to face her, and didn't hesitate to swing my unconventional weapon again, this time doing so side on like I was holding a bat. The force of which ended up breaking her jaw so badly that half of it now hung off the rest of her face. Well, there went her good looks, I thought with a grimace, openly wincing at her.

But amazingly she took a pause and turned her head to look at herself in the mirror in that super creepy way, reminding me of a crazed owl. Her sisters behind her had all paused watching this little scene play out as if in some kind of trance. Then she raised a hand to her hanging jaw and rubbed a finger across a pair of lips that were not really where they should be.

"Yeah, no amount of lipstick is gonna help with that one, blondie," I said, unable to help myself and her response to this was a very permanent way to solve the problem, as she suddenly ripped her jaw off completely and threw it at the mirror in anger, making it splat against the glass.

"Eww," I hissed but then she screamed and when doing so in the ultimate of all-girl paddies, she grabbed a fist full of her hair and suddenly ripped it out, patches of scalp and all.

"Uh…okay, well, that should help," I commented sarcastically, before she suddenly ran at me again. This also signalled the sisters to do the same which ended up in another moment, best described by the next words out of my mouth,

"Ah shit."

Then I ducked out of the way, coming up at the same time she passed, punching her in the gut, one that was bleeding from the impact of my shoe. But then I was dodging another sister as she too tried to get to me, swiping out at my skirt and slashing through the material as I jumped back. Well, lucky for me there were enough layers in this baby to withstand a slash happy maniac. Especially one that didn't seem too hot and high on the brainpower scale right then.

But at least this move put me on the door side of the

bathroom and I intended to bloody use…or at least try, as the second I nearly made it to the handle, it opened and Liessa was stepping through the door.

"What the fuck?!"

"Welcome to the party…Ah!" I said which ended with me being grabbed from behind and thrown into a cubicle, making me twist as I landed against the back wall awkwardly over the toilet. Then the cubicle doorway was being filled by the redhead, only this time she looked solely intent on finishing the job the other two hadn't yet accomplished. Which, I was pretty sure, was to rip my head off and use it as a cocktail bowl for three!

Either way the second she lunged for me she was suddenly being dragged backwards, disappearing from sight… *Thank you, Liessa.*

"Come here, Bitch!" I heard my new best friend growl as she started fighting with the red-headed rogue by the door. I quickly got my bearings and the second another one was coming for me, I looked up at the cubicle frame. Then I grabbed the bottom of my skirt and tucked it down my cleavage and made a quick decision to jump for it. I swung myself forward like a kid on the monkey bars and let my feet fly. They both hit the dark-haired chick in the chest and made her go flying back, where she fell, cracking her head on the edge of the counter before knocking her unconscious.

"One down," I said after letting go and falling back to my feet, where I found a broken faced blondie crouched low to the ground as if ready to pounce.

"You need to get out of here!" Liessa warned and I took a quick glance to see her now fighting the redhead, and in doing so having no choice but to snap her arm before getting her in a headlock.

"Yeah, I will but first, me and blondie got shit to finish," I said then I turned back to her and said,

"My turn." I said rolling my neck and nodding for the bitch to step up. She snarled a demonic hiss at me before she made her move and attacked me. So, I sidestepped, grabbing her arm in time to twist it behind her and not hesitating to break it, making her howl in pain the second I snapped the bone. Then, with her trapped in my hold, one that wasn't easy given a vampire's strength, I watched as Liessa grabbed hold of the redhead's jaw, forced it open and at the same time used her teeth to pull off her glove. Then, once free she held it above the redhead's open jaw and bent her hand back so the poisonous ink could drip down the inside sucker on her wrist and force the bitch to swallow it down.

"Damn it, now why don't I have that?" I said making her wink at me, before I decided to improvise yet again, doing so quickly before blondie slipped free. So, I grabbed her by the hair, kicked out her legs and slapped her head against the countertop at the same time, allowing both the force of gravity and my strength to do its job. Then I quickly kicked my leg up backwards and grabbed my shoe, before raising my hand up and bringing it down full force into the side of her head.

The second it struck, landing inside her ear, she exploded into a cloud of red ash and I took a step back in time to see that the redhead also did the same after first falling forward, choking on the venom.

"Well, I wasn't expecting that," Liessa commented staring down at the red ash floating around her feet.

I walked towards her, fully intent on getting the hell out of there when the black-haired one started to moan on the floor. So, without thinking I picked up the sink that Lucius had knocked free when he was…well, *knocking me*. One hard yank was all it took, and I was using all my strength to lift it off the counter before I literally dropped the whole thing on her head, making her instantly burst into a cloud of crimson dust.

"That's what happens when you forget to wash your hands, bitch," I said before stepping over the gathering pile of ash and walking to the door with Liessa behind me, chuckling at my parting line. But then when we walked back out into the main hall, my satisfied smug expression ended with my mouth dropping open. Because what faced us now was nothing short of utter chaos!

"Oh shit." I heard Liessa say beside me at the sight of all the crazed vampires now attacking anyone that was closest to them, making me realise that the three bitches of Eastwick in the bathroom weren't the only ones that had turned rogue. So naturally, my hands flew to my mouth as I uttered in gut-wrenching devastation,

"What have I done?"

Because the horror of what had just happened started to infiltrate my mind the second I saw the whole room fighting. There were groups of masked people all trying to hold back different snarling wild vampires. Whilst others weren't trying to contain them, but outright kill them. And well, considering what I had just done in the bathroom, then I wasn't exactly one to judge.

I instantly went to where Lucius and I had been sitting to see it empty. Thankfully, I didn't have to look around for long until I saw him cutting through the rogues that surrounded him with frightening ease. Okay, so there was one thing that became very apparent with Lucius in that moment and that was the man knew how to handle a sword...*Mighty lords in Hell, did he just!*

I saw him driving a group of five rogues back to the side of the staircase, as each tried to dodge his advances, meaning they were now cornered. Which I assumed was Lucius' plan all along. But then the biggest of them, a man dressed in a medieval-style tunic, jumped up like a fucking cat intent on taking Lucius out from above. However, before he could land on him, Lucius merely caught him by the throat at just the right moment. Then, whilst dangling him by the end of his arm, Lucius slammed him back down on the spanking bench, holding him prisoner there by his throat. Knowing that Clay was nearby swinging his own heavy weapon, Lucius held out his free arm behind him and shouted,

"Axe!" Clay not thinking twice, kicked the rogue he was fighting, and threw his axe to Lucius as his master requested of him. Lucius grabbed it without even looking and the second he had it in hand, he let go of the rogue's throat, took a step back so as to hammer the axe's blade down, severing the rogue's head in one go.

The body of the rogue burst into red ash, like all the others and I could then see the axe swinging back to Clay just in time. As he too grabbed it and at the same time spun out of the attack of the rogue he had kicked as he lunged for him with claws out at the ready. But Clay brought his weapon back up, slicing up the rogue's torso with a bloody spray that turned to ash in the air, before the body joined it. After this he grabbed one back from joining the group

Lucius was fighting by the back of her dress, yanked her hard to him and at the same time headbutted her with his helmet, knocking her unconscious before she too got the axe.

"Get someone to that fucking bathroom, NOW!" Lucius barked the order at the same time as kicking a rogue so hard that this particular one ended up flying through the air and landing against the St Andrews Cross. Once there Lucius wasted no time before driving the tip of his sword into its infected heart, one that burst like the rest of him.

"On it!" Ruto said, releasing a set of metal wings and after pushing his husband behind him, he started to make his way over to us when another group of rogues descended on him. This meant he had no choice but to deal with them first and his way of doing this was more than a little effective, as he threw his wings forward releasing a shower of blades that all flew from the shards of feathers, cutting through the crowd of rogues. One of which managed to get Caspian in his shoulder. Caspian turned back to snarl over at Ruto in anger before yanking the metal feather out of his flesh and using it to stab a male rogue in the head.

"His bad!" Pip said laughing before snapping her leg right up like some deadly ballerina, catching a male rogue dressed in a tux under the chin. He stumbled back into Adam, who easily snapped the rogue's head, breaking its spine and making it burst into a red cloud in two seconds.

"Aww, it's kind of pretty," Pip commented before Adam nodded behind her and said,

"Try to concentrate, petal." Pip winked at him before spinning quickly to gut punch the female rogue trying to sneak up behind her, then she grabbed her head and slammed her down on her knee making her nose burst. Then, just as the screaming rogue was bent over double, Pip jumped up and hammered her elbow down into the back of the rogue's neck, making her hit the floor. After that Pip stomped on the overhanging edge of a discarded silver tray the waiters had been using, making it flip up off the low table so she could catch it. Before the rogue had chance to get up, Pip gripped the tray with both hands raised it above her head, at the same time coming to stand over her. She then proceeded to smash it down into her neck, severing her head instantly.

It was, without a doubt, utterly badass!

Especially when she looked back at her husband, who currently looked close to drooling over his wife's actions, and spotted another female rogue coming up behind him. Pip, as if acting on instinct, looked down at all that was left of her victim and yanked the embedded tray from the stone. Then she threw it with such precision that it was inches from hitting Adam's head but instead missed him and hit the rogue so hard that she went flying backwards, crashing into a table. After this she skipped over to Adam who was looking behind him to see what had just happened and patted his chest before saying sweetly,

"Try to concentrate, flower bee." Then with a smirk walked past, found the girl, and stomped on her head snarling down at her,

"He's taken, bitch!"

Now that really was badass!

CHAPTER NINETEEN

RISE OF ASHES

I looked to Liessa and the first thing that came out of my mouth was the immeasurable amount of guilt I felt. As there was only one possible reason this was all happening now.

"This is all my fault," I whispered, and without saying a word in return, she took my hand in her gloved one and gave it a squeeze. It was a small comfort in light of what I had done, but it was a comfort all the same. Because the night before, by giving that box my blood, I knew what I was witnessing now could be no one else's fault but my own. I had caused this. There was no doubt in my mind.

But this self-pity was cut short, as my 'oh shit' moments of the night were just about to get even worse, upgrading into what I uttered,

"Oh fuck." This was said because the first rogue suddenly got wind of the only mortal in the room and well, for them I was an easy kill and more importantly…

An easy meal!

Which was now why about eight of them all raised their heads up in the air and started snarling as soon as the scent of mortal blood started to caress their senses. That was when they started to come for us and in turn Liessa turned all business the second she let go of my hand and said,

"Never mind that now! Here, I take it you know how to use this," Liessa assumed after ridding someone of the weapons they wore as part of their costume like Lucius had done. And it wasn't as if they were going to deny her, not when it was me she was protecting, as saying no would have meant a death sentence had Lucius ever got wind of it. So, I caught the sword she threw at me by the handle and said,

"Fuck yeah, I do!"

"Good, then follow me," she said, coming in front and protecting me the best she could as we made our way into the fray, as it was clear she was trying to get me back to Lucius as quickly as she could. I didn't know how many rogues there were that had changed, but there seemed to be enough that it was a group effort in trying to get them under control.

It was also easy to recognise some of the faces I had walked past when being led to Lucius' council seating area that were now part of the unfortunate souls to be infected by whatever this sickness was that turned them back into rogues. Because it was obvious that certain vamps were being turned back to what they once were before Lucius had gifted them his blood. Only it must have been in a more mindless, bloodlust kind of way, because surely such a creature couldn't function in the mortal world like this. As there was blood lust and then there was a rabid dog, foaming at the mouth and out of his mind, crazed with aggression and hunger type of lust.

Of course, it wasn't exactly the best time to be trying to work out all the reasons or coming up with theories. Not when right ahead of me was the sight of Lucius commanding his people with a sword in hand. One, that I noted was bloody and coated in red ash. This wasn't surprising as he was still surrounded by rogues intent on killing him. But then he suddenly found me across the room and for a single moment I froze unable to do more than mouth to him,

'I'm okay,' knowing this was what he would want to know. But then it looked as though I was about to speak too soon.

"Fae, look out!" Liessa shouted and I quickly reacted when I saw a blur of motion in the corner of my eye. So, I spun on one bare foot after already using my shoes as weapons and losing them to the cause of survival. But I didn't need them in this fight, not when I finally had a weapon in my hand and it was one I knew well.

Which was why, the second I saw the rogue coming at me, it didn't take me long before I put him on the ground. I slashed the sword up the length of his body with a roar of my anger. Then not taking any chances I finished the kill by thrusting the length of the sword into his neck, taking an appreciative moment to note the quality of the blade.

On hearing a growl behind me I spun, wrenching my sword out of the spine of the rogue, who like the others evaporated into a cloud of red ash. But with this next one, I just had enough time to see myself being surrounded by more rogues, which I knew made sense seeing as I was the only human in the room. So, I took my defensive position, remembering my training so my footing was my strength as well as the way I held my sword across my body.

"Let's do this," I said to the one snarling at me, bent over and claws at the ready, taking in the seven rogues all spaced out behind him. Each looked beyond all reason of sanity, as the only thing they wanted right now was the taste of my blood.

And how I did enjoy disappointing those that underestimated me and wanted me dead.

"COME ON!" I screamed in anger as the first one lunged, making me bring my sword up the second he did, catching him up the belly as I ran into the move, before spinning quickly and bringing my blade up again at the same time slicing up his back. The second he went down, I was ready for the next, bringing my blade back up and quickly finding myself going down on one knee. This was so I both dodged an attack and could swipe out my blade at the height of my shoulders, slicing through a rogue's belly. The strike ended up cutting so deep this time there was no chance for blood to spray, so instead of getting a face full of blood, I was momentarily consumed by a cloud of crimson ash.

However, this was obviously the point when Lucius had fought enough rogues off around him to do something. And well, let's just say on finding that his girlfriend was surrounded herself, in a ballgown with a sword in hand, battling rogues was probably the last image he expected to see.

So, it was little wonder that seconds before the next rogues attacked, I suddenly found myself being captured around the waist and pulled away, before Lucius was suddenly standing in front of me. Then, in a blurring flash of motion, Lucius managed to take down all the rogues that had been trying to get to me.

For the next few seconds Lucius was nothing more than a blur of motion as he spun from one enemy to the next, slicing through his victims with startling ease and deadly beauty. But then the more he killed, the more he became consumed by clouds of ash that only grew thicker with each rogue that fell by his sword.

This meant that by the time he was finished, he was walking back towards me, emerging like the Devil from a portal in Hell itself. This was thanks to the fog of red mist that shrouded his masterful figure before he stepped free of it and it floated to the ground behind him. It was also when I finally took note that it was Clay who had me in his arms, still holding me from behind no doubt to prevent me from running into danger to assist.

But Lucius looked like a man possessed and with only me in his sights, then it was no wonder why I tensed in Clay's hold, unsure on how those next few minutes would go. Did Lucius blame me as I blamed myself for what had happened? It wasn't as if I could blame him if he did. Because there was no mistaking it, Lucius looked beyond furious and the murder in his eyes was painted crimson and black. He stormed right up to us both with purpose and growled low in his throat before saying in a deadly tone,

"I like you, Clay, but if you don't take your fucking arm off my woman right now, then I will fucking kill you with it and..."

"You got it, boss!" Clay replied quickly and at the same time letting me go before Lucius had time to finish his entire threat. Which was only when Lucius placed his sword back in the sheath that I noticed had been buckled back around his waist. One minus the other smaller sword and dagger.

"Just keeping her safe for you, Sire," Clay added as way of explanation and Lucius nodded, for it was clear he understood this. But still, seeing another man's arm around me must have flipped something inside him, because suddenly the sword I was still holding was snatched out of my hand and tossed angrily to the side before I was tugged towards him. Then, just before making impact with his chest, he bent and I found that impact on his shoulder as he stood with me over it.

He clamped my legs to his chest in one arm, along with the length of my dress before he nodded to Clay. After this he walked over to Adam, who had just snapped the head off one rogue that had tried to lunge for Pip's back who was busy fighting another.

But Pip's style of fighting looked more like a gymnast going through a routine on the mats, as she looked nimble and twice as fast. To the point that the male rogue she was fighting couldn't actually get a hold on her and before he knew it her legs were around the top of his head. And then with a squeeze of her thighs, she let her body fall backwards off him. As she fell, she did a backwards handstand, managing to take the guy somersaulting over her head, causing him to be thrown backwards until he smashed into the far wall. To say it was impressive was a huge understatement. I just wished I had seen it the right way up.

"Report!" Lucius snapped at his right-hand man.

"Most have been dispatched or detained. I ordered those captured to be taken to the cells below as I knew you would want to ascertain as much information as you could from the ones who were weak enough to be subdued. I ordered Ruto and Caspian to do a sweep of the entire castle just to be sure there are none of the turned hiding...Hakan has been on the hunt for those that fled since the first of them changed," my uncle said making Lucius nod in response, making me realise why Adam held the position he did. *Damn, he was good.*

"Good, I want every fucking person not on my council detained and on lockdown in their assigned rooms. Then I want you in my office and Pip in my quarters as soon as it's done!" Adam bowed his head and replied,

"It will be done, Sire."

However, Lucius never heard this respectful response, as he was currently walking through the destruction left in the wake of such a short battle, as I couldn't tell how many rogues had turned in total. But by the look of all the red ash that now coated the floor, then I would have to say it had been more than enough to turn this night into a nightmare.

Lucius walked with purpose, creating footprints in the layer of death, with ash still floating to the ground like blood-soaked snow. But then I watched as his discarded Devil's mask came into view on the floor, and I wasn't sure if he saw it too, as he simply stepped on it, crushing it under his boot. I had to say it ended up being a symbolic sight for how this night had ended and I couldn't help but feel so badly for him. It just seemed that his world was crumbling around him, first with the attack on his club and now his home, making me wonder what was next?

Of course, I also knew that, yes, as much as the box had been the start of all his troubles, I also knew that it wasn't the only common denominator in this equation.

I was.

I was the other end of that blame and I knew that. And really, when all the reasons he'd explained had been why he had kept me at arm's length, were starting to come true, then could it really be argued against anymore? Not after all the things that had happened since I had been forced into his life had been nothing but one disaster after another. Gods, but why, oh why, did I have to open that stupid box!?

I had been so foolish.

Too arrogant in my own ego by believing I knew what was best and allowing my knowledge and intelligence in my field of expertise to convince myself that I had been right. When thousands before me had also been foolish enough to believe them right in their findings. Science was only as strong as its believer at the time until the next belief came along and destroyed theory with fact. It was like American Astronomer Carl Sagan once said, 'Science is a way of thinking, much more than it is a body of knowledge.'

Needless to say, that my mind was at its height of self-torturing mode by the time Lucius had made it to the top of the steps before he reared back and kicked open the doors. Something which jarred me from my self-pity. It also meant that the second he walked a few steps into the hallway, after first checking it was clear, I was near bursting with guilt. He suddenly pulled me forward, letting me slide down his body and pinned me to the wall, looking beyond furious.

So, I blurted out at the same time he did,

"I am so sorry!"

"Are you alright?"

After this we both looked at each other for a few still

seconds before we both spoke at the same time, and once again, mine was a statement and his was a question,

"It's all my fault!"

"You blame yourself?"

"Maybe one of us should pause before this conversation gets too confusing," I suggested making him release a sigh before nodding and telling me in a tense tone,

"Then you can answer my questions, starting with the first, something I consider the most important to me right now." It couldn't be denied that to witness his concern for me, even over everything else that had just happened, was like a gift and one I treasured. Which was why I let my head fall forward, leaning my forehead to his chest as I told him on a murmur,

"I am fine, just ashamed of myself for what I might have caused." I felt his hand cradle the back of my head, his fingers embedding themselves in the mound of curls amazingly still pinned there. A testament to Pip's hairdressing skills no less.

"You're not hurt?" he asked, as if needing to confirm it. So, I lifted my head and told him,

"No, although I can't say the same for the bitches of Eastwick." He raised a brow in question adding to it a questioning,

"Bitches of Eastwick?"

"Erm, I hate to break this to you, as much as the bitchy jealous side of me doesn't, but your triplets turned rogue and attacked me in the bathroom." He closed his eyes and took a deep breath and for a moment I thought this must have upset him. As well, they did all have history, and a lot of it, according to Pip.

But then he said,

"First of all, they are not *my triplets*, for they mean nothing to me and haven't for a long time, and second, they fucking attacked you!?"

"Yeah, but don't worry, they went poof," I said, even using my hand to gesture the effect by joining my fingertips before suddenly spreading out my fingers in an exploding motion.

"They went *poof?*" he asked with a twitch of his lips at the terminology I used and after watching my hand add to the explanation.

"Yeah, and lucky for me before they had chance to do anything more than shove me around a bit, even though I was pretty sure they wanted to do a lot more than that, namely rip off my head and use it as…"

"Yes, yes, I am getting the picture and not one I fucking want to ever have, so get to the point where they went *poof*," he said mocking me by using the same word and making me smile.

"Well, me and Liessa handled it," I told him and again, this prompted another eyebrow raise,

"Handled it how exactly?"

"How?" I repeated, wondering what he wanted here, like a play by play action replay or just the highlights?

"Yes how, as last I checked, sweetheart, I didn't exactly leave you in that bathroom with a fucking axe."

"No, but you should probably do that from now on," I joked, one he didn't see the funny side of if the low growl was anything to go by, especially when it was added by the reprimanding tone of him saying my name.

"Amelia."

"Okay, so let's just say there is a reason I am no longer wearing shoes and I also have to thank you for loosening that sink bowl, as it came in handy…but I might need to add that some remodelling costs may be in your future." At this Lucius took a step back, looked down at my feet a moment and dragged a hand down his face in frustration before admitting,

"I seriously don't know where to fucking start, for I have no words."

"Well, it looked as though I wasn't the only one who had problems," I said trying to steer the conversation back to his fighting.

"I am not sure what triggered it but my people they… they just started to turn back to their natural vampiric state, only it was worse, as if it was even before they had stepped foot in the mortal world," he told me making me frown.

"You mean like when they were first spawned in Hell or something?" I asked and Lucius thought about it for a moment before agreeing,

"Yes, exactly that. It was as if they had forgotten everything about themselves…so many people and all of them with me for so long…in fact…" Lucius stopped mid-thought and looked away as he was clearly trying to piece together something important.

"In fact?" I asked, trying to nudge him into continuing, something he didn't do but instead stepped into me and once again I found my back against the wall. Then he tipped my chin up and said,

"Thank the Gods you weren't hurt." I would have pushed the matter on what he was about to say only moments ago but was stopped in my tracks the second he suddenly crushed his lips to mine. His kiss was hot and heavy. As if the thought of me fighting three against one and with vampires no less, well it was as if he needed to reassure himself that I was still alive and well. Something I happily allowed him the time to do, especially seeing as it came in the form of him kissing me, which was nothing short of toe-curling blissful and utterly divine.

But then, just as I was happily getting lost in the act, I saw a flash of something creeping up behind his back and my instincts kicked in quicker than even I knew possible. Because I suddenly had my hand around the handle of Lucius' sword, drew it from its sheath and drove it forward the second the rogue lunged for Lucius' back. However, I wasn't the only one to react in time as Lucius twisted at the right second and slashed out with what was now a demonic hand cast in Hellish armour. One that I had become used to seeing these days.

It was so powerful a strike that the rogue's head literally severed from his body and as it flew to the floor it burst into a small cloud of ash the second it hit the ground. Lucius then spun back around to find my arm out straight behind him and he turned in time to see the body part of our victim break away into the same red ash. Only now doing so around the blade I had imbedded into his gut.

Then he looked back at me in what was a mixture of shock and open awe.

"I think that's what we call a team effort," I said needing to break the silence and get an idea of what he was thinking. Thankfully, I didn't have to wait long as he suddenly had his hands framing my face, including his Hellish gauntleted hand that, granted, was extra gentle with me. Then he tipped my face up so he could tell me on an aroused growl,

"Gods, but you're fucking magnificent!" Then he kissed me, doing so to the sound of the clatter as his sword fell from my fingers. Fingers that quickly gripped onto him to hold him to me as if I never wanted to let go. And if I thought the first kiss had been a passionate one, then compared to this, it could have been classed as an entrée! As this, well this was most definitely the main course!

But then, like most delicious feasts, it had to come to an end, as Lucius was a King and necking his girlfriend all night after his people had just suffered a tragedy meant only one thing, Lucius needed to focus on damage control. I knew this when he swung my legs from beneath me and started carrying me in the direction I now knew was towards his private home.

"That's okay, I can walk, just..." His pointed look was what killed this sentence dead in the water.

"Not when you don't have shoes, you can't," he told me nodding down to where my feet were currently hidden by layers of material, a dress that had mainly survived other than for the claw marks slashed across the skirt. Something he growled at the moment he noticed it.

"Do I want to know?" he all but snarled.

"Not really no, but if you like I can really embellish reality and say a ginger pussy cat didn't take kindly to me gut-punching her sister after first knocking off her jaw with the back of the toilet or when I stabbed her in the gut with my shoe for that matter... so naturally, I got her claws." Lucius stopped walking and stared down at me before asking,

"And exactly which part of that story is the embellishment?"

"Err, the part where she is a cat," I answered cautiously.

"That's what I thought…Gods alive, woman, is there anything you do by halves?" I rolled my lips inwards and finally gave in to the urge to bite my fingertips, before saying,

"Not really, no…although I should point out that Liessa was the one to break bones this time."

"And you didn't?" he asked as if he knew the answer already,

"Well, yes I did but she did it first and besides, I needed some way to get her to her knees and let's just say that extreme pain really helps in getting what you want."

"On her knees?" he asked, clearly very interested to know.

"Yeah, well it was easier that way when smashing her head onto the counter before I stabbed her in the head with my other shoe." Lucius cursed through his teeth before saying,

"So, you stabbed her twice with the same shoe?"

"No, different shoes, as it's how I lost them both and to be honest, looking back now and blondie really did get the worst end of the fighting stick." Lucius' eyes widened before he shook his head as if he was trying to picture everything I'd just described but was still coming up empty.

"And the other two?"

"Liessa took care of the redhead by forcing her to drink her ink and the black-haired chick, well I kind of might have dropped a sink bowl on her head."

"Ah, hence thanking me for loosening it," he surmised before saying,

"I think it's safe to say that you are the most resourceful person I have ever met." I smiled but then the reality of the reasons why hit me, and I swallowed hard before saying,

"Yeah, that might be true, but Lucius, what if by me opening the box caused this…those three sisters would still be alive…all those people…your people…what if I am…?" Lucius again stopped walking so he could lift me higher to his face and whisper down at me,

"Don't go there, sweetheart."

"Don't go there?! How can I not? Hell, here I am making jokes about killing them and…"?

"They did try and kill you first, pet, so it's not like they didn't deserve it," he told me making me scoff,

"Yeah and what if the only reason they turned that way was because I opened that fucking box! What then?"

"I said don't go there, Amelia." I released a shuddered breath before sucking one back in again, the moment I felt the tears of guilt rising.

Then, as the first tear fell, I told him honestly…

"But I am already there."

CHAPTER TWENTY

LUCIUS

AN ERA TO ASHES

"How is she?" I asked Adam the moment he set foot in my office. This was once the rest of my council had been given leave and after an hour of me being beyond pissed off and barking orders at everyone! Adam shrugged his shoulders first of all, and said,

"She blames herself and as you know, guilt is a torturous emotion to live through." Fuck, but he had that right!

Adam was one of the only beings alive that knew the full extent of the guilt I had good reason to feel and the main reason why I had kept her at arms-length for so long. Something he had even had to keep from his wife. A feat in itself, as it was to date the one and only thing he had ever kept from her.

But, if such a thing was possible for a being like me, then

Adam was what convention would class as being my best friend, however juvenile that sounded. But then he was my right hand for a reason, as he was loyal to the very core and even had he been without the gift of my blood, making him what he is today, then I knew without a doubt he would still have my back no matter what.

But our genuine friendship was one that others rarely saw for what it truly was, as in front of the rest of the world he seemed to be the most cordial servant. However, behind closed doors like this time, he was simply a friend who was free to give me shit and speak to me however he damn well pleased. And I wouldn't have had it any other way. Because I needed that honesty in my life and being King, and one with an often deadly and icy temper, well let's just say there weren't many brave enough to challenge me.

But well, Adam was...*different*. And that was putting it mildly considering he was the most powerful being ever created and created he was. Lucifer's idea of an experiment gone wrong and when I say wrong, what I mean is the destroying all of Hell variety.

Before he merged with Adam, the man before me now and the mortal vessel the beast lived within, he was actually a colossal beast, by the name of Abaddon. For many years Lucifer managed to contain him, first needing to give him his own level of Hell to roam as an unsuspecting prisoner. But Lucifer's beast would grow irritated and if such a word could be used to describe such a creature... *he also grew bored.*

So, Lucifer, not wanting to waste his beast, put him to good use as the final punishment when passing the cruelest of judgements. The same punishment that was cast upon a fortunate Pip, after first being tried for the part she unknowingly played in bringing the black plague to London, causing the deaths of at least 40,000 people.

This meant she soon found herself being given to Abaddon as a plaything, one he usually ate after he was done amusing himself with them. However, what no one expected was that the beast would never get bored of Pip and in fact, beyond all comprehension, actually fell in love with the Imp.

But when Lucifer got wind of this, he feared the power she would hold over Hell, knowing that Abaddon had the ability to destroy his Kingdom, should she merely ask her beast to do so. Which meant that what he did next was the grave mistake of having her taken from him. Or at least they tried, for the moment Abaddon discovered her gone, his rage ended up causing the 1667 Shamakhi earthquake that killed about 80,000 people, ironically double the death toll his little Imp had accidentally caused.

What came next was time for Lucifer himself to pay her a visit, when he tried to convince her that if he revoked her sentence then in return, she must control the beast to his needs. But what he didn't count on was that Pip had also fallen in love with Abaddon and utterly refused to allow anyone to use her beast.

This naturally didn't go down well with Lucifer, so as a punishment for disobeying him, he revoked her sentence anyway, doing so in such a way that Pip had no choice but to be sent back to the mortal realm. In doing so he believed he could then use Pip as bait, controlling Abaddon by threatening to keep her from him for eternity if the beast refused to do as he commanded. Needless to say, that Lucifer, also known as my father, was a bit of a bastard in this regard.

Unfortunately for the Devil, Abaddon didn't take too kindly to this and quickly started to destroy Hell, despite Lucifer's armies trying to stop him. Which meant that he had no choice but to plead with the Imp to find Abaddon a host and one strong enough that he could accept such a beast out of Hell and contain him in a mortal body.

Lucifer then called upon his good friend, King Asmodeus who rules over the Circle of Lust and just so happened to be the father of one Dominic Draven. Seeing as at the time I was Dom's right hand, I was then commissioned to find the shadow Imp and help her in her mission to find a host. One who, to survive the transformation, would first have to die whilst being turned into one of my sired. And furthermore, at the same time Pip had to bring forth Abaddon, drawing him out through Hell and fusing him inside his new host. The only way it worked was because it had simply all been fated to happen this way, as my abilities to sire a human can only achieved if it has been granted the power to do so by the Fates themselves. Which I assume was how the past version of me was able to achieve this with Keira. For I have no knowledge of the act other than what Keira has conveyed to me herself about the events that happened all that time ago.

But as for Adam and Pip, the pair never left my side other than for the last thirty years or so that they have been at Afterlife. Something at the time I encouraged at first for Keira's sake due to the deep friendship she and Pip had forged. Then secondly, after meeting Amelia for the first time and discovering who she was to me. Well, then it served its greater purpose by having the most powerful being alive, one loyal to only me, situated where my Chosen One resided.

Which also meant that Adam had been the first to discover my true feelings for the girl and had aided me in keeping tabs on her since the tender age of sixteen. Pip, of course, eventually learned the truth of my feelings for her 'niece' as it became harder and harder to keep my obsession from her, especially when I had her husband doing my dirty work for me.

Of course, eventually this knowledge also got back to Keira and made for somewhat of an awkward conversation to say the least. But then she admitted that there was always a part of her that knew this would happen. And it was like she had said, 'who was she to get in the way of what is fated to be'. Of course, since being the one fated to prevent the end of days, then let's just say that Keira's 'personal thoughts on the Fates and their plans' had changed somewhat over the years.

"Yes, I am somewhat familiar with the sentiment." I said drily in response to his guilty comment, as he walked to the opposite side of my desk and help himself to a seat.

"She fears that you blame her too," Adam informed me making me rub a hand down my face as was a habit when frustrated.

"I blame the fucking box, the bastards that want it and a fucking witch I want to see burn by my feet for manipulating her into opening it!" I snarled.

"Are you sure she did, and our girl wasn't just too curious to stop herself?" he asked, playing Devil's advocate as he usually did behind closed doors. For Adam would never question me like this in front of anyone else.

"She planted the fucking seed and that is enough for me!" Adam smirked at my response and replied,

"It's good to know you don't have it in you to blame her." I rolled my eyes and snapped,

"Do you blame your wife for half the shit she does?" Adam rolled his wedding band around his finger, whilst smiling down at it and said,

"Oh, I blame her, only in a way she enjoys. But out of the bedroom, no, not ever. To begin with, you know full well the beast won't let me, for in our eyes my Winfred can do no wrong." I walked over to the wet bar, grabbed two glasses and the only bottle that would do. Then I walked back to my desk, having good memories infiltrate my mind and unable to help myself when my lips twitched in a knowing grin that wanted to emerge at the sight of the damage I had done to the desktop. Claw marks I purposely kept there as a reminder of taking Amelia on my desk. Then I wisely poured us both a drink and left the bottle within reach.

"You soft sentimental bastard, you." I said on a laugh after passing him a glass of Henri IV Dudognon Heritage Cognac, one aged for a hundred years and worth every single penny of the expensive price tag it came with. But let's just say that tonight, it was a two-million-dollar drink moment. Of course, the drink itself wasn't worth the majority of the expense. No, that was mainly down to the bottle it came in which was dipped 24K gold and sterling platinum and decorated with 6,500 brilliant-cut diamonds. A drink fit for a king I thought with an inner roll of my eyes. Fuck, but I hated all that king shit sometimes, and thought back to the easier, simpler days when I left all that up to Dom. Meaning I was then free to take on the assassin role I was most comfortable doing.

"Yes, and I welcome you to the club, my King." Adam

replied raising his glass to me before taking a sip as if he had just known exactly where my thoughts were. But that was Adam, he often knew what I was thinking even when millions of others wouldn't dare to try and guess.

"Well, you can do this sentimental bastard a favour and cut the king shit, yeah?" I said, re-taking my seat opposite him at my desk. He smirked again and nodded his head.

"So, what are you going to do?" he asked making me relax back into my seat, rubbing the day's growth of stubble at my jaw before telling him,

"Hope you have some ideas and they don't start with the one I refuse to do," I said making him shrug his shoulders before saying,

"Then my advice is not to ask me, for you won't like my reply, Luc." I groaned and hissed a venomous,

"Fuck!" Then I downed the drink in one, before swiping the bottle for a refill.

"Did you get the names of all the fallen?" I asked, quickly changing the subject.

"I did."

"And is it as I suspected?" I asked offering him a top-up in a silent gesture but with a shake of his head he declined and told me,

"All that turned rogue were the first of the new kind, the oldest of your sired, like you thought." At this I lowered my head a moment and hissed an ancient Persian curse. I thought back to all I had sired in that time, knowing that most of the ones here tonight we'd had no choice but to take out and turn to ash. Something, I had never seen happen before and had to wonder at its cause. Was it a curse of some kind? Was this the witch's doing for looking at the box's contents, being that it held nothing more than a seemingly pointless map, then I had to question why? It had held nothing suspicious or anything to make me believe that Amelia was the cause of this by opening it in the first place.

Or perhaps Adam was right, and I was looking at this with a biased mind. Either way it didn't change the outcome, as nothing could be done to change it now, so why torture the woman I loved with a guilt my words of reprimand would only make worse. She had already received my disappointment and annoyance when first hearing of her actions, she didn't need more.

However, when I thought back to all that had been lost tonight, and in all honesty, my only thoughts had centred on Amelia. Barking orders at my council in getting to her, for she needed to be protected. Orders I knew should have been centred on the safety of my people. But then I had failed in my duties as King, for I knew in that moment I would have sent any of my people to their deaths in order to save her from her own.

But then this was the power of a Chosen One, as I remember what Dom had been like all those years with Keira, something he remained to this day, extending it now to his precious daughter.

"I need as many of my youngest turned on the hunt, for it is possible that right now there are thousands of rogues out there hunting the mortal world like mindless, rabid dogs out for blood," I told him and he informed me,

"It has already been done, but you know by doing so it will not be long before he hears of what has happened and my suggestion, don't wait for him to call you," Adam said, referring of course to Dom, who was essentially the King of

Kings, the first and overlord of all supernatural life, despite us being on equal footing. Although, when it came to his daughter, then I doubted he would see it that way.

"Point taken. Now, what of the others, are there any showing signs of turning, ones not quite as old but close in age all the same?" I asked.

"Nothing as of yet but seeing that we have no clue as to what this even is, then it could be hours, days, weeks, or even never, and just the oldest were targeted because they were of the weakest you turned at the time," Adam replied and it was true, as at first, I wasn't exactly picky who I turned. Besides, I was put there to do a job and that was to change the first of my kind. Savage beings that were unruly and often too bloodthirsty to see sense. However, they were nothing like the mindless beasts they had turned into tonight. But then they'd had years to adapt to mortal life and even managed at times to keep their existence hidden. Of course, there were those of them that were sloppy in that one rule Lucifer had set, hence why he deemed it necessary for a change…*cue me.*

But since then and as time continued on, I preferred to turn only demons, angels or other subspecies who were the strongest of their kind. Morphing them into something so much more and tapping into their potential, doing so by enhancing their abilities and strengths. But then I thought about all my people inside these carved walls and now every single one of them became a potential threat to Amelia. Which now begged the question, where the fuck was safe for her next!? Well, Adam had his ideas about this, and they were ones I didn't want to fucking hear right now, even though I understood his reasoning.

"So, what is our next move?" Adam asked making me hammer my glass on the desk after I had downed the last of the expensive liquid making it crack, before saying,

"The fuck if I know!" I snapped in frustration and about five seconds away from ripping my fucking hair out! Because it was true, I had no clue where to go from here. I literally had nothing to go on. I had already been down to my dungeon, one kept at the lowest level of the mountain and was cut off by a large body of water that continually seeped down the large crack at the top of the castle as snow melted or rain fell. It created a waterfall that ran down the centre which fell into a pool by the cells, the constant sound of running water often driving my prisoners mad. Nature's natural torture if you like.

However, the twenty or so rogues imprisoned there now were already lost to madness and the sight took me back to my first day setting foot into the mortal world once more, in my new body. It had been the time of the great Cleansing, as all that wanted to survive it had to kneel to their new master before accepting my blood. An act that brought about their change.

They would then grow stronger, but the price was doing so under my control, for I could literally command them to do as I wished and they would have no choice but to obey. But, like the two rogues I'd faced back in Munich inside that mansion, I hadn't been able to control their minds, just like the snarling mindless prisoners that had faced me inside the cells.

I couldn't see anything inside their minds other than rivers of blood and rage. It was as though whatever had done this to them had infected their minds to such a degree, that they no longer had the knowledge of who or what they were. Had mortals witnessed such a being then the terminology they would have used to label such beings would have been mindless zombies, for right now it was a fitting description. As they had been stripped of all personality, leaving nothing behind other than their most basic instincts...*their need to feed.*

I had even ordered some blood to be given to them in hopes of calming one enough to get a read on their mind, or in hopes even a primitive level of communication was possible. But unfortunately, this merely seemed to drive them into wanting more. Which I believed if allowed to, all that would eventually happen was they would simply gorge themselves to death.

Either way, unless I found a way to stop this or at best case scenario, reverse the effects, then these poor unfortunate souls would be sentenced to death. And in all honesty, it was doing them a justice, for being left down here to die was no way to go. Not after over two thousand years of fidelity to me and such loyalty.

My added frustration quickly came when thinking of all the rest I had turned over the years, wondering which would be the next wave of people it would affect. I thought about those closest to me and the council I had surrounded myself with, which had essentially become family. But then, with these thoughts attacking my mind like a never-ending river of questions flowing through me like acid in my veins, the worst of it hit my heart the second one name slipped through my lips,

"Keira." Adam straightened in his chair and asked,
"What is it?"

"Fuck!" I was up and out of my chair, this time raking a hand through my hair and growling like a caged beast, only hearing my name being spoken bringing me back from the blinding rage brewing like a storm in my mind.

"Luc?"

"What if this is all about time?" I said as my thoughts all travelled at such speed, I was surprised it allowed enough energy left to form fucking words.

"What do you mean?"

"The first of those I sired, they were the first to change. Well, what if it doesn't stop there but starts to change the next of those I sired and so on, and so on and doesn't fucking stop!"

"You mean it is like an infection travelling along a family tree of those you sired," Adam deduced and I nodded, making him now look grave, for that would only mean one thing.

The eradication of our entire race.

"I had assumed that whatever was inside the box had the strength or means to end my life, which was how we interpreted the end of all vampire life, seeing as each is tied to me and my blood, but what if we were wrong."

"You believe the eradication of our kind now has nothing to do with your death but instead, is death itself?" he asked forcing me to admit the severity of what could be our future.

"Yes, for after tonight's events it would make sense, seeing as I am still standing and yet the first of my people to turn are not and now nothing more than ash coating the floors of Blutfelsen," I replied giving him food for thought as he raised his glasses further up his nose and asked me,

"Then why is it this witch and whoever she works for,

want it so badly?" It was in that question that the answer started to really hit me, and I hammered a fist down on the desk, and swore viciously,

"FUCK!"

"What is it?"

"I have been so fucking blind! They don't want the box to kill me, they never did! Gods, how blind I have been."

"Then why do they want it?" he asked placing down his own glass and doing so with far less anger than I.

"The same reason we now need it, to stop the end of our existence." I told him, for it seemed so fucking obvious now!

"You believe the box will lead you to the way to stop it?"

"It has to, for that can be the only reason for it in the first place if not to destroy us," I replied, for it was true, what other reason could there be!?

"I hate to play Devil's advocate here, Luc, but don't you think it's possible that this infection could have been released when she opened the box?" I thought about that and told him,

"No, because such a thing would not have been able to focus on vampires of age. No, it has to be something else driving this and I think that box is the means of stopping it. Why else would Amelia have found a map inside when she opened it?" Adam looked thoughtful a moment and I continued on to say,

"And I will remind you that there were nearly twenty hours in between her opening it and the first wave of deaths to infect our people. It wouldn't make sense for it to take so long and target only a certain age of vampire, for why didn't it target me first and what was its purpose to do so if its reason was complete eradication?"

"Put like that, then yes, I have to agree, but what now, for didn't you say that the map is useless?" I leant my weight back against the desk as I ran a hand at the back of my neck, looking up to the ceiling as I tried to think what it could possibly lead to, as like Amelia had pointed out, it seemed utterly useless.

"I don't know what the map is trying to tell us, but I now know one thing and that is whoever is pulling the strings to all of this, is not telling his rogues the truth of why he wants that box. I would bet my fucking fangs that he is simply trying to find a way to save his own ass!"

"You think he's maybe a rogue of age and one that has gone under the radar for that long?" Adam asked now clearly coming round to my way of thinking.

"It is possible and their desperation in retrieving that fucking box would certainly suggest so. A desperation that has now become our own, for I fear time is not on our side here," I told him making him nod before asking the hardest question of all,

"And what of Keira, surely she is safe for she was turned less than thirty years ago?" Adam said forgetting the biggest part of that turning… the fact that it wasn't the 'me' he saw standing here now who actually had sired her.

"You're forgetting one important part about that, my friend," I said making him raise a brow in question, so I told him the severity of the matter,

"Keira was sired by me yes, but by me in the past…"

"Two thousand years ago,"

CHAPTER TWENTY-ONE

SNAPPING THE CORD

"How is she?" I asked as soon as I finally made it back down to my quarters, looking down at Amelia from above the living area. Pip had known I was there, hence why she came up to meet me, and I had to say the grave expression on her face wasn't one I was used to seeing. This alone told me it wasn't good, something her words only confirmed.

"She blames herself." I released a deep sigh as I took in the sight of my girl, who was currently still in her dress. Only now instead of the regal rose she had been when entering the grand hall, she now looked more like a wilted flower. She was currently sat on the floor, shoulders slumped as she concentrated on building something on the coffee table in front of her. Her glasses now replaced her contact lenses and they were currently sliding down her nose as she fitted what must have been a tricky piece.

"What is she doing?" I couldn't help but ask.

"I don't know, but she isn't even following the instructions, so that just goes to show how upset she is!" Pip exclaimed dramatically, still giving me no clue as to what Amelia was doing. But then I noticed all the torn boxes and clear plastic bags around her and through the power of deduction, I guessed it was making her precious Lego sets I had asked Pip to bring her.

I knew then that what she was doing was deflecting, trying to take her mind off the night's events. I had to confess that the sight of her forlorn face caused my heart to ache. I just wanted to go down there, pick her up off the floor and carry her to our bed, simply to hold her until she slept. She had been through so much since I had stepped into her world and commandeered every aspect of it. But then she had stepped into mine willingly and that had been the last of my restraint, for it snapped declaring that she would never leave my side again.

Well, now I would have no choice but to break that vow, for I knew I would soon have to leave her. This was so I could discover who or whatever was causing the death of my people. And I couldn't risk her safety by taking her with me, not when my blood mixed with hers simply made her a target. Unknowingly, I had done this to her when binding myself to her, making her a living, breathing key to the box, and one that could potentially be used at any moment to destroy my race. Because, after speaking with Adam, I now knew that it was possible that the reason the box existed was as a safeguard in case this ever happened. Something that would only come to light once it was needed. Now an army of rogues wanted it before they lost their lives to the crazed sickness that consumed those of them that had turned tonight. And what if they got their hands on the way to stop this epidemic first, as let's just say that I doubted they would be inclined to share.

No, my guess was that as soon as they found the cause or antidote, it was one they intended to use against me, trying to overthrow my rule with one of their own. After all, the one who had the power to reverse the infection or offer a cure of life held all the cards and what good was I, as their ruler, if I was no longer the one to save them?

Of course, I couldn't be certain on this plan of theirs, but it stood to good reason, as what else would there be? Very little else made sense. So, after this discovery, it was time to get plans in place, which first of all meant getting my Chosen One to a safe location before I had to leave to deal with this shit storm!

Now this thought didn't exactly fill me with joy, as leaving her would be like willingly tearing my fucking heart out and handing it to her on a platter for her to keep until my return. So, agonising was the consensus on that one.

But it was a necessary evil that had to be done, for there had been far too many attempts on both her life and stealing her away from me so far. I wasn't about to let it happen again! Which was why I had Adam working on some alternative locations where keeping her safe would be possible. Something that, putting it mildly, I knew she would not like.

She hated to be made to feel weak and not be included in everything, something I knew was a by-product of being made to feel isolated and segregated from her father's world. And truly, I hated the idea of doing it to her, knowing it had the power to affect our relationship and the solid foundations

I had near broken my fucking back trying to cement between us!

So, unless she was suddenly willing to see reason and not let her stubborn beliefs overrule what I deemed was the best for her, then maybe I had a shot at keeping the peace between us…but let's just say that I wasn't holding my fucking breath with that one!

Which was why I had made the decision only to tell her my plans to leave once I had gotten her to wherever it was that I decided was for the best in keeping her safe. Of course, I knew where Adam had tried to convince me would be safe, but I had not wanted to hear of it so I told him to keep looking.

"What will you do?" Pip asked in a small, sad voice that I hated hearing on one usually so full of life and exuberance. But then again, Pip had been with her since the day she was born and thought of her as the daughter she never had. So, having to witness her heartache was one that would only end up mirroring her own because of it.

"Whatever I have to in order to keep her safe," I told her with a nod towards the door, telling her that I was here now to relieve her in protecting Amelia for me and adding to the silent order,

"Go and aid your husband and tell him that once he has researched all options, for him to come and find me." Pip released a deep sigh and leant her head against my folded arm, asking me,

"It will all be okay…right?" I tensed before forcing myself to relax before turning to Pip, and it was very much like being a father to a child, despite how old she was. Her innocence was something that she never outgrew with age or by her years of experience, but instead only seemed to nurture it. Which also made it increasingly difficult to ever be angry at her. Meaning that out of all the people under my rule, without a doubt, she got away with the most.

Besides, I fucking hated seeing her upset and she knew it!

So, I took her chin and raised her endearing face up to mine and told her,

"I am not worthy of being King to my people if I fail and seeing that saying I would die trying is out of the question, then I will say this instead, for as long as there is breath left in but a single vampire upon this Earth, then I will not give up trying to put an end to this." She blinked back the tears forming in those deep forest green eyes of hers before she finally graced me with a childish grin I secretly treasured.

"Now go to your Khuba, whilst I go to mine," I told her nodding to the exit, something she did but not before grabbing me by the lapel of my waistcoat and kissing me on the cheek, telling me,

"Sure thing, boss man." Then she skipped off to the door but before walking through it she paused and called my name,

"Oh, and Luc..."

"Yes, little Imp?"

"I know you won't let us down and die." Then she winked at me before skipping through the tunnel entrance. I turned back to the sun in my life and muttered,

"I sure hope not, Winnie. *I sure as all of Hell hope not.*"

As silently as I could, I walked into the living space and simply watched her until she realised she was no longer alone. She was so deep into her activity that this took her nearly five minutes. But I found her utterly captivating to watch. I was fascinated by her level of concentration. I could imagine the same level of commitment in her work and could even picture it for myself. Her sat at a desk scrutinising and analysing over every inch of some ancient artefact she would have sat in front of her. That same adorable look on her face where her glasses continually slid down her nose. I fucking loved it when she did that, like some damn librarian that made me hard at just the thought. The idea of taking her up against some bookshelf, with a hand over her mouth in order to keep her abiding to the rules of her workplace. Just the thought of feeling every breathy moan or captured scream of pleasure against my palm…Gods, but it made me want to build a fucking library just so I could act out the fantasy.

But then it was also the way her big, beautiful blue eyes widened one moment and started narrowing the next as she came across something new in her discovery. Gods, but I confess I didn't know what the sight of her made me want to do first, bend her over as I had done in my office or simply pick her up and bury my face in her neck, holding her to me. However, then those big blue eyes finally found me standing there, leaning casually against the single stone wall near the living space and just seeing the redness in them, then I knew she had been upset. Which was why I went with the latter option of the two, knowing that comfort was what she needed right then.

However, as was usually the case being around Amelia, she surprised me when she suddenly raised her palm to me and shouted,

"Stop!" Instantly annoyed and narrowing my eyes, I said in a warning tone,

"Excuse me?" As let's just say nothing and no one kept me from my Chosen, not even her and I didn't give a fuck how barbaric it sounded.

"Don't come any closer!" she said again and I swear I could feel the rage of such a demand building up inside me, with my demon leading the way. Which was why the next sound from my mouth was her name said as a firm warning against whatever reason she could have to try and keep me from her.

"Amelia." I took what I knew was a determined step towards her, one that probably looked quite menacing considering the furious mood I was now spiralling towards. But then the moment she said her reasons, all my anger evaporated in an instant and was replaced by nothing but awe.

"Please, I haven't quite finished yet and I don't want to ruin the surprise," she said, getting to her feet and rushing over to me, despite first struggling with her large dress. Which meant that by doing this, there was no reason for me to continue to be angry with her. Not when she was now freely giving me what I wanted, which was her body in my arms. She placed both her hands on my chest and looked up at me in that beseeching way of hers and one that rendered me powerless to say no to her.

"I won't be long, I just need a few more minutes and then I can show you. So, just close your eyes and I will lead you…"

"I have a better idea," I told her after she had grabbed my hand and started leading me away from the living space. I released my wings, summoning them from both realms of Heaven and Hell, before picking her up by the waist and flying her over to the bedroom. She squealed in surprise but was back on her feet again in seconds and before the breathy sound had ended.

Then I took her hand and led her into the bedroom, happy to see that Nesteemia, my witch, had cast her wards along each of the bedposts like I had commanded she do. In fact, I could even feel the strength of them the moment I walked inside, knowing that it would take me a while to grow accustomed to the dark signature she had used in binding the protection spell around where we slept.

At least tonight I might have a chance of getting some fucking sleep, as I hadn't since she had been lured to the silent garden for fear that it would happen again.

"Where are we go…?" she started to ask before she soon found the answer, as I then led her inside the dressing room. I had to say, it still warmed my heart when seeing one side full of her stuff, knowing that I had finally made it happen, despite the underhanded tactics I'd had no choice but to use to make it so.

"I want you to get out of this dress, get yourself into something comfortable and whilst I have a shower, you can finish your surprise," I told her, knowing that since she first sat down between my legs at the ball, she had been uncomfortable. And no matter how utterly breath-taking she looked in it, she had been in it far too long now, and it was bound to start making red marks against her skin. I knew this for a fact as I could feel the metal boning beneath my fingers when having her against me in the grand hall.

"But I…"

"No buts," I told her firmly before letting her go and walking away to give her privacy when suddenly her words stopped me.

"I can't get out of it." I frowned before looking back at her,

"Come again?" She took a deep breath and released a heavy and embarrassed sigh before admitting again,

"Pip wasn't here long and all the time she was, she was busy in the kitchen forcing me to eat the sandwich she made me before you showed up. So, even though I tried to ask her, she was…kind of in a talkative mood, so I didn't really have chance to explain…"

"You can't get out of the dress yourself?" I concluded making her blush and I swear the sight made me want to fucking howl, as it was delectably cute.

"No…but it's because Pip got me in it and no matter how hard I tug at the cords, I can't get it loose enough…I was even tempted to try and take a knife to it at one point…" My growl of disapproval made her frown before snapping,

"I obviously didn't."

"I am glad to hear it, as it would have been a sure way to make me fucking furious," I informed her, hoping the threat would resonate into making future decisions that included any type of blade coming into close contact with her skin.

"I gathered as much…hence my aching ribcage," she said making me sigh, before walking back over to her and cupping her cheek, caressing a thumb across the blush of her skin.

"My poor baby," I teased making her give me an adorable pointed look which made me chuckle before telling her softly,

"Turn around, pet." She did as she was told, along with keeping still when I warned her of such. Either way, just to be sure I placed both her hands together on the black marble top of the centre island. Then I held them there with my right hand. After I was satisfied she wouldn't move suddenly, I pulled on that Hellish side of me, summoning the true nature of what my hand had become thanks to decisions made in the past. Then, once my fingers were now tipped with a demon's razor talons, I simply dragged two claws down the centre of her back, being cautious of her flesh so as not to catch her skin accidentally.

The second the tight cord started to snap back, freeing her of her constraints, Amelia took in a large gulp of air as if she had wanted to do this all night before releasing a big sigh of relief. Then, holding the corset to her front, she turned around and threw her arms around my neck, meaning I had to quickly hold my left hand away from her so as not to catch her. I would have growled in warning, but she started kissing my jaw and cheek in thanks and I didn't want to ruin the moment.

"Oh Gods, thank you, that feels amazing!" she said making me grin and instead of my reprimand, I wrapped my right arm around her waist and told her gently,

"You're welcome, pet." Then I released the power of Hell I had summoned so the threat was taken from her, and now I could use both hands when removing her dress completely.

"Uh…I think I can manage it from here," she chuckled making me grin down at her before explaining,

"Call it my payment and we are even." She looked

amused before brazenly holding her arms out to the sides and saying,

"Alright, handsome, have at it."

"Mmm, now that is an offer I wouldn't ever refuse… *don't mind if I do."* And 'do' is precisely what I did…

Twice.

CHAPTER TWENTY-TWO

THE GIFT OF BAD DECISIONS

A little time later I got out of the shower still thinking about Amelia in that little scrap of lace that granted, hadn't survived long in the grand hall's bathroom but was enjoyable all the same. And it was like I told her, they had been my spoils of war, for I still had her torn panties in my pocket. However, it was what had come after ripping them off her that was the real treat and it was one I made sure to savour. Something I got to do again when cutting her free from her pretty dress and finding her bare and ready for me.

Which meant that Amelia had no choice but to join me for the first part of my shower. This was seeing, as per usual, I had made a mess of such beauty, marking her body in the most dominant and primal way possible. A sight I fucking loved, for there was nothing else like the sight of my release dripping from her abused pussy.

But once in the shower I had tenderly washed her perfect

little body, banding an arm around her the whole time and keeping her tucked tightly against my frame. Then I cared for my Chosen One, as any mate should do, making sure to soothe out the red marks the dress had caused. Ones that now matched the light bruising finger marks my aggressive hold on her hips had caused. However, I knew at the time that the small bite of pain it caused only managed to drive her hurtling deeper into her release. And besides, with my blood inside her merging with her own, then her body would start to heal, meaning the slight bruising would be gone within the hour.

What's more, when she kissed me in thanks, my knowing grin developed because I knew she was remembering my grip in her mind and enjoyed the replay. I knew this just from her eyes alone, and the heat in them that only made me want to take her once more. But then I knew that after fucking her as hard as I had done both times, that she would also benefit from the hour's respite on her pussy as well. So, I let her leave the shower, smirking down at her when she told me to take my time, for she had a surprise for me.

Strangely, I felt myself almost excited as to what this surprise of hers could be and be assured that it was a sentiment as foreign to me as it would be for Pip to be depressed.

But, however sweet and thoughtful this gift of hers was at its core, I also knew that its focus was a tactic of hers, as it was clear she didn't want to get upset in front of me. I knew this when in the shower I had tilted her head back to look up at me and asked her if she was alright. She nodded her head a little and told me that she was fine. However, the second her body tensed against my own, I knew she was just putting on a brave face.

She still felt guilty.

And knowing Amelia as well as I did, I also knew she wouldn't want to burden me with the worry of knowing her feelings, as she had no doubt assumed I had far bigger problems on my hands than having to deal with her feelings. *But she was wrong.*

Amelia didn't yet fully comprehend the fact that no-one in this world meant more to me than she did, and she was my first and main priority in all things. Admittedly, even that of being King, which was why, instead of simply ordering one of my men, or even Pip or Adam, to take her back to my private quarters, I had done so myself. Even though I was letting my people deal with the fallout of what had happened in the grand hall.

However, she was my Chosen One and my people knew this and therefore expected nothing less, for the claiming of your Electus took precedence over all else. Yet she failed to understand this or maybe it was that such a being as one fated to another was something that had never been fully explained to her before. Something I intended to rectify should this be the case.

Either way, she had been busy making something as a way to channel her mind and keep it from wallowing in self-pity by the time I arrived back. It was what was commonly known as a coping mechanism. Well, if it helped ease her wounded soul, then I would naturally indulge her, which was why I took the time she'd asked me to take and got ready without haste. After first assuring her with my words, then before she left the shower, I grasped her chin and forced her to look up at me. Then I gently ran my finger around where the lace mask had once been over her face, something she must have removed after the first time I left her. I took my time into doing this and finally when I knew I had her full attention, I told her,

"It was not your fault, none of it was…do you understand, Amelia?" She rolled in her lips and nodded as much as my hold would allow. Then I pulled her into me, plastering her naked front against my own and held her until I was assured that she had gained the comfort in both my words and my body.

After this, she had left the shower to dry herself and dress, and in turn I concentrated on washing myself and taking my time to do so.

Then, once finished, I got out and was ready to dress. I ended up grabbing a pair of soft flannel trousers that I rarely wore, as let's just say that at the end of my day, I found myself naked in bed, not lounging on the couch in front of a TV watching Sci-Fi, like my little geek did.

However, doing so with Amelia tucked up tight against me, entangled with me in some way, was quickly becoming my new favourite pastime and well, if truth be told, it was something that was starting to make me feel, *unnaturally human.*

I decided to forgo the T-shirt as I knew Amelia liked the sight of my body and her reaction to seeing it always amused me. She would blush, fidget, bite her fingertips without knowing or I would simply feel the heat of her eyes on me whenever she thought I wasn't looking. And well, I wasn't a fucking saint, which meant I took full advantage of this and did so feeling smug. Arrogance came with the territory of being King, and even though I'd had no problems in getting a woman into my bed in the past, now that there was Amelia, then there was only one I intended on keeping there. Something better achieved when attraction fuelled the flames of desire from both sides. Which was why her reaction to me being near-naked was something I relished.

Meaning of course, the moment I appeared back in the living space, and she took one look at me, her reaction didn't disappoint. The very visible gulp she took was a start and the blush that quickly followed was utterly charming. Then she added to this endearing sight as she had to clear her throat first before speaking, a single word that ended up becoming a high-pitched sound.

"Hey!"

Fuck me, but she was adorable, something that was only added to by the sight of her in tartan pink pyjama trousers and a white tank top that I thanked the Heavens for being tight across her ample breasts. Although what a snickerdoodle was exactly, I had no clue, but on her then it was most definitely something I wanted to pinch, as the shirt claimed I would. Especially as there seemed to be two cookies over her breasts, giving me a clue as to the delicious parts I would be paying most of my attention to.

But then I liked that my girl had curves, as I enjoyed the feel of them in my hands, hands that fucking itched to take hold of her again. Gods, but I was like a man possessed, for the more I had of her, the more I fucking wanted! Making me wonder if my desire for her would ever be sated?

Naturally, I wouldn't be making that bet anytime soon.

"Fuck me, you're cute," I told her letting her know my thoughts and doing so in order to see that blush deepen. I also drank in the sight of her squirming from the compliment, after muttering a quiet,

"Thank you." She shyly pushed a damp strand of hair behind her ear and pushed her glasses up her nose.

My beautiful, shy little geek.

Gods, but how I fucking loved her!

I looked beyond her just to save her from her clearly embarrassed state, to see something large now hidden under a throw that had been on the couch or what she called the 'sofa'.

"Is that for me?" I asked looking back at her and catching her gaze travelling the length of me,

"Um?" she said telling me her mind had been elsewhere. Good, then the obsession wasn't as one-sided as I often believed it to be. I gave her a knowing grin in return and then grabbed her hips, enticing a breathy gasp from her before I leaned down a little, getting closer to her face and dominating her personal space as was my right to do so. Then I said,

"Under the blanket, sweetheart." She rolled in her lips, which was another endearing habit of hers before nodding, adding to it a little unsure,

"Oh…oh right, yes, yes, of course." I smirked down at her and let her go…*begrudgingly.*

But I was also curious to know what she had been working on, as it wasn't exactly often that I received gifts, unless they were from Pip. If they could be called that, seeing as they were often something ridiculous and completely impractical. Like a book featuring toilets around the world or the donut shaped soap, labelled 'for your dick'.

She had even bought me a puppy once, a pug she named

Mr Little Fangy Pants. My response had been, 'Am I expected to kill it before I eat it?' Thankfully, this had been a sure way for her to take the dog away and become its new owner, as I knew it would. It wasn't that I disliked the animal, even if this particular one looked as if it had been hit in the face with a frying pan. It was just that I hardly had time for a fucking pet and even if I had, it most certainly wouldn't have been a fucking lapdog!

So, like I said, I was curious as to what she had been doing and now that I did look intrigued, she, in return, looked unsure. Because she hadn't yet moved towards it and was biting the tips of her fingers. This being the reason why I took them from her lips, brought them to my own and started nibbling on them myself in a teasing way, before asking her,

"Come now, you're not shy, are you?"

"No, it's just…well…" She started to struggle to find the words and I leaned closer to her lips and whispered in a teasing tone,

"Well, what?"

"I am worried you might think it's lame," she said making me jerk back a little as it never occurred to me that this would be her main concern. It was in that moment that I realised how much my opinion was going to matter to her and it warmed my heart to know she cared for my approval as much as she did.

"You made this, yes?" I asked confirming as much when she nodded.

"Yeah, I did but still, it's not exactly your thing. It's just that when I heard it was your birthday, I wanted to get you something but…well, I just…okay, so I doubt Amazon would successfully deliver here," she said struggling with her words at the end making me grin before assuring her,

"Anything you give to me will not be ridiculed, sweetheart, I can promise you that." She gave me a shy smile in thanks and finally nodded before walking over to the throw that was peaked in several places from what was hidden underneath.

"Okay, so just remember, it's not something I am expecting you to keep or no way display or anything…it was just mainly for a bit of fun and well…"

"Amelia, my Šemšā, show me," I said prompting her to continue, as it seemed to feed my soul to see her so concerned as to whether or not I would like it or how much my reaction to such would mean to her. At this rate there could have been a collection of empty bottles under there and I would have thanked her, for disappointing her wasn't something I ever wanted to do.

"Okay, here goes!" she said, lifting the throw carefully with both hands and revealing something it took me a moment to fully comprehend. But then I stepped closer and really started to take it in, realising suddenly what it was she had made me.

I was in awe.

"You…you made this?" I asked stumbling on my own words this time, unable to help the moment as I took in the extreme detail of the model she had built. I walked closer still and sat down opposite it just to see it better.

"I did…do you like it?" she asked rolling on her heels in an endearing way as she awaited my reaction.

"Like it, I fucking love it! How could I not, Amelia…? You made a model of our home," I said making her blush again, only this time there was something more there as unshed tears glistened in her eyes. That's when I knew she liked the sound of me calling it 'our home'.

"Phew, I am so glad you like it," she said and I couldn't help but growl a command at her in a raspy tone, one that let her know exactly how I felt,

"Come here." She gave me a shy grin but did as I asked, coming to sit next to me. I leaned back and framed her waist with my hands so as I could lift her to straddle me. Then with her knees either side of me, I ran my hands up her back, my thumbs framing her spine before resting my fingers at her shoulders. I applied pressure so she was forced to lean into me, something she did eagerly.

"I don't just like it, *I love it, my darling sweet girl…* thank you for such a thoughtful gift…I will forever fucking treasure it…now kiss me," I told her before showing her just exactly how much I appreciated it, *with my tongue.*

A while later, and only when I was ready to do so, I released her so she could show me her creative little world in more detail. She explained that she had used all the Lego sets Pip had bought her so she could create the exact replica of the Heart of the Mountain. Something she remembered, for the words, 'Our heart of the mountain' was on a flat, miniature brick plaque at the bottom.

The surrounding base was the peaks I had seen under the throw, where she had built up beige coloured rocks mimicking the ones that indeed framed our living space. Then, in the centre, she had recreated small platforms with block made furniture in each room, trying to match it the best she could. She had even managed to make our bed swing, but it was what was next to it that made me throw my head back and roar with laughter. My hilarity was also one I had found myself unable to get a hold on for a quite a while.

For next to our bed were two small figures, one was the female with dark hair, who had been bent over the end of the bed, whilst the male one, which I noted had blonde hair to represent myself, was stood behind her giving her a good time. And if the cartoon grin was anything to go by, it was a very good time.

Gods, my girl was fucking funny!

"But seriously, I am not expecting you to keep it," she said making me shake my head at her before saying,

"Not a single fucking thing will ever make me part with it." At this she melted into me and gave me another gift,

"Thank you, that means a lot that you think that way… although, I am not sure where you would put it," she finished looking around the room.

"I will have a glass case and stand made for it," I told her as I most certainly would and again, because of it, she was beaming up at me. I was just about to kiss her once more when I sensed one of my own entering my domain and I tensed before discovering it was only Adam. I gave him a knowing nod, silently telling him he could approach, seeing now that he too had changed from his earlier attire worn at the ball into something more casual.

He stepped forward and when Amelia finally realised we weren't alone, she looked up.

"Uncle, is Pip alright?" she asked making Adam grin,

"She's fine and currently passed out after overdosing on jellybeans." Amelia laughed and I automatically squeezed her when she made the sound. She had a comical laugh, and you couldn't help but smile yourself whenever hearing it. It had different layers to it and would change often depending on what she found amusing at the time.

"But what is this, did you make this, my niece?" Adam asked coming over to see the model and Amelia beamed, telling him proudly,

"Well, it's no Picasso, but he's having it put in a glass box and on display, so I must have done something right." I laughed giving her a firmer squeeze this time and telling her,

"Picasso is overrated, Lego is clearly where it is at," to which she burst out laughing and as usual, I congratulated myself on being able to make her laugh. I liked that she found me funny in return, something I knew she had been shocked to discover after spending more time with me. And it was of little wonder really, considering my past treatment of her. When I think back to how stern I was with her, it made me feel ashamed of myself. Even despite wishing that I had the freedom to be as I was now, I had still maintained the belief in keeping her at arm's length. But after spending even such little time with her, I knew it would become an impossible task.

"Little Bean, would you mind if I stole a moment of my master's time?" Adam said, calling her this for the second time and I had to force down the urge to growl, as I didn't like anyone else having a pet name for her. But then I also knew it was a feeling born from an irrational jealousy and served me no purpose right then. So instead, I granted myself one last touch before I let her go, doing so the moment we rose from the couch when I pulled her to me.

"Go to bed and wait for me, I won't be long, sweetheart," I told her making her grin back up at me and answer sweetly,

"Alright, honey." And Gods, but I fucking adored it

when she called me that or any loving endearment and I didn't fucking care if it made me sound anything but the hardass I was!

"She is a sweet girl," Adam commented once I had watched her leave, making sure she was safe on the steps, seeing how clumsy I knew she could be. And had it been anyone else to say these words, I would have knocked them unconscious, or ripped their throats out, depending on the level of my mood. But Adam was like her family, so I let his words flow over me.

"That she is...so tell me, where are the safe options for my sweet girl to be when I have no choice but to leave her?" I asked fucking hating the thought already of what I would soon have to do.

"Like I said, you're not gonna like it, Luc." At this I slashed a hand down in the air, wishing it was about to land on someone's head instead of the nothing it cut through.

"Fuck!" I hissed, making sure at least to keep my outburst low enough not to be heard by Amelia.

"There is only one place on Earth that can protect her and that is the one place no one else lives but a single soul that was sired by you...but you know this," Adam said and I growled, knowing it was fucking true and he was fucking right!

I swear just the thought of taking her there was like swallowing fucking acid. Besides, not to mention it fucked with my future plans in a big way, as I had been fully intent on keeping her here for as long as possible. Or at least, keeping her by my side or safely hidden in one of my many domains and untouchable from the memory of the life she had before me. I knew it sounded barbaric and yes in many ways it was, but it was not my intent to do this forever. Only until I was completely assured and could trust that it would never be a life she wouldn't want to return to.

She was mine.

But now, after what had happened, I knew Adam was right. I couldn't afford to take the risk, as it wasn't safe for her to be around any of my people. Even Adam and Pip were pushing it, and as for the rest of my council, then they had each been forbidden to go near her.

So that obviously left me little options here and knowing that Amelia's safety came first, I had no choice but to tell him,

"Make the arrangements and have the jet ready to go as soon as I give the word."

"And the destination?" Adam asked, needing it confirmed. So, I released a growl of resentment and said the very last place I wanted to and the one I was most loathed to say…

"To Afterlife."

CHAPTER TWENTY-THREE

WITCH EVER REASONS

The moment Adam left with my reluctant orders given, I joined Amelia in the bedroom, expecting to find her in bed waiting for me. When in fact, she was simply stood at one of the end posts, shadowing her fingers along the scorched markings an inch from actually touching them. These were the ones Nesteemia had made when casting her wards. I could tell that her natural curiosity had drawn her to them, and that she was no doubt in that very moment trying to decipher what they meant. In fact, she was so deep in her concentration that when I wrapped my arms around her, she screamed in surprise before her natural instincts took over. And when they did, two things happened to me that in all of my two thousand years plus on this Earth, had never happened before.

The first was being so startled, that it stole my breath. And the second was the reason for the first, as I suddenly found myself on the floor, being put there on my ass by a female mortal!

She did this by suddenly stepping out with her right foot into a crouch, before her left foot stepped behind my right leg. Then she stretched her left leg out, creating a barrier for me to fall over, as she grabbed the backs of both my thighs. Then, at the same time, she let her left leg go straight at the same time her right squatted down before falling to the side. This defensive move ended up taking me down with her, slamming me to my back. Then she rolled quickly into me and had her elbow at my throat applying pressure, until she realised that it was me.

"Shit! You scared me!" she accused releasing her hold on me and looking both embarrassed and guilty that she'd attacked me. On the other hand, I was equally impressed, shocked and fuck me but I was turned on! Gods in Hell, but her skills at fighting were more remarkable every time I was forced to witness them! And now she had managed to take *me down*, which was utterly unheard of. And really, how could I reprimand her for doing something like that, for accomplishing such a feat should only be rewarded and praised.

She quickly got off me and held a hand out to help me up.

"I guess I am a little jumpy after tonight and well, I didn't hear you and kind of reacted without thinking," she said giving me her reasons and obviously worried about what my reaction to her attacking me would be.

"Remind me never to piss you off, sweetheart." I said after taking her hand and getting up, making sure not to rely on her to take too much weight, for I wasn't light at over two hundred pounds of muscle.

"Erm okay, so this is me reminding you that by you getting pissed off at me for mistakenly putting you on your ass…will piss me off." she replied straightening her glasses and tightening the tie in her hair that kept it all back from her face. This also made me smirk down at her. Gods be worshipped, but for someone so cute, she was surprisingly ruthless when she wanted to be. As I couldn't help but recall her recap of events when taking out the triplets in the bathroom, and my shock on hearing how she had killed not one but two. And without being hurt at that! Well, it was nothing short of astounding.

Even some of my own people had their difficulties in accomplishing such a task. I had even found myself asking Liessa about her account of events, once I had carried Amelia back here and begrudgingly left to have a meeting with my council. Liessa had naturally shown her own astonishment at seeing the way Amelia had handled herself, admitting that by the time it had taken her to kill one of them, my Chosen had managed to knock one unconscious and stabbed the other to death with a shoe…both killed in Liessa's word…*brutally.*

And I could believe it too after seeing for myself how well she handled a sword. Her moves had been precise and fluid, obviously doing so after years of training with her father. And after seeing her with the particular weapon, quite possibly Takeshi as well. A being who was Dom's own seeker. But Takeshi had once been known as Grand Master, Miyamoto Musashi, before he was turned and made into a member of Dom's council. Of course, I too had learned many skills from him.

But before he'd died and was reborn, he had been known as one of the Rōnin, who was a samurai without a master during the feudal period in 1185–1868. They were known as the wanderers, who were forced to live with great shame upon their name. As those who became the Rōnin, were those who did not honour the Bushido Shoshinshu code. This code was when a samurai committed seppuku upon their master's death, which basically meant to fall upon your own sword until disembowelment. As for Takeshi, he only did this after first meeting Dom and being convinced to do so, knowing what was to meet him in his Afterlife.

A higher calling.

Naturally after this, he became mine and Dom's teacher in the art of the samurai at the start of his rebirth back in 1630. And well tonight, it had been easy to see some of the skills I myself had learned from him coming out in Amelia. Especially when taking down the rogues with a blade in her hand.

"That's good to know," I told her in response to her 'pissed off' reply, deciding in that moment that before we had to leave, some of our time would be spent tomorrow down in the lower level of my home. As it was about time I introduced her to my training room and after the move she just pulled, well I knew I wouldn't have to fight fair. Besides, with this firecracker, then I didn't think it would bode well on me to go too easy on her. After all, if I did that then I doubted I would manage in getting her pinned to the floor like I intended to do. Mmm, but the idea made my cock hard at just the thought of what tomorrow would bring!

"I really am sorry, but then, you should really learn to be heavier footed, unless you enjoy the idea of being put on your ass on a daily basis by a girl," she commented in a sassy tone, adding a wink. I couldn't help but grin, knowing now was the time to give my girl a little insight as to what awaited her tomorrow.

So, I held my hand out to her, and the second she placed her own in mine I yanked her to me, and performed a shoulder toss, making her land on the bed with a bounce. In doing so, she landed in such a way that it put her head staring directly up at me from the bottom of the bed, with her feet next to the pillows. I smirked down at her, bent down to kiss her forehead before telling her,

"Oh, but so trusting, pet."

"You cheated," she grumbled making me laugh.

"All's fair in love and war, sweetheart," I told her quoting a proverb attributed to John Lyly's Euphues.

"Yes, well let's leave the Anatomy of Wit out of this, should we?" she replied making me smile as she had obviously heard of the 15th-century poet. Reason being why I teased,

"Ah, there she is, my clever little scholar." Then I tapped her on the nose, before leaving her on the bed growling. I walked into the dressing room and as I was about to remove my trousers, I heard her shout from the bedroom,

"So, these are the wards you mentioned your witch casting...oww fuck!?" she yelled suddenly, and I stopped just with my thumbs hooked inside the waistband before I ran back in there to find her cradling her hand, sat on the edge of the bed.

"What happened?!" I asked sitting next to her and taking

her hand in my own so I could see it for myself. Then the bed shifted with the extra weight, swinging ever so slightly as she turned to face me.

"I don't know, I just touched one of the markings and something sparked and felt like it burned me, but there's no mark, just a tingling up my arm…it was so strange, almost as if it was calling out to me." I looked for myself to see that she was right, there was no mark there. But the fact that Nesteemia's power had been drawn to her was concerning, as there was no reason for something like this to happen.

At least, *not to a mortal.*

My witch's power was one used to ward off, not only my own kind, but any supernatural life that was not granted access to our bed. This was as literal as it sounded, for even I could not have had access, had my sigil not been added to the castings, allowing me to be the only one near it.

Unbeknown to Amelia, it was practically a cage without bars, and not one I was about to admit to. But once she was in bed, nothing could release her from it but me. Which meant that if the rogues' witch managed to access her mind again, then it would be no use as she would not be able to slip out of it without my knowledge. This was because the wards cast were linked to me, and my control on them allowed me to be aware of when they were trying to be breached.

However, should my girl wake in the night and take it upon herself to get up for a drink or need the toilet, then I would automatically wake, sensing her breaking the ward and instantly allow it to happen. Or at least this is how it should have worked, but after what Amelia had just said, by it connecting with her…well, now I wasn't so sure.

"I want to have my witch check for herself that it is nothing more than a charge of leftover power, if this is alright with you?" I asked, making up the reason so as not to worry her or give her any hint as to what these wards really meant. As let's just say, I think Amelia would have found a problem with me imprisoning her in my bed. Meaning it was a fact I wanted to cover up for as long as I could.

"Okay, all things considered lately, I don't think being overly cautious is a bad idea."

"I have to agree," I replied, not revealing the fact that I had been overly fucking cautious in all things Amelia since the day I first met her!

"I won't be long, I will come and get you when she arrives if you want to rest?"

"That's okay, I'm not that tired anyway, besides, I could do with a cup of tea."

"Ah yes, caffeine usually helps when you're trying to get to sleep," I commented, teasing her with a knowing grin.

"Maybe not, but I hear it's good for the soul...maybe you should try some, Vampy," was her playful response and I snapped my fangs by her neck and whispered by her ear,

"Why would I do that when I have my favourite beverage right here." Her breathy sigh and increased heartrate was all the reply I needed in making me grin, doing so after kissing her neck against her perfect sun-kissed skin.

However, Amelia almost always came with a sassy response and she didn't disappoint.

"You know, if I ever walk back in this bedroom and find a giant-sized teacup for me to sit in, then me and you are gonna have problems," she said the moment I released her and found myself laughing at her quip. What a witty

Chosen One the Gods had granted me, and I had never found myself enjoying someone's sense of humour as much before. There was just so many layers to Amelia that it made me question whether or not I would ever get to the core of them all. I adored our playful banter just as much as I loved having the ability to render her speechless and shy.

She could be fiery one moment and submissive the next and I found myself enjoying the fact that I didn't know which side of her I would be on the receiving end of next.

"Don't tempt me, sweetheart, as swap that teacup for you naked in a giant champagne glass and it will be here before you can say cheers," I told her making her laugh, another fucking sight I adored! Gods, but I was fucking lost to all that was her and quite honestly, I found myself asking how this had happened so fucking quickly.

Yes, she had always been my obsession, ever since I first laid eyes on her that night, even at the young and naive age of sixteen. Because I knew instantly who she was to me. But I had wisely been cautious. Not only due to her young age, but also to the dangers my world represented. At the time however, I had been led to believe that she was living the life of a spoilt, sheltered princess, when in fact, only one of those was true. And Amelia was far from spoilt.

She had been sheltered and so much so, that it had naturally made her resentful, for it was easy to see that her relationship with her father was strained at best and no doubt they both suffered from it. However, as much as it pained me to say it, I had to admit that from Dom's point of view, I was somewhat inclined to agree with him on many aspects of her upbringing. And I too had to thank him for protecting her so well…unbeknown to him, *doing so for me…* I thought with a hidden grin.

This had me wondering for many years just what the bad-tempered royal bastard would do when he discovered the truth and who his precious daughter was to me. For not even he could stand in the way of the Fates, as he had tried that once before and look how that had turned out for him. Besides, I would go to fucking war before he tried to attempt taking her from me, even if the act would be fucking karma after I had once done the same to him.

"Ha, you and champagne, I don't think so, more like being trapped in a giant beer bottle like a genie in the lamp!" she responded making me chuckle this time.

"Oh, I will rub you to wake you up any hour of the day, sweetheart," I said with a wink before grabbing her hand and pulling her up.

"Now come on, all this talk of drinking has given me a *giant thirst*…so unless you are willing to…"

"Slit a vein?" she interrupted, this time making it hard not to laugh again, but instead I held it in, grabbed her by the hips and pulled her hard into my body. Then I growled down at her,

"…Become my willing victim." She feigned a casual look, with an added tap to her lips with one finger. But she couldn't hide her first reaction to the idea as she shuddered in my hands. Oh yeah, my girl liked screaming her release to the feel of my fangs latched onto her flesh, as I sucked back the sweetest, most divine blood I had ever fucking tasted. Addiction wasn't the fucking word for it!

"Umm, can I think about it over a cup of tea first?" she teased making me kiss her forehead and say,

"Alright, seeing as I am a gentleman and such." She chuckled and teased,

"Uh…my ass disagrees, especially when in your office."

"I bet it does…well, I'd better not disappoint then," I said before slapping her biteable ass and making her yelp as she started to walk away, teasing me with it when rubbing the one cheek I had abused. Gods, but how I wished she was still wearing those tight yoga pants when I had done that, although, if she had, then I doubt she would have ever got her tea.

I shook my head and tried to rid myself of the sight, one now with the power to give me a constant hard-on and not something I wanted when I was about to speak with Nesta, a shortened name for my witch. So, I reached out with my mind and summoned her to our private quarters once more, giving her all she needed to know by allowing her to access to the memory of what had just happened. I also added my concerns so as not to speak of them in front of Amelia. Her reply was a simple,

'Five minutes.'

And like she said, down to the last seconds, it was five minutes later that Nesteemia was walking up the steps to the kitchen where Amelia and I were currently stood. Or should I say, where I was busy kissing her neck after first ridding her of the danger of hot tea so she couldn't burn herself again this time.

"My King, you summoned me." I turned to face her and in doing so gave Amelia a view of her for the first time…or so I had thought had been the first, as the second she saw her, she suddenly said in an accusing tone,

"It's you!"

"What do you mean?" I asked Amelia, not Nesta this time, as I wanted to know how she knew her, especially when I had never given the witch permission to approach her. Something all of my people would have needed to get close to her for doing so without my consent and behind my back was a rule I set to be punishable by death. Needless to say, if this was true, then Nesteemia was on thin and deadly ice right about now.

"I remember seeing you once, you were outside my school." I turned my own accusing eyes on my witch and said in a tense tone,

"What?!"

"My Lord, I can explain," Nesteemia started to say but Amelia continued.

"You convinced me to go on that school trip to London, even though my dad wouldn't let me go…you even forged his signature for me…I was sixteen," she finished this when putting her hand on my arm, and the moment she told me her age, I quickly pieced it together.

"You were the reason we met?!" I asked, now in a less stern tone but one that was pissed off all the same. After all, I should have been informed of this long before fucking now!

"I might have had my hand in it, yes… but it was fate that brought you together," my witch replied making Amelia scoff, making me shift my gaze back to her, annoyed that she would snub the idea.

"Erm no, fate had nothing to do with it. I, on the other hand, did." I frowned down at her before asking,

"Someone please explain this and fucking quickly before my patience snaps."

"My dreams are what told me to go to London, you

turning up at my school just gave me the small nudge I needed," Amelia told me, while still looking at Nesta.

"Your dreams?" Okay, so this was the part that I knew I had missed a big fucking thing here and one look at Nesteemia and the guilt was plain to see. But it was Amelia's next confession that rocked me to my core.

"I have been dreaming of you for years, Lucius."

"For how long?" I asked, relaxing somewhat for I knew I had been playing a cruel part in her dreams after we first met, doing so more frequently as she grew older. Dreams that dominated her thoughts and ended up granting her, her first sexual experience, as was my right to do with both her mind and the taking of her sweet flesh.

But her answer was not what I expected.

"Since I was seven years old and…"

"Since the first time I met your witch."

CHAPTER TWENTY-FOUR

BOUND TO DREAM

"Explain to me just what the fuck you think you were doing!?" I snapped the moment I was alone with Nesta, after first asking Amelia to give us a moment, something she agreed to considering how angry I looked in that moment. The witch at least had the good graces to look guilty.

"I can only apologise my…"

"Fucking explain!" I snarled cutting her off, for I didn't want her apologies right then, I wanted her fucking reasons!

"It was never meant to happen," she said and when I started growling, she started fidgeting with the many bangles that covered her wrists. As always, she was dressed in the typical style of a gypsy, with multiple scarves wrapped around her head in reds, yellows and purples. This matched a heavily embroidered sleeveless, cropped jacket and long skirt in the same burgundy design.

These were worn over an off the shoulder shirt with a

tasselled edge that clinched at the waist from a thick black belt, adorned with coins. However, her physical appearance wasn't always what it appeared to be. Her vessel looked old and haggard, with yellowing teeth as if she chain-smoked and tanned weathered skin awash with so many wrinkles, that her eyes and cheeks almost folded over themselves. One red star was tattooed close to her right eye and it was one that hid the mark of true power.

Because this worn appearance was the creation of deception and projected to the rest of the world by the power she possessed. For in reality, she was actually quite beautiful. However, she had also been the target of a particular Goddess' wrath thanks to the wandering hands of an unfaithful husband and therefore she used this physical mask as a way to hide her true identity. Something I aided her in since becoming her master. My payment of course was an eternal life of loyalty.

"Nesteemia, you are on my last warning, now fucking explain!" I snapped, finally getting somewhere with my threat as she started speaking,

"You charged me with finding the King's Chosen One all those years ago when she was but a child, so you could keep watch over the development of her life and therefore know the moment she found her fated mate."

"I fucking recall the past, Nesta, so kindly get on with the parts I don't fucking know!" I snapped, as it was true, back then I had ordered her to do this. Although my job of keeping Keira safe until finding Dom hadn't exactly gone to plan considering the trauma she had suffered.

"Well, in order to find her as a child, I had to first be granted the powers of the Janus, and as the God of past, present and future, I was then able to locate the right girl. This however came with a price."

"What type of price?!" I asked.

"I was granted this gift only if I swore to find all of the fated Chosen Ones and set them on the path of finding their Kings. The easiest and kindest way to intervene was to simply make them dream. That way, by the time they are found, they subconsciously feel the connection, even if they don't fully understand it." I ran a frustrated hand through my hair and growled,

"Why the fuck am I only hearing this now, Nesta?"

"Because until I was asked, I was not allowed to speak about it…you know the Fates, my Lord, you know whatever they grant, they seek in return and they cannot be denied," she told me in earnest, and it was right, the Fates were as she said they were, which made me speak out my next thoughts,

"And now? Why are you free to do so now?"

"Well, seeing as you are the last King to find his Chosen, then now my promise to the Fates is complete."

"And Keira? I don't recall her dreaming of…" I asked but she quickly interrupted me,

"Her mind, as you know, could not be touched, which was why I granted her the sight of our kind, thinking this was the only way I could prepare her for the life ahead," she replied with something I actually knew.

"But Amelia's mind is just as powerful as her mother's, for I, nor any other, have the power to access it," I reminded her, and as frustrating as this fact was, I was glad for it, as it meant none of my kind could feed from her essence.

"Ah yes, all but one," she said, reminding me of the night before and making me curse,

"Fuck! You mean the other witch?!" My tone was venomous.

"Her power is unlike anything I have ever come across before and as you know, I am no stranger to power." This was true, as up until recently there had only ever been a small handful of witches that rivalled her gifts and one was her cursed daughter.

"And the dreams?"

"As your intended mate, it was something her mind welcomed naturally, so I didn't have a fight on my hands as I did have with Keira, a child who knew nothing of the world she was being thrown into."

"And because Amelia did, you say that her mind was more open to the idea?"

"Precisely, my Lord." Well, this certainly made sense and as much as the idea of her mind being manipulated angered me, I also couldn't argue too much against what the Fates had deemed a necessity, especially in bringing her to my attention. It is true that I had seen her once before the age of sixteen, as it had not been long after she had been born. A time I barely remembered at the time, if only at all thanks to that one moment that ended up changing everything for her.

But at the age of an infant, then it was never a time when a Chosen One was to become known to you, as even Dom wouldn't have known had he found Keira at that age. This was understandable, seeing as the temptation to influence such a young life would only end up being detrimental later on. For lives first needed to be lived, along with experiences gained. The Fates made it this way for good reason. For example, had I intervened in Amelia's life then she wouldn't have been the person I fell in love with today. All her personality traits I adored, all came from her passions, her loves and her hates, her intelligence and so forth...all gained through living her own, free life.

Who an Electus became in both nature, heart and personality was a gift to her intended King.

"And London?" I asked, intent on hearing it all.

"Like she said, Sire, simply a little nudge to get the erm...ball rolling." I frowned before saying,

"Indeed."

"And what of my next possible annoyance, does this mean your wards won't work on her?" I asked seeing as she knew that which I spoke of having seen it all for herself in my memories. The ones I allowed her access to when reaching out to her over what we called, the Void.

This was an astral plane of sorts, where the conscious mind could access others, along with memories if such were shared between two beings. It was also a tool we used when teaching at the academy, for the once young and Chosen souls that the Fates had selected long ago we mentor and guide into their new roles.

It had been a safe way to channel their new powers and energy when in training. Aiding them to contain those gifts until it was safe to use them in, for lack of a better term, the 'real' world. It had worked quite well for all the teens back then...well, all but one, I should say, as nothing it seemed could contain his power or his demon.

"She is...different," Nesta said with some caution and for good reason.

"Of course, she fucking is...you think after all this time I would have forgotten that!" I snapped because any reminder of that day and let's just say it was a sure way for me to lose my temper.

"Then it stands to reason, my Lord, that the more you exchange your blood with her, the more chance it will be in bringing that side…" I cut her off with a growl.

"Enough! Just answer me, will the fucking wards hold or not!?" I snapped, interrupting her and the shit she didn't need to say. As now was not the time for me to worry about that, as well as everything fucking else I had going on.

"In all honesty, I have no idea, for her connection to you, her blood now mixed with yours, means that she is recognised by your sigil. However, it should still mean that no one else can gain access past it, so even if this particular witch tries again, she will not succeed." At least hearing this took some weight off my mind, for that was what was most important. So, it wasn't the cage I had hoped for. Which meant I had no choice but to trust Amelia not to go wandering off on her own at night. But then, if she woke and this other witch was waiting for this moment, she would then possibly be able to lure her out that way.

"I want the wards cast at every exit, at least that way if she wakes and I do not, I know at least she is safe within our home." Nesta bowed her head and told me,

"It will be done within the hour, Sire."

After this I left her to do my bidding, making sure it was safe for Amelia as I refused to allow what happened that night happen again, for nothing or no-one was going to try and take her from me again. I would see to that!

But then, after our conversation it had left a sour taste in my mouth as it did whenever the past was brought up, something only Nesta and Adam knew the full extent of.

This was because after the day it happened, I had sought out her help in trying to fix it. Something she had been unable to do.

After that, I had no choice but to put the event to the back of my mind, seeing as little could be done. But then, when I had found out that she was my Chosen One, then by the Gods, it had felt like Janus, the Fates and fucking karma had played one big fucking joke on me!

Because what I had done to Amelia as a child could never be undone. Because I had bound her to me long before she had taken my blood. Bound her to me in such a way, that not only was she tied to my life, but also, she was eternally...

Bound to my curse.

CHAPTER TWENTY-FIVE

AMELIA

MUSCLES AND A PUNCHBAG

The next morning I woke briefly to a gentle kiss on my forehead, making me moan from both being woken and how sweet the gesture felt.

"Ssshh, my sleepy little Šemšā, find your dreams once more and I will see you when you wake," Lucius whispered down at me and I snuggled closer to my pillow mumbling some response which made him chuckle softly.

After that brief moment, I had no idea how much longer I slept but when I woke, I did so feeling refreshed after what I knew was my first good night's sleep in a while. But then again, just waking up and not being outside in the snow, being lured by a witch and surrounded by hungry hellhounds was what I classed as a bonus these days.

But as I stretched out my arms, I felt a piece of paper that was folded and wrapped up in something black. This was, of course, instead of finding my boyfriend, who I would have much preferred. But then I remembered him saying goodbye to me and grinned at the sweet memory. Then I rubbed the sleep out of my eyes, gave a yawn and reached for my glasses off the bedside table that was as natural to me as breathing.

Then I grabbed the note and frowned down in question at what it was that was tied around the square paper.

"Oh, you naughty bastard!" I said on a laugh the second I saw that he had used my torn lace panties to tie the note. The very same ones he had pocketed in the bathroom back when I took advantage of him last night at the 'disaster ball'. Although, this was an unfair name as up until everyone turned into attacking zombie, vampire hybrids, then it had been a pretty good night and had been well on its way to being ranked as one of the best nights of my life.

But then I had to think back to the other 'almost contenders' and frowned, starting to think I was cursed on dates or something. I mean the first on the rooftop had ended with being shot at, and pretty much beaten up before I jumped from a crashing helicopter. And now this one, where it ended with me losing my awesome shoes, killing a couple of Lucius' ex-girlfriends and then heading into battle in a corset.

Seriously, at this point I was wondering if even going to the movies was safe or was some axe murderer going to jump out of the screen and start taking out anyone not sharing popcorn.

I decided it was best not to think about it and instead focus my attention back to the note that was wrapped up in

Lucius' sexy humour. I pulled on the end, unravelling the lace and unfolding the note.

It said,

> My sleeping Angel,
> Get ready for payback, Pet,
> For this time, I am aiming to get more than
> just the spoils of war...
> So better dress for battle.
> Love, your warrior. x

After this I released a deep sigh, held the note to my chest and looked down at the torn panties, wondering now what was in store for me? Which was why only one thing was uttered past my lips,

"Heaven help my girly parts."

About an hour later I was being guided down into the lower levels of Lucius' castle by Pip, who was currently talking about the walls. This was because in this particular section of the castle the walls were utterly breathtaking. This was due to the large chunks of deep aquamarine colours, of sea blues and lagoon greens embedded in the stone, reminding me of the colours in a peacock feather.

"It's called Kupfernickel which means copper demon, but if you wanna get all techno and shit, then Azurite and Malachite are the better-known names, which are copper-based gemstones giving it that razzle-dazzle mojo," she said making me grin...she certainly had a way with words, that was for sure. But then she was right, as the second she flipped a switch on the wall, the whole tunnel lit up and suddenly it was like walking inside a giant geode.

"Cool, huh…last time I was here they didn't have electricity installed in this part of the castle…any woo, we must Star Trek on, I doubt Lucky Luc will wait all day," she said directing an arm in front as if she was leading a bus full of tourists, minus the flag. Although, what she was wearing had enough colour to make it impossible for you to lose her.

Her leggings were a pretend knitted pattern in different colours reminding me of a rainbow scarf. And her yellow T-shirt was a take on the 80's kids show, He-Man and She Ra. Only her version was obviously her tribute to Gay pride, as across her chest she had the two swords pointing in different directions in an equals sign and in the same font it said underneath,

'She Man, Shim Ra …Mistress of her Own Mastered Universe.'

It was brilliant and as soon as I told her so, she tilted her head right over to one side, tapped her temple and told me,

"Mental note for Christmas," which meant I was now to expect the same one under the tree this year. She was also wearing cyber knee-high boots that looked mirror shiny and very space-age, with I don't know how many pink straps across the front. To this she'd added edible candy jewellery, which I knew was a favourite of hers, she had used a bra as a headband to push all the tight curls back which created a colourful afro. Painted flames over her eyes and lips covered in cake sprinkles completed the look.

"Is it much further?" I asked, knowing we had already

gone down one spiral staircase and I don't know how many tunnels and hallways.

"Nah, just one more level down and we will be at the snack smack whack happy place!" Pip exclaimed excitedly with a clap of her hands, her pointed neon nails tapping against each other. I looked down at myself and tugged at the high waistband under my breasts, hidden by the zip-up I wore, suddenly feeling self-conscious for when I had to take it off. My plan, when getting ready, had been to look more sexy than practical but then, what if Lucius was in the mood to take this 'battle' seriously? Either way, surely the power of distraction was a weapon...*right?*

Well, I couldn't change it now, not when I was nearly there. So there I was, wearing a pair of cut off yoga pants that again, were super tight around my ass. They were also in a cute light baby pink camo pattern with a thick, strappy waistband under my belly button. To match was a two-tone top of light pink and darker dusky pink, that was also strappy, low cut and only covered my breasts.

But it was after Pip's wolf whistle that I grabbed the zip-up hooded top to cover myself up. It was black and didn't match but at least it did the job in covering my breasts.

A pair of sneakers later and I was ready for what was to be my 'work out'. Honestly, with the amount of gym wear I owned, then anyone would have thought it was my favourite place to be. When, in actual fact, I only ever bought them for the comfy pants and half the time, the skimpy tops just came with the set. Which was why this was the first time I had worn the complete outfit, matching the look with my hair in a high ponytail and of course, contact lenses. A swipe of pink-tinted gloss later and Pip declared it was, in her words, 'time to guide you to a different kind of ball, the one where there are two of them, that I should try and kick em, to make the boys go down'.

My answer had been,

"But I like Lucius' balls." She had howled with laughter.

"And here we go!" Pip announced getting to a pair of double doors that looked made of bamboo painted in a black glossy paint. Pip pushed open the doors and the first thing that came to mind wasn't exactly what Pip muttered in a breathy tone,

"Holy Uncanny Photographic Mental Processes, Batman!"

On the other hand, I went with something a little less confusing,

"Holy mother of Gods in Heaven…"

Both of these breathless reactions were at the sight of the living God that was Lucius, who was now stood with his back to us, looking utterly exquisite and beyond sexy. He was topless, with only a pair of loose black training pants, and was currently pounding into a punchbag that looked seconds from exploding, given the battering it was receiving. But as hot as this was, it was more about what the exercise was doing to his body, as every single muscle was now tensed and readily on show, covered by only a fine sheen of sweat that I swear I just wanted to lick off him like a damn candy bar!

His hands were wrapped in red strapping, one of which was strapped over a single glove, and one in a long combat style that he wore concealing the whole of his left hand and forearm like usual. Oh, and did I mention the muscles…so many muscles! Gods, but what was this man going to do to me?

In fact, this was exactly the point when I started to get nervous and nudged Pip to say,

"Psst, I think he's a bit busy, maybe we should just go and…"

"Whoohoo hunka, hunka, burning lover boy!"

"…leave." I whispered this last part as the end of the sentence I never got to finish properly, as I had already started moving backwards towards the doors in hopes of making my escape. Well, thanks to Pip she kind of made this impossible, as the second she opened her mouth, Lucius caught the punchbag on its swing back towards him instead of punching into it as he had been doing. Then, with the bag in his arms, he turned his head to see us both standing by the door.

I swear that his grin was pure undiluted, bad to the bone and spoke only of all the despicable things he wanted to do to me.

"Oh lordy, boy am I getting some mega fuck me like, you Jane, me Tarzan vibes coming from him and sending solely your way, chickbee," Pip said fanning herself as Lucius left the bag and rubbed a hand through his hair, brushing the longer strands back.

Gods, but I was never going to survive this!

"Erm, you were saying something about holy uncanny photo…something or other…" I mumbled the minute he twisted his torso and snagged a towel so that when he started to walk towards us, he was wiping down his large defined chest and too many abs to count. Every single muscle was now tensed and at the ready.

"In season two, episode 'Batman's satisfaction,' Batman notices that three distinct letters are missing from a bowl of alphabet soup. Robin is so impressed with Batman's mental acuity that he lets him know it via his "'holy uncanny photographic mental processes' statement…or at least that is what it says here on Wikki," Pip said and I finally tore my eyes from Lucius long enough to see her reading this from her phone. One that, I should mention, had a rubber dick on the back as a holder, meaning she looked like she was currently giving her phone a handjob.

Great, because something to remind me of sex was all I needed right then. Gods, but I was the one trying to look sexy but right now, in front of Lucius, then I had no hope! Hell, I couldn't even be sure or not that I wasn't drooling at the sight of him. As he didn't just walk closer to us but looked more like a wild jungle cat stalking me, as he cut through the distance between us.

The room looked exactly what it was, with its huge open space that had been sectioned off by the different equipment on show. There was the gym side, where machines and heavy-looking objects sat on rack shelving along the floor. There were also bars and railings above one part probably used for chin-ups and other muscle building things.

A row of punchbags hung from where he had been stood and another piece of equipment I recognized and knew well, having spent many an hour in front of it. A wooden post on legs, known as Mook Yan Jong. It was basically a wooden free standing dummy with thick branches sticking out to help train those who wanted to master the art of Wing Chun.

Which is a traditional Southern Chinese Kung fu and a

form of self-defence, also known as 'beautiful springtime'. I used to smile at the name seeing as it always seemed too pretty a name for what was essentially a tool to learn how to kick ass. But then I learned to appreciate the fluid beauty of it and the story that, according to legend, was created by Ng Mui. She was an abbess who taught it to her student Yim Wing-chun as a means of defending herself against unwanted advances.

Although the idea of a load of nuns all practising how to kick a man's ass before prayer did make me giggle. But to be taught this by Takeshi did make me question it to my dad once, as he was Japanese. His answer had been, 'Only a narrow mind doesn't embrace diversity.'

There was also a large open arena-style space at the very back of the room, that looked to be surrounded by weapons all hanging on the walls. This was above the panels of bamboo that, like the doors, were painted black, with a warm tan tone bare concrete above. The flooring was solid hardwood, but not one of the highly polished kind. Instead it was more worn, rough and rugged, with knocks, and dark knots in the wood, which most definitely went with the vibe of the room.

But then the room beyond faded into insignificance as Lucius took the last steps needed to bring him only a foot away.

"Finally, my sparring partner has arrived, *I was getting lonely.*" Lucius said raising a strapped hand to my cheek and running two fingers down my skin. He also only acknowledged Pip with a brief head nod as his eyes were solely on me, currently scanning the length of me with a knowing grin.

"Yep, all ready and primed with a kick-ass sexy little number hiding under there…"

"Pip!" I shouted making her fake a 'what did I say' look but then it was Lucius' response that said it all, especially when it was nothing more than a short,

"Goodbye, Pip."

She smirked and gave him a salute before replying,

"Ay, ay captain, gonna get me some…little toots, have fun, kicking and all that jazz!" After this parting goodbye she skipped out of the doors singing 'I'm sexy and I know it, but Fae be the girl to show it!' and my only response to this was to groan out loud.

But then these embarrassing thoughts fled me the second Lucius quickly tugged me to him, igniting a yelp out of me, Then, he grabbed my ponytail, wrapping his fist around the length of hair near its tie at my scalp. This was so he could yank my head back in a possessive, dominant manner. I couldn't help it, but his name left me on a breathy whisper,

"Lucius."

His response to this was only spoken after he lowered his head to my ready lips, growling as he said,

"My time to play."

CHAPTER TWENTY-SIX

ALL'S FAIR IN LOVE AND WAR

After Lucius had let me know what he had in store for me, he then kissed me deep and just as I was still in the euphoria of it, he released my lips far too suddenly. Then he grabbed my hand and started to pull me towards the back of the room as my head was still spinning.

This meant that I was only semi-aware that I was being pulled towards the back of the room, where half the floor was covered in training mats. They were large interconnecting slabs that were black with a red border running around the length. The walls were also decorated in every type of none firing weapon known to man and I couldn't help but tease,

"Wow, you and my dad must have the same decorators." Lucius growled playfully at this and warned,

"Behave, my little student."

"Uh, who are you calling student here, mister?" I asked with my hands on my hips.

"I would think that's obvious, seeing as you are here to learn," was his cocky reply.

"I think I know all I need to know, Lucius and I believe that recent history proves my point," I told him making him raise a brow at me.

"Is that so?" he asked in a knowing way. I didn't answer but instead let my body language do it for me when I folded my arms and gave him a pointed look.

"Well, you won't have any trouble putting me down then, will you?" was his cocky reply, so I shrugged my shoulders and reminded him,

"I think I already proved that I can do that just fine, or are you forgetting things in your old age?" I bantered, making him smirk before pointing a finger at me and saying,

"Oh, but you will pay for that one, sweetheart."

"What's the matter, old man, you touchy about your age?" I replied again feeling overconfident. Then I watched as he kicked off his shoes and motioned for me to do the same. I didn't walk towards him like he wanted but instead kicked my sneakers off where I was, slipping the sports socks off with them. Then I watched as, with a knowing grin, he walked into the centre and motioned me forward with a few jerks of his straight fingers. Gods, but why did he have to be so fucking sexy!

"Oh come on, can't you at least put on a t-shirt or something?" I confessed making him chuckle.

"What's the matter, sweetheart, am I distracting you from kicking my ass?" he teased, making me think, well alright, if he wanted to tease me in that way, then two could play that game. So, I shrugged my shoulders before I unzipped my hoodie, hoping that what he found beneath it meant that I wasn't the only one affected. And I had to say, I wasn't disappointed by his reaction. A response I received the second the zip was down and I opened it up before slipping it from my shoulders. I dropped it to the side with confidence and the hissed curse word coming from between his lips told me all I needed to know. Which was why I smirked when I heard it,

"Fuck."

"What's wrong, *sweetheart*, am I distracting *you* this time?" I asked in an overly sweet voice, making sure to emphasise the sweetheart and you part of that sentence.

He looked down and chuckled to himself whilst shaking his head, muttering,

"Damn." Then he rubbed a hand at the back of his neck, before looking back at me, and with a bite of his lip, he told me with a grin,

"You don't play fair, pet." I couldn't help but start biting the tip of my fingertip as I shrugged my shoulders again before reminding him of his own wards last night,

"All's fair in love and war." He smirked back at me and said in a knowing tone,

"That it is, pet, that it is."

It was at this point that I winked at him before I quickly made my move, running at him before he knew what was coming. Then I sidestepped one way and then the other and just as he went to grab my arm, I slid down the middle. I managed to get in the centre of his legs, so I could catch him behind the leg, trapping one and scissoring both, so I could sweep his feet from under him. Like I predicted, he went down, landing hard on his back. The shock on his face was pure astonishment and as I crouched over him, I kissed his nose quickly and said,

"That's one for me, handsome!" Then I spun away to the sound of him groaning.

"And that's the last one you will get, beautiful," he vowed after kicking his legs up and flipping back to his feet, which was an impressive move for a man of his size.

"We will see about that," I said feeling pretty damn good about myself. But then again, the both times I had taken him down had been using the element of surprise on my side and now, well now he was most definitely ready for me.

"Okay, how about we set some ground rules...huh?" I asked making him grin.

"What do you have in mind?" Oh, I don't know, how about I tie you to a chair and have my wicked way with you, I thought with a cheeky grin.

"Naughty thoughts, pet?" he asked as if reading my expression that obviously gave me away. So, I ignored his very accurate comment and instead said,

"No super vamp speed, no using your enhanced strength or anything else I don't have, for that matter," I said making him shrug his shoulders this time, before saying,

"Suits me." I nodded wondering if he would actually stick to these rules or not. Well, there was only one way to find out and the second he stepped into the first attack, one that could probably have killed me had his full strength been used, then I got my answer.

Which meant I was able to block it with my forearm before punching him in the gut, something he too blocked before my fist made impact with his abs. He then grabbed my wrist, and tried to put me in a lock, which I slipped out of before he had time to apply too much pressure. And this was how the fight continued, and I had to say, hell but he was impressive. As, other than that first time, I was yet to get the upper hand on him again. And it was as he had said, that was the last time he was going down...*or was it.*

I finally managed to get a kick to his side, before he grabbed my ankle on the return and flipped me so I landed on my front, with my palms flat to the mat and hands tucked in beneath my chest. I felt him lean down over me before saying,

"That's one for me, beautiful." I growled in annoyance before hitting the mat in anger. Then I rolled over, ignored his offered hand and flipped up to my feet just as he had done, making him smirk at my stubbornness. Then we went after each other again, only this time I increased my efforts and at one point thought I had him in a lock, but it lasted a mere few seconds before I was gripped in a lock myself and thrown over his shoulder to the floor, landing with a bang to the mats. Again, he offered me his hand and again I ignored it, knowing I was being obstinate, but I hated being beaten in a fight.

So, I got up, ignored his grin and said,

"Again." He nodded and once more came at me. This time when he had me in a double arm pin from behind, he whispered in my ear,

"Had enough yet?" I made sure to put a foot back in between his own stance and say,

"Why, you getting tired, Vampy?" Then I twisted side on into his torso so my arm slipped free of his hold, and I could then spin round so I was behind him. Once there I delivered a kick to his lower back. This made him stumble forward a little but not as much as I had hoped. But then he spun and the next set of moves I could barely keep up with, as I was left with nothing else to do but block them one after another. It was exhausting but I managed to keep up without getting hit...*barely.* Then, as if sensing that I needed a moment to catch my breath, he took a step and said,

"Good, that was good." I stood there panting and he wasn't even taking a single deep breath! But instead he just motioned me forward after about thirty seconds and said,

"Again."

I felt like snarling at him, but instead I did as he said for me to do and I gave it to him again, only this time going in for the attack. I was just hoping I could keep it up a little longer than before. So, I started with a couple of combinations to his torso, every one of which he blocked, be it my fists, elbows or my knees.

He was like lightning and I knew that he wasn't even using his added vampire gifts to do this. The natural skills of this man were astounding! Even so, I still gave it my all and just as I kicked out at him, he grabbed my ankle and spun me. But this time before I could land fully, I pushed up on my hands, and finally caught him with a kick to the chest. This was before flipping side on, twisting to my feet and kicking out again, catching him as he blocked it with the top of his arm. Then I really went for it, changing my style and punching him in the face, barely just clocking the side of his chin before he blocked the next one.

One two, one two, and each one blocked, before I then kicked out at the back of his knee, trying to take him down. However, the second I got him in a bit of a chokehold, he slipped out of it with ease and spun now having me in the same hold but obviously trying to show me how to do it right. Because no matter how I tried I couldn't get free. Which was when I remembered what he had said last night. So, I decided enough was enough of fighting fair.

"OWW!" I shouted making him quickly let go and as I stepped away, he lowered his guard coming towards me to make sure I was okay.

"Shit, Amelia I am sorry, where did I…" He never finished as I grabbed his outstretched hand as he had done with me yesterday and I yanked it down, stepped an arm over it and used my body's weight and momentum to roll to the side and take him with me, slamming his body to the mats. I moved with him, which ended up putting my crotch to his neck, where I sat on him.

The look of utter shock was clear to see, and I was most definitely claiming this as a victory, especially when I mimicked his words last night and said,

"Oh, but so trusting." At this he grinned up at me and it was one that only spoke of the trouble to come. And I was right as he grabbed the tops of my thighs and as he gained leverage with feet to the floor, I soon found myself flipped to the side, landing on my back with Lucius now on top on me this time.

"That was a dirty trick, pet," he said down to me with his palms either side of my head. I shrugged as if relaxed before I joined my hands together around his one arm in a gable grip and forced my arms down suddenly. This made his one arm bend at the elbow, then I quickly grabbed his wrist and was about to grab his elbow so I could tuck my leg in and roll out of the hold. A move that would have taken him down and to the side. But he was too quick and jerked his arm backwards out of my hold. Then he grabbed both my wrists and pinned them above my head.

"Oh no you don't, you are right where I want you for the time being, my little fighter." But I wasn't done yet, and I raised up my knees under his ass. Then I started to slide one arm he had pinned to the side of my head up ever so slightly so it was positioned further above. A move he didn't seem too concerned about. Then I raised my head up at the same time so I could whisper,

"Is that right?" His cocky smirk told me his overconfidence would be his failing, as the second he lowered his head to reply, I stamped my left foot down on the mat and pushed up at the same time, cocking my left hip up and taking him off to the side, before rolling with him until I was on top again. Then I placed my forearm against his throat and applied pressure.

"You were saying?" I said winking and making him laugh, despite the weight against his throat.

"You're just full of surprises aren't you, pet?" I sat up a little on his abs and said,

"Never underestimate your opponent," I told him, and he just answered with a single,

"Indeed." Then just before I could respond, he snapped a leg up and twisted his hips so the back of his leg went across my chest and ended up pinning me to the mat with it after first pushing me backwards and off to the side. Now this time he really had me pinned and this wrestling match of ours had quickly come to an end, as this time he wasn't going easy on me. I knew this when he said,

"Do you yield?" I shook my head as I still tried to get out

of the lock. But then he grabbed my wrist and forced my arm to stretch out as he held it in such a way that I knew with barely any pressure at all that he could have snapped it.

"Ah!" I said, not really from pain but from knowing it would be easy should he decide to inflict it.

"Now do you yield?" I groaned before growling at him in anger, knowing he would soon beat me.

"Stubborn girl," he said squeezing my torso with his leg and making me moan before he clearly had enough waiting and stated firmly,

"You yield." Then he let me go and stood, with me still flat on the ground. I rubbed my face with both hands, holding my palms to my forehead as I panted, making him stand to the side of me and bend over slightly before saying,

"It was a good fight, partner." I nodded a little, before suddenly taking him off guard, twisting my hips, and swiping my foot out which took him off his feet completely. He landed on his back, with an echoing thud, lying over my outstretched leg. Which was when I said in a breathless tone,

"Yeah, it was." He then burst out laughing and I was soon doing the same and I continued to do so until the muscles on my stomach started to ache. He sat up and extracted my leg from under his before offering me a hand to do the same, so now I was sat facing him. I then had my elbows to my knees and held my head in my hands as I tried to catch my breath.

"I think it's safe to say that you most definitely have skills, my girl," he praised, making me grin and I let a hand fall from my head to point at him without looking, telling him the same,

"Right back at you, handsome." He chuckled before

getting to his feet and then before I knew it, I was being lifted off the floor and put over his shoulder.

"Hey!" I shouted before I was slapped on my ass, making me follow up this complaint with a yelp of another,

"OWW!" This was also one he ignored as he started walking with me towards a different part of the room, towards a door at the back. But it was one I could hardly see, so I pushed up on his lower back and looked around him as he walked through into this new space of darkness.

But then he flipped a switch and just as my eyes took in the rest of the room, one now filled with equipment of a very different kind, I asked in panic,

"What are you doing!?" Which was when he suddenly pulled me forward, dragging me down the length of him before he growled down at me only three words…

"Spoils of War."

CHAPTER TWENTY-SEVEN

SEXUALLY SUSPENDED

The moment Lucius put me down on my feet, he started walking me backwards with his hands framing my hips. I looked around the room seeing bars, ropes, benches and other equipment I couldn't name. Which was why, at first, I thought that he had brought me into some kind of sex dungeon. However, it was then that I realised this was just an extension of his training room, obviously used so more aerial activities could be practiced. A space, no doubt, used solely for those who had wings.

It stood to reason seeing as in this part of the gym the ceilings stood so high, that it looked as though it could have been at the bottom of a massive hollow peak in the mountain. Even though the walls were smooth at this level, it was halfway up where they were jagged, and decorated with stalactites. It was also a roundish room, reminding me of some naturally formed castle tower.

But right then, all that concerned me was the section in

the room Lucius was walking me towards. One which strangely held lengths and lengths of red straps that curled as they gathered on the floor. There were so many, that it formed a sort of curtain, and each was a different thickness. But every one of them rained down from the high frame of bars they were fixed to above.

I opened my mouth to speak but stopped when a stern looking Lucius shook his head at me, telling me now that the masterful dominant Vampire had come out to play. And from the looks of things, I was his intended toy. Or should I say…*his spoils of a battle won.*

After we reached the curtain of straps, he raised my arms above my head, telling me exactly what he meant to do with them. So that when he grabbed a thicker length and started wrapping it around my wrists, I wasn't surprised. No, I was just incredibly turned on!

Once secure, he took a step back and took his time scanning the length of my body, even going so far as to walk around me, dragging back the rest of the hanging straps as he did, so it opened up for him to pass through. I turned my head one way and then the next trying to keep an eye on him behind me, that was until he snapped an order,

"Eyes in front!" I did as I was told because gone now was the playful Lucius and behind me was the man I could do nothing but obey.

"Good girl, now this sweet ass, the one that has been teasing the fuck out of me this last hour, will tease me no more," he said, before taking hold of my hips and yanking me back hard against his erection. I moaned at the feel of it, getting high now from his control over me, as back on the mats I had wanted nothing more than to beat him. But now, well now I wanted nothing more than to become his willing slave, his submissive little pet for him to do as he pleased. All with the promise of making me come screaming his name.

I felt his fingers caress across the thick waistband of the pants, teasing just beneath the stretchy material as if any minute he was going to rip them from me.

"These fucking skin-tight pants of yours…Hell's Blood, but do you know what this ass does to me!?" he snarled in my ear and I shuddered in his hold, now gripping on tighter to the strap that bound me above. And it was a good job too as he suddenly yanked them hard and rough down my legs, ridding me of them and leaving me in nothing but a thong and a crop top.

He caressed a gentle hand down the curve of my ass, being a total contrast to how he got it bare in the first place. He then hooked a finger under the band of my thong and he followed the thin strip of material down, pulling it out from in between my cheeks before he fisted it suddenly. This made it twist and as a result, the front part tightened over my pussy.

"Ahhh," I moaned making him grin against my neck, before biting it playfully without breaking the skin.

"Fuck, but I just love this racing heart of yours, this delicious pulse I feel just beneath my tongue…this life I own…this blood of mine…just waiting to be tasted…waiting to be consumed…*it drives me fucking wild…fucking insane with my need for you!"* Lucius said on a growl and I swear his words made my arousal start to pool at my opening, before I felt it soaking into the material of my thong. One he still had pulled tight over me, in his unruly grip. He then tugged at it, and with his fist still wrapped in the back section, I had nowhere to go, but on my tiptoes as I was rocked back towards him.

"I can wait no longer!" he snarled before he banded an arm around me and sank his fangs into my neck, making me cry out and this time, with the pain subsiding into screaming pleasure almost instantly. I was coming quickly, as it gave me no time to build up to it. Not as the orgasm ripped through me, exploding my senses with the first few pulls of my blood being sucking and swallowed down by him.

He didn't take much, just enough for me to come and him to have a taste without making me pass out on him. As it was clear that he needed me conscious for what he had planned next. I knew this as he quickly yanked at my thong, ripping it from me. This was before taking hold of my hips and spinning me around to face him, making the straps above me twist. After that he took hold of the back of my thighs in his large hands and hoisted me up, stepping into me at the same time. Then with my arms still tied above me, I had no choice but to rely on him to take my weight so my wrists didn't suffer from no longer having my feet on the ground.

But Lucius had other ideas about this as well, as he reached up to grab another length of strapping before he began wrapping it around the top of my thigh.

"What are you doing?" I couldn't help myself from asking, and this time instead of commanding me to be silent, he simply answered me,

"What does it look like, I am tying up my winner's prize, my conquered prisoner, so she can't escape me." I released a shuddered sigh just as he started to do the same to the other leg, taking his time in wrapping the strapping around the different parts of my body. Winding them around me, so that eventually when he took a step back, I was now hanging there unaided, with my legs spread wide and ready for him. It was as if he had made a sex swing, only one I was actually tied to.

All along the upper parts of my legs were wrapped in red straps all the way to my knees. This also included two straps at my waist and even more around my arms, for extra support. There was even one around my neck, which he did solely for the look he wanted. I knew this when he said,

"Time to collar my wild beauty," making me gasp.

After he was satisfied, he made short work of opening up his pants and stepping back into me, his large cock now straining forward ready to take me and glistening at the end with precum I was near desperate to lick.

But he took his own length in hand and instead of guiding the tip to my opening, he teased me with it, getting it wet from my earlier orgasm, and rubbing it up and down through the soaked fold of my sex and playing special attention to my clit. I let my head fall back, making the strap tighten around my throat as I let loose a moan of pleasure. One that was strangely enhanced by the slight constriction around my neck.

"Gods, you have no idea how you look right now, so perfect, so fucking beautiful all wrapped up and nowhere to go. No way of escape, I could do anything I fucking wanted to you and you would take it...wouldn't you? You would take it for me, like such a good girl," he said making me moan again and rub myself against him with the small amount of movement I had.

"Words...give me your fucking words!" he snarled, making my head come back up and tell him,

"Yes, I would take it all for you." At this he growled and suddenly reared up inside of me, making me grip the straps tighter just for something to hold to as he pounded into me with speed. Then he growled down at me and told me,

"I want all of your fuckable body wrapped up for me, every bit tied so you know exactly who owns you!" Then without further warning he ripped open my yoga top, freeing my breasts and letting me know now what he meant by that statement. Watching him now when he reached up and grabbed hold of one of the thinner straps before he started wrapping it around each breast. Then making me cry out when he yanked on the end so it tightened and at the same time he thrust up harder inside me.

"Lucius! Gods, Lucius!" I said in a pleading tone, but then he grabbed my ass, holding me to him, as he leaned down and told me in a stern tone,

"You can take it!" And he was right...*I could.*

After this order he lifted the end of the strap still attached to my breasts making one rise to his awaiting mouth. There he sucked in a nipple and used his teeth to create that delicious pain I fucking craved! Meaning that seconds later I was coming once again. I ended up shaking in the straps from the force of it hitting me, making me swing, as I continued shuddering in the lengths of material holding me captive and suspended in the air.

In fact, the only thing that grounded me was the length of Lucius' cock seated inside me, thrusting and still doing so at a maddening pace that it soon had me building up the next wave of an orgasm. Only to then have it coming crashing down around me, even seconds after the last one had barely left me.

But then I knew he was near as there was one last thing Lucius wanted of me, and I knew this when I felt him cupping the back of my head. I looked up at him through hooded lids, so close and on the cusp of passing out from what I knew would be a mind shattering last orgasm.

"Not yet, first you feed," he told me on a demonic growl he had no way of controlling. So, he guided my face to his neck and when I was about to ask the obvious question, he told me,

"This time, you pierce the flesh...now bite me, bite me fucking hard, my Khuba and mark me as yours...claim me!" he ordered and the second he shouted this last order I did as he said, biting down as hard as I could, and feeling his flesh giving way to my teeth. Now feeding me with not only his blood but also with the power I felt in doing so.

As he was right, it felt as though I was claiming him this time!

And I wasn't the only one who felt this way, as Lucius roared out his own release seconds later, rearing up inside of me and going as deep as I was physically able to take it!

But the more I swallowed him down, the more it started to affect me, making me feel drunk off him. I was dizzy, and I wanted to know why I was suddenly spinning by the cords above. But then the moment I thought it, the spinning stopped as well as everything else. Including my mind, as it seeped quietly into a beautiful darkness.

A darkness that was thanks to Lucius'...

Demonic wings.

CHAPTER TWENTY-EIGHT

BOUND TO DREAM

"I can't help but think this is a bad idea," I muttered the second we pulled up to a private hanger and facing us now was a sleek looking Gulfstream G550. Which was basically one of the most expensive private jets money could buy and one that only yesterday I'd been informed exactly where this particular one was taking us to. I shook my head just thinking back to last night…

"Are you going to eat that?" I asked leaning across the table and stabbing my fork into a crispy potato and doing it quickly before Lucius had chance to answer.

"Hungry per chance?" Lucius asked with a hidden grin.

"Yes, and I wonder why?" I replied making his lips twitch before he answered with a cocky,

"No idea."

"I'm not exactly a gym bunny you know," I told him, making him laugh before saying,

"No, you could have fooled me, although I am thinking a 'gym bunny' should most definitely be your next outfit choice for round two." Needless to say, I nearly choked on that stolen potato. And speaking of being back in that gym, I had once again passed out on Lucius after mind blowing sex. But this time it had been the moment his demon side had burst through, wanting a taste of what I had been offering… or should I say…*more like taking.*

Lucius had told me not long after waking, that the moment I'd bitten him, his demon had also recognised the claim and Lucius had no choice but to allow him to surface. His demon had, in fact, been the one to carry me back to our living quarters once I fell unconscious, and in doing so, first covered my naked form in his arms with one of his wings folded over me like a blanket.

This meant that when I woke up, lay with my head in Lucius' lap, I was instantly confused. What was even more confusing though was that I found Lucius sat on the sofa, watching TV, with me spread out next to him, wearing one of his oversized T shirts. Then, the second I shifted my gaze to what it was Lucius was watching, I could barely believe my eyes. To find him currently sat watching the third episode of Star Trek Discovery, season one on Netflix made me believe at first that I was still dreaming.

But he was also playing with my hair and it felt way too nice for it not to be real. Which was why I muttered a sleepy,

"I think someone has been converted." He chuckled making my head jiggle thanks to it resting on his lap with my legs folded, and on my side lay out next to him. Five minutes later he explained to me how I'd got there, hence the conversation about his demon. But it was also when I sat up and because his tee was pulled tight and tucked under me, it meant that it stretched the neck, so I could now see for myself the bloody teeth marks I had made low on his neck by his shoulder. Marks he had purposely not allowed to heal so he could keep the scars!

To say I was a little shocked was an understatement but his only explanation to this after he rose from the sofa was a firm,

"You claimed me." Then he left me sat there with my mouth hanging open in utter shock. A little time later, I still found my eyes wandering over to the sight, even though it was once again hidden under the neck of his black t-shirt. It was also one that had me smiling the second I saw it, as it had the red Transfusion club logo across the chest. I didn't know what shocked me more, the fact his club had merchandise available to buy or that he was wearing it himself.

He explained that it had been Liessa's idea a few years ago and had actually been quite a profitable one, seeing as it also advertised the club as well. This made sense and was actually something my own father had allowed my Aunty Sophia to do, seeing as the running of the club was mainly her doing.

But the one Lucius now wore was also the same T-shirt he had put on me and I had to grin knowing that we matched. Although, I had to giggle in the dressing room, wondering that if I wore an Afterlife one, would that mean it would end up being a battle of the clubs?

I laughed the silly thoughts away and finally forced

myself to change, now opting for a pair of jeans and long-sleeved navy-blue top. One that had white flowers sketched across the hem and bottom of the sleeves.

But just because I removed the Transfusion T-shirt, it didn't mean I wanted to part with it. So, I walked out of the bedroom waving it around before asking him, the second I made it to the kitchen, if I could keep it. His answer had been a chuckle before he gave me a soft look, pulling me towards him after first hooking his fingers in my belt loops.

"You own my heart, Amelia, and with it comes everything else I own."

"So, is that a yes?" I asked thinking his words were sweet, but as for owning everything he did, well that was a little much seeing as we were only still classed as being at the dating stage. Even if being each other's Chosen Ones meant so much more.

"It's a Hell yes," was his response making me melt into him. But then, thinking about our relationship, I was leaning more towards his view on it, than my own. As according to Lucius, he wasn't my, *and I quote,* 'fucking boyfriend'. As he thought the term sounded too juvenile. Oh yeah, but eternal life partner sounded so much better I had thought with a smirk.

Although being unable to think of anything else but those marks on his neck, the ones he purposely wanted to scar, well, then I had to say how he labelled our relationship sounded a lot more apt for that type of commitment. I mean, it was like getting my name tattooed on his body or something!

So naturally I was fascinated, as I had never heard of this before. Of course, claiming a Chosen One was something well known for the Kings of my father's world. But as for having their Chosen One's teeth marks scarred there purposely like a badge of honour…nope, this was the first I had heard of it.

But I also knew that he was fully aware of where my eyes would wander to, if his trademark knowing smirk was anything to go by. However, surprisingly he didn't comment, not even when he watched me as I cooked our evening meal.

I had decided on a typical English Sunday dinner of roast chicken, stuffing, yorkshire puddings, roast potatoes, vegetables and homemade gravy…which unfortunately turned out to be a little gloopy. But hey, my roasties were the donkey's bollocks, as Pip would have said. Fluffy on the inside and golden and crispy on the outside. The trick was two things, part boiled and shook in the pan to rough up the outsides before placing into the hot oil in the oven. The second was roasting in duck fat which, when I found it in the fridge, had been the whole reason I had decided to make the meal.

But then Lucius hadn't complained as he had pointed his fork down at them and said,

"Now these are the stuff of legends and I'm sorry, but they blow your chilli fries out of the water, love." I laughed and secretly congratulated myself on the fact that he liked my cooking. But then our meal had finished and without making anything for dessert, I ended up grabbing a tub of chocolate ice cream out of the freezer. One I had discovered when trying to decide what to make. I also took two spoons with me and was just about to dive on in there when his words made me take pause. Pause with my spoon suspended mid-air.

"I am afraid we need to talk, pet."

"Erm…that doesn't sound good," I remarked, leaving the ice cream and putting down the spoon. Lucius, for the moment, looked both frustrated and awkward, even unsure, and it was then that I started to panic.

"I'm not even sure how to say this or even approach the subject, but…" I never let him finish as I bolted from the table and said in a pained voice,

"Oh Gods, this is it, isn't it…?" Lucius frowned at me and also rose from his chair, doing so as it must have been obvious I was about to run out of the dining room any minute and he wanted to be at the ready to prevent this or even chase me. Although, after what he was just trying to say, I wasn't sure why he would want to stop me from doing anything.

Especially leaving.

"It is…unavoidable, pet," he told me and I gasped, taking a step back as his words started to sink in, holding a fist to my heart as I felt it start to break.

"But why!? I don't…don't understand…I mean, we have been getting on fine here, great even! I thought…well, I thought that you…*that you wanted me here!"* I said my voice trembling and Lucius hissed a curse before dragging a hand through his hair before telling me,

"Of course, I fucking want you here! But it just isn't possible anymore…not now," he told me and I swear my whole chest felt like it was cracking wide open and I was drowning on his blood I'd recently consumed that was pouring out of it.

"Why, is it because I opened that fucking box?!" I snapped, hating the tears I could feel coming. Gods, but how could he do this to me and why now?! He closed his eyes in frustration and told me,

"I just can't do it…I can't chance…"

"You fucking coward!" I shouted at him, suddenly so angry! Unbelievably so! Which was why I cut him off, making him growl at me for the insult.

"Careful, pet, for I am not accustomed to such disrespect," he warned and I swear the bastard had some gall!

"Fuck you! Actually, you know what, screw you and screw your fucking castle!" I yelled at him, as I stormed off despite the growls behind me.

"Gods, give me fucking strength!" I heard him mutter as he followed me into the dressing room, where I went straight over to my clothes and started stuffing everything back into the empty boxes still left there in the corner. Gods, I had been so fucking stupid to trust moving in here! I was an idiot for trusting him with my heart and I knew once the anger had subsided, then what would be left of me I had no clue. Because Lucius had the power to totally fucking destroy me!

"What the fuck do you think you are doing?!" he snapped and I slammed the armful of clothes I had ripped off the hangers into the box.

"What does it look like I am fucking doing! Packing of course and getting out of your hair, seeing as you no longer want me!" Lucius seemed to take a few steps back as if I had just slapped him, as he looked totally dumbfounded. A reaction that started to confuse me.

"Say that again?" he asked in a deadly tone and a disbelieving jerk of his head, telling me that I was possibly missing something huge here. Either way, I continued down

the road he himself had set me on, so I wasn't backing down now.

"Gods, I just don't understand, I mean you were the one who forced the issue of me moving in the first place! I just cooked you dinner after we had the most amazing and hottest sex of my life, where you asked me to claim you, for fuck sake and now you tell me over ice cream that you are breaking up with me and after you told me my potatoes were the stuff of legends! What else do you expect me…?" It was in this moment that Lucius didn't just growl, no, he sounded like a vicious beast on the verge of losing it completely. Which meant that I suddenly screamed when I found the box being thrown back against one wall and I was being pressed against the other!

"I don't know what fucked up shit you just got from my words down there, but let me be perfectly clear and I suggest, sweetheart, you fucking listen and listen good, because what I tell you now *is fucking law!"* he said after first raising my arms above my head and making it impossible for me to escape him or his anger…something that was terrifying. So, I wisely let him say his piece until he got the hell off me.

"You and I are for an eternity! There is no fucking breaking up and there is no ending this relationship. *It is for life…* and soon I will seal that fucking vow with a ring on your finger and a title of both wife and queen! But until then, you DO NOT get to throw that fucking shit in my face ever again! Now, do you understand or do I have to remind you who owns you by chaining you to my fucking bed this time and sleeping with my cock deep inside you?!" he snapped in a way that I had never heard him so angry before. But then his words started to finally seep in and the main part I got from it all was what I blurted out in a quiet voice,

"You want to marry me?"

After this he growled low and pushed himself away from me. Then he raked an angry hand through his hair and snapped,

"I will be in my office and for your sake, Amelia, I suggest that by the time I come back, your shit had better be out of that fucking box and back on those hangers or so help me my girl, I will not be held accountable for what I do!" he roared before he suddenly turned and stormed out of the door, leaving me to slump to the floor and ask the empty room,

"What just happened?"

A few hours later and Lucius still hadn't returned. However, he must have told aunty Pip to come to me as the second she turned up I burst into tears and told her everything that had happened. Because since he had left, I had started to replay the whole thing in my head again and that was when I stupidly realised that I had totally overreacted, as he hadn't once said anything about breaking up with me.

In fact, it all became clear the moment Pip filled me in on what he had been trying to tell me and it had been the very last thing I had accused him of, meaning that I was feeling like shit and guilty as Hell, begging Pip to take me to his office so I could apologise. Because no matter how scary his reaction had been, or how aggressive he had turned, he had never hurt me. Shocked me, yes, but then his anger had been fuelled by being accused of something that he could barely even fathom. That obviously cut to the core and hurt him deeply to even think about.

No, he hadn't just been angry.

Lucius had been...*upset*.

Which was why Pip finally caved in and took me to him, although she must have had her orders not to let me leave at all. But she took the chance and did it anyway. I knew this the minute she knocked on the door and the first thing she shouted was,

"She was crying and upset, there were tears everywhere and I couldn't say no...okay, bye!" Then she pushed me through the door and slammed it shut behind her. Which was how I found myself in his office for the second time. But just like the first...*I was in trouble again*. Which was why I found Lucius sat at his desk, looking beyond pissed off, with a nearly empty bottle of some expensive drink within arm's reach. The glass in his hand looked to have been a permanent fixture since entering the office hours ago. I decided that it was best I say what I came here to say and to do so quickly,

"Okay, so turns out I'm rather A, an idiot, B, about to get my period and therefore way, way over sensitive or C, foolish enough to still fear you're gonna leave me and I have a bit of a hang up about it due to what happened in the past..." I paused taking a deep breath and, pushing my glasses back up my nose, decided to carry on, seeing as he hadn't yet said a word. No, he just continued to watch me, so I added,

"Of course, you can also choose option D, which is a combination of all three. Either way, I just wanted to come and tell you that I am sorry...I, don't know what I heard but I realise now it wasn't what you were trying to tell me, *admittedly too late*, but had I just shut up and listened then… well, we would probably be in bed together right now discussing how the hell we are going to face my parents tomorrow. " The moment I finished and he still hadn't said anything I was seriously starting to panic, so said in a pleading voice,

"Please, Lucius, say something." Lucius released a deep sigh and downed his drink before placing his glass back on the desk. Then he ordered in an even tone I couldn't yet detect,

"Come here." I swallowed hard, knowing that I wanted to go to him as much as I didn't. However, I also didn't think it wise to let him wait. So, I did as he asked and walked over to him, pulling the side of my white hooded sweater over my shoulder as the large neckline kept slipping. It was one I had grabbed to put on as walking around the castle was definitely on the chilly side of comfortable.

He watched me as I fidgeted in an unsure manner, as I approached. But when I reached his desk, now stood opposite him, I swear it felt as though I had been called to the headmaster's office. However, I obviously wasn't where he wanted me to be as he turned side on in his chair and pointed directly in front of him, telling me without words where he wanted me.

So again, I did his bidding and walked to his side of the desk and over to him. Then, the second I was within reach, he framed my hips with his large hands and did something uncharacteristic of him. He leaned forward and placed his forehead to my belly and breathed deep. I didn't know what to do at first, just holding my arms up without touching him, but then I heard his deep sigh and decided to take a chance. So, I ran my fingers through his sandy blonde hair, amazed as I always was at how soft it was. Then I held his head to me before telling him again.

"I am really sorry, honey." This was when he moved back, straightening but still gripping my hips, he tightened his hold enough that when he suddenly stood, he lifted me onto the desk. Then he looked down at me,

"I know you are, sweetheart," he told me as he brushed one side of my hair back behind my ear, as it was currently loose around my shoulders and flowing passed my bra line.

"Just so you know, I wouldn't have got so upset if I didn't love you so much," I pointed out, making him get closer to my face, grip my chin between his thumb and forefinger and this time whisper,

"I know this too."

"So, does this mean we have made up...'cause I remember that part going particularly well the last time you called me out for acting insane?" I asked waggling my eyebrows in a comical way. I knew this the moment he started laughing, before pulling me into his chest for a hug and muttering,

"Gods, but what am I going to do with you?"

"Erm, take me to the Himalayas, so I can be a goatherder as I hear it's a safe enough occupation...you could even give up being King and join me." At this he burst out laughing and muttered,

"I will think about it."

"It's all I ask," I replied keeping up with the joke. Then I looked down at his desk and could now see for myself the extra copies of the map he must have had replicated, along with the original folded next to the box.

"You planning on setting a really crummy treasure hunt where the winner gets to kill a Merc, a witch and find out there's no Narnia through the wardrobe after all?" I asked making reference to the book. His lips twitched before he told me,

"I have had a few copies made for the Kings in hopes they have more luck in deciphering its meaning."

"Ah, but of course, let me guess, a meeting of the Table of Kings." I said with a sigh, knowing exactly where such a meeting was going to take place. Lucius then raised my face to his, applying a slight pressure under my chin and told me,

"It is the safest place for you to be right now and trust me, you have no fucking idea on how much it pains me to say so." This was true for I could see it in his eyes and the tension and obvious burden there. So, I raised my hand to cup his jaw and said,

"I know."

After this we both spent some of our time looking at the map and once it drove us a little mad, I walked around his office asking him about the things I found. Like the books or collection of different globes, and even the winged brass figures I found on one shelf. He told me of the things he had collected over the years, many of which were spread out in the different homes he owned and in the different places he had lived throughout the years.

But then I came to a painting on the wall above the

fireplace and was about to ask him about it when suddenly his phone started ringing. The moment he then hissed a curse I looked back at him in question.

However, when I heard him answer with a particular name I froze, knowing exactly what fate held in store for us next…

"Hello, Dominic."

CHAPTER TWENTY-NINE

GUNG HO HAPPY

A plane back home.

This was what faced me now. I was about to walk on to what I knew was a state-of-the-art luxury jet, and I swear my feet didn't want to move an inch. Because ever since that phone call in Lucius' office I couldn't stop thinking about what would happen next. I had been so hot and bothered about it that I had needed to take off my hooded sweater and lift my hair off my neck to fan myself. Lucius had known exactly why I was having this reaction, because he gave me a tender look before silently beckoning me to go to him. So, I did and the second I heard my father's voice on the other end, I tensed in his hold, which made his arm tighten further around me.

"Yes, I am listening, Dom," he had needed to reply when I heard my dad snapping at him. I hated the sound of him being so angry and taking it out on Lucius. Which was only one of the many reasons why I had released a silent sigh knowing that my dark fairy tale was cracking around me and would possibly shatter the moment Lucius took me from his castle.

But then Lucius had made the phone call short and I had a feeling this was more for my benefit than his. He did this by telling my father that what needed to be discussed was to be done in person, for we would arrive tomorrow and yes... *daughter in tow.* This had been one of my father's first questions, along with wanting to speak to me. I had shook my head, when Lucius looked down at me in question. Then he told him flatly,

"She is currently otherwise engaged." My dad had argued at this, and started to make his demands when Lucius suddenly snapped,

"Very well, I believe she said she was going to have a bath before calling it a night, but if you insist I go in there and...No, I didn't fucking think so," Lucius said ending this last part after my dad rescinded his offer for fear that his daughter's precious modestly would be in jeopardy of being violated by a Vampire King. Ha! Gods, if he only knew the half of it, then I think even the Heavens would shake from the force of my father's rage.

And after Lucius gave him the details of our flight and when we would be arriving, he hung up, signalling for the next awkward conversation we needed to discuss. The talk on what we were going to do about my parents. Lucius hadn't hesitated in this, wanting to tell them both the second we arrived. On the other hand, I had given him a look of disbelief before explaining that giving my father a heart attack in the first five minutes probably wasn't the best of ideas. To which I received a pointed look in return.

Hence why this conversation turned heated before it turned pleading. The pleading part coming from me in the form of me begging him not to say anything.

Not until I was ready.

Something I wasn't sure I would ever be, which was why I was staring at the jet now as if it was a wild beast that wanted to eat me up before spitting me out into a place I didn't want to be…like the doors of Afterlife.

I was also wondering if I could get away with being 'ready' in about fifty years or so, because it wasn't as though they would have aged. On the other hand, I had no clue what would become of me. It was said that taking the blood of your Chosen would extend your life, and for at least one of the other Kings I knew about, then this was true.

Not that it had happened like that for Ella, my cousin. Who'd had a complicated time to say the least seeing as it was obvious that she was destined for Jared Cerberus, who was King of the Hellbeasts. But once again, that was a whole supernatural can of worms right there.

Thankfully though, Lucius had agreed, but in his words, 'for only so long,' which in Lucius speak, meant until his patience snapped. And considering this secret relationship of ours meant not being able to touch each other in front of anyone, I couldn't see it lasting long. Not whilst we had to act as though we were nothing more than friends. Let's just say then, that I would be surprised to find it lasting even a whole day.

Which was precisely why I flinched the second I felt Lucius' hand at the small of my back, guiding me towards the steps of the aircraft.

"Come on, heart of mine, let's get you on board."

"You mean before I pull an Iron Maiden and I *'run for the hills'*?" He chuckled and said,

"Something like that...not that you would get far with the *'number of the beast' chasing you."* This last part was growled in my ear playfully as he had used another Iron Maiden song in return, making me grin back at him over my shoulder. Then I told him in an impressed tone,

"Oh, now that was smooth." He smirked down at me and teased,

"What can I say, you and your wit must be rubbing off on me." But then, as we walked on board and took our seats next to each other, I looked down at my lap and confessed,

"I'm going to miss this." Lucius didn't allow this for long as he raised my face to his in his usual manner and told me,

"Then let us tell them." I released a deep sigh and said,

"We can't...not yet."

I also wanted to add to this that it was because I liked him handsome and didn't particularly want to see him and my dad tearing into each other in their demon forms.

Lucius allowed this, no doubt not wanting to go over the old grounds of last night, as we had finally left his office still arguing about it. Although, we did so a damn sight milder than the explosive argument before it. But then I had excused myself and told him I forgot my sweater, so ran back into his office and grabbed it, doing something I knew I shouldn't have done in the process.

I watched as Adam stepped inside with the box with a guilty, sinking feeling in my gut and one I couldn't help. Of course, the rainbow in his life quickly followed, bouncing up the steps like an excitable puppy. Adam and Pip were the only two of Lucius' council that were to accompany us there. And as the lockbox in his hand suggested, Adam had been charged with looking after the box. One which was now secure in a wide metal looking briefcase.

Before we left Lucius' office I had watched as he placed the original map back inside the box in which it came and sealed it, using his blood on the lid this time to lock it. He then explained to me how he thought this was for the best, at least until they were safely at Afterlife.

So yes, I had a lot to be nervous about, which meant that before long we were up in the air and being asked if we would like a beverage by a pretty brunette in a blue flight attendant's outfit. I opted for champagne, whilst Lucius order his usual beer.

"YEY, it's like a road trip, only without the road...' Where we are going, we don't need roads. Ha, classic drop the mic moment, once again, Winifred!" she said congratulating herself before continuing to inform us,

"In fact, we named our first goldfish Doc Brown...didn't we Pookie?!" Pip said leaning into his arm and looking up at him in that adoring way, making Adam grin back down at her before agreeing,

"That we did, my Little Bo Pip." The second he said this nickname she purred at him before walking her fingers up his arm and shaking his glasses, telling him,

"Mmm, you liked that outfit if I do recall, Mr Ambrogetti." Adam actually blushed at this, making me laugh.

We had been up in the air for about ten minutes with the drinks still not in sight. This was also when Pip started complaining. So, I told her,

"She might be getting snacks or something else ready for us...relax." This pacified her for the moment until Adam informed her that he needed to use the restroom and would be back in a few minutes, making her embarrass her poor husband further by throwing a hand up in the air and shouting,

"Okay, enjoy your poo, honey POO bear!" The she sniggered the moment she heard him groaning his reply.

"He really hates it when I do that," she said leaning over the centre aisle to whisper this behind her hand. I rolled my eyes making her laugh before sitting back in the luxury cream leather seats, that looked more like double armchairs for two people. They were situated along the plane rather than positioned side on, facing the windows or like the ones we were sat in now, that were two facing each other with a walnut table in between.

I hadn't been left to wonder for long why Lucius opted to sit next to me rather than face me, as his hand was held to my thigh. Then he squeezed to get my attention and let me into his thoughts,

"Not touching you will be difficult, pet," meaning that he was now getting in as much of it as he could before we landed and had no choice but to act as friends and unfortunately, not the kind with benefits.

I had been giving it some thought on what the next week, or however long we had to stay for, would be like when I noticed a serious lack of comical catchphrases that usually surrounded Pip. I glanced over to her and I don't know what caused it, but she just seemed really agitated and I was starting to question why. She kept scratching at her skin and shifting in her seat as if uncomfortable.

"Aunty Pip, you okay sweetie?" I asked making her give me a vacant look before answering,

"Uh, yeah...yeah, I am okay." I frowned and turned back to Lucius to whisper,

"Something's not right, she seems on edge." Lucius, who had actually been busy reading what looked like emails on his phone, looked first to me and then over my head to Pip. Then the moment he did, the stewardess appeared, with a tray of drinks and, just like I thought she would, *snacks*.

"So sorry about the wait, your drinks will be with you shortly," she said sweetly and I smiled at her before turning back to Pip and telling her,

"See...*snacks.*" I mouthed this last word at her and motioned to the stewardess who had her back to us as she was busy preparing our drinks at the small wet bar. She was currently pulling the bottle of champagne from an overly large silver ice bucket, one that held three bottles. Personally, I thought it was a little overkill, as what did she think the four of us were gonna have, a party and spray it all over each other!

I mean, I know there were some eccentric billionaires out there but please, you had Lucius in a dark grey suit with red tie, you had Adam who looked like his travelling accountant. Then me, who could have been his unprofessional looking PA in my skinny jeans and black sweater over a white shirt and flat boots. Needless to say, I was going for the smarter side of casual seeing as I was going home and all.

As for Pip, well then yes, she could have passed for a party girl in her roll neck, knitted sweater dress. One with stripes of pastel colours and covered in coin sized plastic lips sewn in a particular pattern. It was a dress that was also pulled in at the waist with a Kermit the frog belt, that looked like the actual muppet had been wrapped around her, with his hands holding his own legs.

Her hair was twisted up into a retro rockabilly roll, with a bright pink bandana wrapped around her head. So, all in all, we were a pretty mixed bunch.

"Hey, what are you doing…no, no, no, chickee…" Pip said when she noticed the stewardess struggling with the champagne bottle, now getting up to show her how to do it.

"Nah, you are opening it all wrong… see you twist your…wait a minute, my Spidey sense is doing the whole shiver me' tinglings thing here…shouldn't you know how to open one of these by now?" she asked and I had to say, she had a point. The stewardess looked sheepish but shrugged her shoulders and said,

"I confess, I'm new at this." This peeked Lucius' interest and now he asked,

"And what of Freda? She is my usual…"

"Oh her, yes well she couldn't make it today, her kids are sick," the girl said, before adding,

"It's just me and Tammy in the back, she's getting your…" She was quickly interrupted.

"Freda doesn't have kids." This came from Lucius who obviously knew his human staff and the second he said it, the stewardess shot us each a look of panic and just as Pip went on to say,

"Who in the Donkey's…" she was suddenly stopped when the bitch suddenly blew something in her face that she must have had concealed in her hand. But then at the same time, she also brought up the champagne bottle so hard, it hit Pip square in the jaw, making her head snap back. It even knocked a tooth out of her mouth before Pip hit the floor with the bottle landing intact next to her.

"PIP! What the fuck did you do to her?!" I screamed standing quickly, as did Lucius. I was about to rush towards her when Lucius quickly held me back.

This was now at the sight of our new problem.

As that was just what we needed...

Another fucking gun.

CHAPTER THIRTY

WINGING IT

"NOBODY FUCKING MOVE!" A blonde guy shouted, coming from around the corner, dressed as an air steward and holding a gun to the window, before telling us,

"If you try anything, I will shoot out the window, and I think you can guess what will happen next!" Lucius started to growl low and menacing, as he started to shift in front of me.

"He said don't fucking move, Vampire!" the female said, now producing her own gun from underneath the ice bucket, telling me why it had been so big...big enough to conceal a weapon on board.

"You sure that shit the witch gave you worked?" the guy said to his partner, who snapped,

"She's fucking unconscious, isn't she!"

"What do you want?" Lucius asked, eyeing up the gun and also weighing up his options in getting to both of them in time before a single shot went off. I also knew that, like the others in the mansion, it was obvious that Lucius couldn't control these two.

"Like you don't fucking know!" the woman snapped before the guy started issuing orders,

"Here is what is going to happen, you are going to give us the box and our pilot is going to land this plane where there will be a team waiting for us and will blow this fucking plane up the second they sense any trouble. So, unless you wanna see your bitch die today, then I suggest you'd better not try anything!" the guy said making me look up at Lucius and say,

"Aww, look honey, they actually think this is going to happen." Lucius scoffed and said,

"Deluded humans."

"Shut the fuck up, bitch, and get over here, I have heard about you and want you down on the floor next to your crazy friend here, right where I can keep an eye on you," the girl snapped making me say,

"Nice to know my reputation for killing you bastards is growing stronger by the day." I moved to do as she said because, well I had a plan, but then Lucius' arm snapped out and grabbed me, holding me to his side.

"NOW!" the woman said again, but it was me that he listened to as I looked up at him and said,

"It's okay, all's fair in love and war, remember?" This was when he finally understood what I was trying to say and that he needed to trust that that I could do this. He nodded once and let me go. So, I walked closer to her and when the bitch motioned to the floor with her gun, I got down on my knees and then on my hands, making sure I was positioned close to what I needed.

Then I moved in a way so I could check that Pip was still breathing. The relief when her pulse was still strong was immeasurable. But this was when our biggest problem hit me as I looked first to Lucius side on and then to the back of the plane, telling him with a single name mouthed silently, the real threat in all of this. Lucius looked at me and the second they weren't looking, he mouthed back, 'be ready'.

Because this plan of theirs didn't include one very important detail...*we had a monster on board.*

Oh, yeah and these morons had just attacked his wife!

The moment Adam came from the back of the plane and took in the scene, this became a big oh shit moment for us, and Lucius was the first one to know it.

"Fuck!" he hissed, the second Adam started to lose his shit and when I say this, I mean he suddenly roared like ten fucking lions were all on board with us and it made the plane start to shake. Then his head started shaking, doing it so fast that it was morphing into something else right in front of us. It was as if a monster version of him was trying to break free of his skin. But Lucius and I both knew that if that happened, then it was bye, bye, for all of us. Well, all except for the one who had wings. Although, I liked to think that I would be the first choice of wing buddy. However, it was Pip and Adam that were my major concerns. Which meant taking out the threat.

"What the fuck!" the guy shouted at the sight of Adam desperately fighting his rage and the beast from coming through. So, Lucius made a move to go to him and the bitch shouted,

"I told you not to fucking move!"

Lucius snarled at her, his fangs and crimson gaze now showing her exactly who she was threatening, which was why I said,

"If he doesn't go to him then this whole fucking plane is going to be ripped apart and all because you knocked out his wife, you dumb shits…but hey, I'm sure you two can sprout wings and fly…*right?*" They both looked at each other exchanging a moment of panic before telling him after the plane rocked again,

"Alright go, but don't try anything, Vamp, or I am taking my chances and putting a hole in your bitch's head!" Lucius snarled low and looked ready to pounce on the guy and rip him to shreds just for the insult alone. Which was why to get him back on track I shouted,

"Lucius go, help control him!" This got him moving and now with their eyes firmly on Adam, who was changing bit by bit every second, I could grab the bottle like I had wanted to. I then looked behind my shoulder when another mighty bellow from the beast shook the floor and again the plane dropped from the force of his rage. This made the girl reach out quickly to steady herself. Lucius looked back to me and nodded, indicating with just a look that I should be ready for when it happened again.

But then to help us in this, the pilot chose that moment to shout something from the cockpit, which gained the guy's attention. This was when Lucius made his move, momentarily letting go of Adam's beast and making the plane rock again, only harder this time. Both of them reached out to steady themselves, which was when I jumped up, shaking the bottle as I went. Then, with a little pressure, I made the cork fire off before spraying them both with champagne. Just as the bitch screamed, I quickly kicked the gun out of her hand, and threw the nearly empty bottle at the guy, who was covering his face so as not to get it in his eyes.

It hit him on the shoulder, jarring his arm back, long enough for me to pick up Lucius' beer bottle and throw that at him too. This was something that managed to hit him in the head and smash on impact. But then the bitch was coming back at me, running straight and intent on tackling me down the aisle. However, I positioned my feet to prevent this so that when she did hit into me, I was ready to grab her head. Then, when I got her locked in my arm, I punched her in the face three times with an uppercut, feeling the pain in doing so and quickly ignoring it.

Then I swung her away from me and into the guy who was bleeding in the head and now looking for his gun on the floor. But with blood in his eyes he thankfully couldn't see it. However, once more the plane shook again and this time, I knew Lucius was failing to keep the beast contained. I looked back and the sight of Lucius trying to keep Adam in his own head lock looked to be a sight even the Gods would struggle with. It was like watching someone wrestling with a crazed brown bear!

Which was why I knew I had to wake Pip up, as she was the only one who had the power to control him and this was by letting both beast and Adam know she was okay. So, I crouched down to her with my only hope that whatever had been done to her, was only temporary.

"Pip! Come on Pip, you needed to wake up! Please, oh please, wake up, honey!" I shouted and the second I saw movement I knew I had to put these two down for good. So,

I stood up, and blocked the bitch's attack before kicking her in the stomach so she landed into a wall. Then I was raising my forearm for another block, only this time it was side on as the guy also came at me. But he was clumsy with his vision impaired, which meant I had chance to grab his head and slam his face onto my knee as I brought it up at the same time.

Then I dropped him to the ground and picked up his hand, bent it in such a way, that with one quick twist, it broke his wrist making him bellow in pain. I was just about to kick him in the gut, when I was struck from behind. This was obviously by the bitch who was back for another round. I fell forward at an awkward angle, hitting one of the fancy tray tables with my hip, and banging my head on the side by a window.

"Pip, waking up right about now would be fucking swell!" I shouted before kicking back at the girl and catching her before she could attack. But then the plane shifted way over on its side and we all started to slide making the pilot's shouts grow louder and more panicked. Of course, this finally managed to jar Pip enough into groaning, which I took as my first good sign.

"PIP, time to get up, NOW!" I shouted the second Lucius was thrown off, as even more of the Hellish beast was breaking free. In fact, now one whole arm was forming into the stuff of nightmares and it was growing bigger by the second. And what was that underneath his skin…was that, skulls?

Okay, so yeah, time to wake up the sleeping Bo Pip! So, I thought of the one thing that just might do it.

"PIP, ALL DONKEYS ARE GONNA DIE!" I screamed

and suddenly Pip was lifting herself up and shaking her head, asking in a grumbling voice what had happened.

"Oh nothing, just that we're are all about to plummet to our deaths unless you get your husband under control!" I said trying to help her up, when suddenly I felt a gun pressed into the back of my head and the hammer was being clocked back. Damn it, but the bitch had found her gun again.

"Aww shit," I muttered.

"Amelia!" Lucius shouted and I could see him still fighting for control and now he was unsure what to do, as either decisions might mean my death.

"Back the fuck up, bitch!" I did as she said, seeing Pip looking up at me and quickly taking in the scene. So, I continued back, telling her,

"If you shoot me, you could end up bringing this plane down." However, reminding her of this just made her snarl at me,

"Yeah, but it would be fucking worth it, so time to get on your fucking knees!"

"Alright, okay, I will do as you..." This ended with the sound of a loud dong, before the girl's eyes rolled back up into her head. Then she fell forward and hit the floor, making me have to jump out of the way first. Behind her was the culprit with the large ice bucket in her hands after she had just bashed her over the head with it.

"That's for wasting good booze, biatch!" Pip said making me clear my throat and say,

"Err, Pip."

"Yeah."

"You might want to continue saving the fucking day and go get Adam back." Right in that moment Lucius bellowed,

"PIP, GET YOUR ASS OVER HERE!"

"Eeek, sure thing boss!" Then she dropped the bucket and the second she did, just to be sure, I picked it up and used it on the guy, who was still barely conscious. However, right then, even slight movement was too much for my liking. So, as it had worked well for Pip, I snatched it up and hit the guy at the back of the head with it making another satisfying dong sound.

But it was at that moment that I realised the plane was losing altitude and I frowned back at Lucius to see them both now trying to contain Adam. Something that was only achieved by Lucius holding him in a head lock whilst Pip was holding his monstrous face and cooing at him, telling him that she was alright.

Well, other than the plane about to take a nosedive, at least the rocking had stopped. So, I snagged the gun off the floor and went to see what was happening, knowing from what they said, the pilot was one of the bad guys. The moment I peered inside, I saw his co-pilot was dead and looked to have had his neck cut from behind. Which made me question if this was what the fake steward had been doing before making himself known.

I raised the gun towards the last man sitting and said,

"Bring this fucking plane back up!"

"You can't shoot me, if you do that we will both get sucked out of here!" he said looking over his shoulder at me and appearing confident that I wouldn't.

"Oh, don't worry, I have no problem in getting creative," I told him.

"I was told that I am to bring this plane down in Stuttgart and that is exactly what I am doing!"

"Then you are a dead man!" I snapped making him sneer at me and say,

"You're the one that is dead, as I will crash this fucking plane just to kill every last one of you blood sucking bastards!" Okay, so this was when I knew that this guy was a lost cause, and rather than trusting him not to kill us all, I decided to act. So, after a quick 'creative' think, I ran back into the main part of the plane, briefly noticed that they had finally managed to get Adam under control, and I grabbed what I needed.

"Amelia!" Lucius said my name in warning making me wink back at him. Doing so as I raised the bucket up and shouted,

"I have everything under control!" Then, without waiting for a response, I ran back into the cockpit to see that the lunatic was now close to crashing the plane, if he continued on his current course, as all the instruments were screaming at him to pull up and level out!

"Oh, you are so dead!" I said making him laugh in a sinister way,

"You first, you dumb fuck, as you can't kill me, no one can fly the plane."

"In that case, class this as your retirement and have a drink on me!" I said, then dumped the large ice bucket over his head and before he could struggle, I put my gun underneath it, aimed at his head and fired one shot before a back blow of blood splatted his neck and shoulders. Just in that moment Lucius ran into the cockpit, took one look at what I had done and shouted,

"Fuck! Amelia, what did you do!?"

"I took care of a problem, now quick, get him out of the

seat!" Lucius did as I asked and lifted the dead weight out, as I quickly slipped in the seat.

"Now get the other guy out of here and then take a seat!" I ordered. Lucius did as I told him to and the second the seat was free, he shook his head in disbelief.

"I can't believe you shot another fucking pilot!" Lucius said looking down at me and the second I started to level the plane back out, pulling her back up, I turned to him and said,

"Oh, don't worry…" Then I looked back out through the front window and finished,

"This one, I know how to fly."

To be continued…

ABOUT THE AUTHOR

Stephanie Hudson has dreamed of being a writer ever since her obsession with reading books at an early age. What first became a quest to overcome the boundaries set against her in the form of dyslexia has turned into a life's dream. She first started writing in the form of poetry and soon found a taste for horror and romance. Afterlife is her first book in the series of twelve, with the story of Keira and Draven becoming ever more complicated in a world that sets them miles apart.

When not writing, Stephanie enjoys spending time with her loving family and friends, chatting for hours with her biggest fan, her sister Cathy who is utterly obsessed with one gorgeous Dominic Draven. And of course, spending as much time with her supportive partner and personal muse, Blake who is there for her no matter what.

Author's words.

My love and devotion is to all my wonderful fans that

keep me going into the wee hours of the night but foremost to my wonderful daughter Ava...who yes, is named after a cool, kick-ass, Demonic bird and my sons, Jack, who is a little hero and Baby Halen, who yes, keeps me up at night but it's okay because he is named after a Guitar legend!

Keep updated with all new release news & more on my website

www.afterlifesaga.com
Never miss out, sign up to the
mailing list at the website.

Also, please feel free to join myself and other Dravenites on my Facebook group
Afterlife Saga Official Fan
Interact with me and other fans. Can't wait to see you there!

facebook.com/AfterlifeSaga
twitter.com/afterlifesaga
instagram.com/theafterlifesaga

Acknowledgements

Well first and foremost my love goes out to all the people who deserve the most thanks and are the wonderful people that keep me going day to day. But most importantly they are the ones that allow me to continue living out my dreams and keep writing my stories for the world to hopefully enjoy… These people are of course YOU! Words will never be able to express the full amount of love I have for you guys. Your support is never ending. Your trust in me and the story is never failing. But more than that, your love for me and all who you consider your 'Afterlife family' is to be commended, treasured and admired. Thank you just doesn't seem enough, so one day I hope to meet you all and buy you all a drink! ;)

To my family… To my amazing mother, who has believed in me from the very beginning and doesn't believe that something great should be hidden from the world. I would like to thank you for all the hard work you put into my books and the endless hours spent caring about my words and making sure it is the best it can be for everyone to enjoy. You make Afterlife shine. To my wonderful crazy father who is and always has been my hero in life. Your strength astonishes me, even to this day and the love and care you hold for your family is a gift you give to the Hudson name. And last but not least, to the man that I consider my soul mate. The man who taught me about real love and makes me not only want to be a better person but makes me feel I am too. The amount of support you have given me since we met has been incredible and the greatest feeling was finding out you wanted to spend the rest of your life with me when you asked me to marry you.

All my love to my dear husband and my own personal Draven… Mr Blake Hudson.

Another personal thank you goes to my dear friend Caroline Fairbairn and her wonderful family that have embraced my brand of crazy into their lives and given it a hug when most needed.

For their friendship I will forever be eternally grateful.

I would also like to mention Claire Boyle my wonderful PA, who without a doubt, keeps me sane and constantly smiling through all the chaos which is my life ;) And a loving mention goes to Lisa Jane for always giving me a giggle and scaring me to death with all her count down pictures lol ;)

Thank you for all your hard work and devotion to the saga and myself. And always going that extra mile, pushing Afterlife into the spotlight you think it deserves. Basically helping me achieve my secret goal of world domination one day…evil laugh time… Mwahaha! Joking of course ;)

As before, a big shout has to go to all my wonderful fans who make it their mission to spread the Afterlife word and always go the extra mile. I love you all x

Also by
Stephanie Hudson

Afterlife Saga

A Brooding King, A Girl running from her past. What happens when the two collide?

Book 1 - Afterlife

Book 2 - The Two Kings

Book 3 - The Triple Goddess

Book 4 - The Quarter Moon

Book 5 - The Pentagram Child /Part 1

Book 6 - The Pentagram Child /Part 2

Book 7 - The Cult of the Hexad

Book 8 - Sacrifice of the Septimus /Part 1

Book 9 - Sacrifice of the Septimus /Part 2

Book 10 -Blood of the Infinity War

Book 11 -Happy Ever Afterlife /Part 1

Book 12 -Happy Ever Afterlife / Part 2

Transfusion Saga

What happens when an ordinary human girl comes face to face with the cruel Vampire King who dismissed her seven years ago?

Transfusion - Book 1

Venom of God - Book 2

Blood of Kings - Book 3

Rise of Ashes - Book 4

Map of Sorrows - Book 5

Tree of Souls - Book 6

Kingdoms of Hell – Book 7

Eyes of Crimson - Book 8

Afterlife Chronicles: (Young Adult Series)

The Glass Dagger – Book 1

The Hells Ring – Book 2

Stephanie Hudson and Blake Hudson

The Devil in Me

OTHER WORKS BY HUDSON INDIE INK

Paranormal Romance/Urban Fantasy

Sloane Murphy

Xen Randell

C. L. Monaghan

Sci-fi/Fantasy

Brandon Ellis

Devin Hanson

Crime/Action

Blake Hudson

Mike Gomes

Contemporary Romance

Gemma Weir

Elodie Colt

Ann B. Harrison

Ingram Content Group UK Ltd.
Milton Keynes UK
UKHW041336120523
421648UK00001B/194